Blood, Beasts, and Betrayal

Sharper Than Thorns

Praise for Sharper Than Thorns

"The quality of both the writing and style is spot on and thoroughly enjoyable."

-T.E. Elliot,
Author of *Loved by the Beast*

"An incredible...fresh take on classic tales with each offering their own twist. A must read."
-Miriam Wade,
Author of *One Sword Saga*

Praise for Fool's Honor

"*Fool's Honor* is a magical anthology like no other I've read, full of whimsical worlds and enthralling characters that tug on your heartstrings. I'd highly recommend it for fans of *Six of Crows* or *Caraval*."

- Bethany Meyer,
Author of *Robbing Centaurs and Other Bad Ideas*

Praise for What Darkness Fears

"The spookiness of each of these pieces fascinated and sucked me in—even as I shivered, I couldn't put this anthology down! *What Darkness Fears* is a bright anthology by multiple authors."

- Sarah Sutton,
Author of *If the Broom Fits*

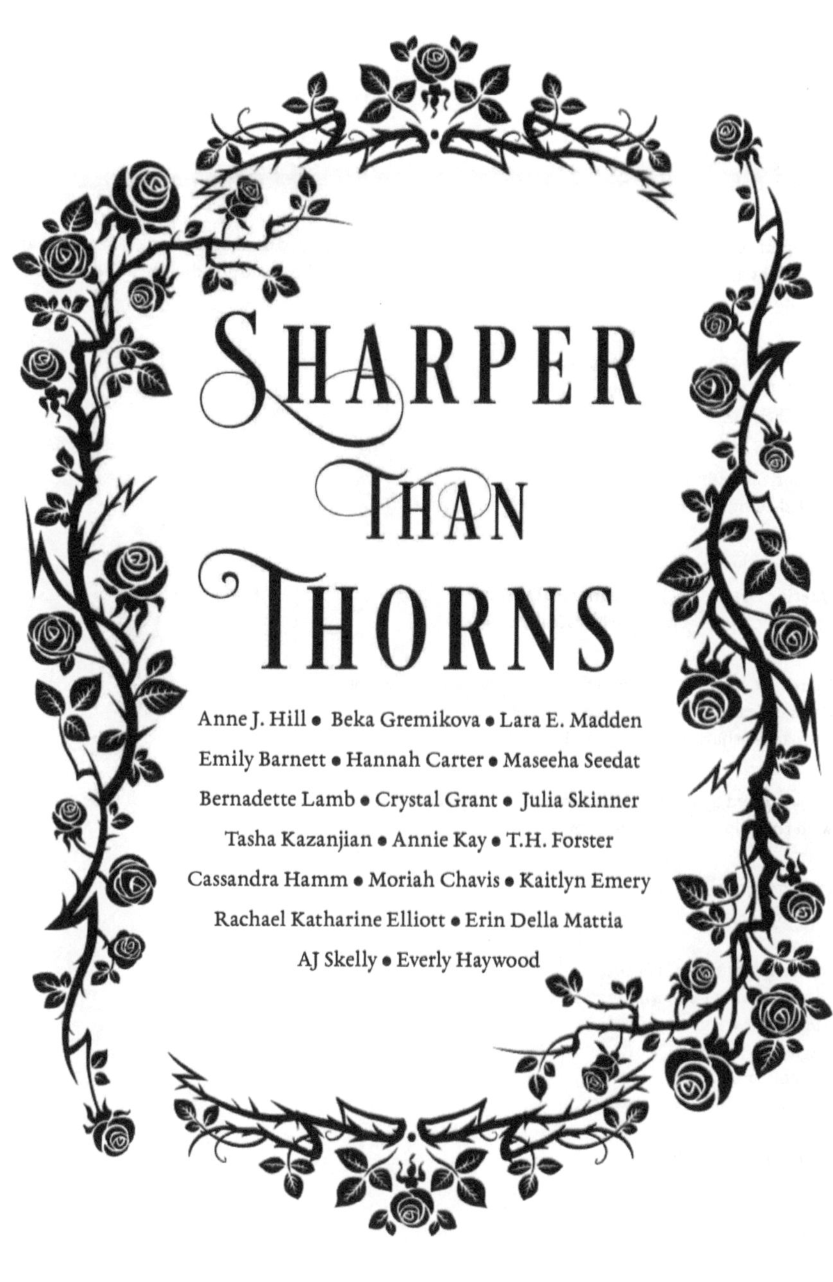

SHARPER THAN THORNS

Anne J. Hill • Beka Gremikova • Lara E. Madden
Emily Barnett • Hannah Carter • Maseeha Seedat
Bernadette Lamb • Crystal Grant • Julia Skinner
Tasha Kazanjian • Annie Kay • T.H. Forster
Cassandra Hamm • Moriah Chavis • Kaitlyn Emery
Rachael Katharine Elliott • Erin Della Mattia
AJ Skelly • Everly Haywood

SHARPER THAN THORNS

Paperback ISBN: 978-1-956499-05-6
Ebook ISBN: 978-1-956499-07-0
Hardback ISBN: 978-1-956499-06-3

Edition one published in July 2022
Published by Twenty Hills Publishing

Cover Art by JV Arts
Interior formatting by Dragonpen Designs
Publisher logo by Nathaniel Luscombe

Edited by Anne J. Hill and Beka Gremikova with help from
Crystal Grant, Hannah Carter, Maseeha Seedat,
Rachael Katharine Elliott, and Emily Barnett

Book created by Anne J. Hill, head of Twenty Hills Publishing,
with the help of Beka Gremikova

CONTENT WARNING:
Fantasy violence
Murder
References to sexual violence
Physical, emotional, and verbal abuse
Suicide ideation
Neglect
Societal prejudice
Starvation/disordered eating
Gore
Violence against children
Death/grief
Mentions of cannibalism and infanticide
Mild language in Thorn Tower *sneak peek*

Beka Gremikova:

For my Saviour, who bore both cross
and crown of thorns to save His roses

Anne J. Hill:

To my brother, Erin, for the long nights
discussing books and writing,
and Lara E. Madden, for the same thing

TABLE OF CONTENTS

PART TWO: PURER THAN POISON

PART THREE: FIERCER THAN FANGS

PART FOUR: MIGHTIER THAN MAGIC

CINDERELLA

SLEEPING BEAUTY

RAPUNZEL

EXCLUSIVE SNEAK PEEK FROM THORN TOWER

Introduction

FAIRYTALES ARE A universal language, perhaps one of the easiest to learn. Most children are exposed to fairytales at a young age, whether through Disney movies or parents who love folklore and myths.

And, sometimes, when those children grow up, they add their own spins—whether by exploring the whimsical worlds of those tales through humor or delving into the deep, dark snarls of the characters' souls.

I, Anne J. Hill, do just that in my upcoming novel, *Thorn Tower*, the first in my debut series: a trilogy inspired by Beauty and the Beast, Snow White, and Little Red Riding Hood, with nods to Cinderella, Sleeping Beauty, Rapunzel, and other tales. To help introduce my debut, Beka and I organized this collection of short stories and poetry that reflect and retell these beloved fairytales. Some of the pieces coincide with my debut's themes, style, or overall feel, while others stand on their own entirely. Several of my own stories and poems in this anthology are about the characters in *Thorn Tower*. To further whet your appetite, a character introduction for *Thorn Tower* is included at the very end of the book.

From tantalizing flash fiction, to poetry, to short stories, you'll find familiar tales told in ways that will haunt you, encourage you, and inspire you. Between Beauties facing off against their Beasts, Snow Whites discovering the poison of regret, and Red Riding Hoods learning the true nature of wolves, these twists are sharper than thorns—and will gladly pierce your heart.

-Anne J. Hill and Beka Gremikova

BRAVER THAN BEAUTY

PART ONE

Lonely Souls

Anne J. Hill

THE GUARDIAN OF the Forest sat in his tower in the trees. Alone. Tracing his palm, he remembered a time when he was able to feel such a delicate touch. He once knew love and held it dear. He once was the elf he wanted to be.

No more.

His harp sat between his feet, ornate roses engraved down the wooden framework. The Guardian rubbed at his temple as he ruminated on past mistakes that made him feel like a monster. He brushed his white, youthful hair behind his ear; the ends trickled over his lap.

Shadows crept along his walls and danced in the flickering candlelight. They closed in on him, ready to smother. And no one would notice....

All alone.

He took a deep breath and plucked the harp's strings. The once numbing pricks were now merely light taps on his fingertips; his sense of touch weakened each day. His eyes drifted closed, and the enchanting melody filled his soul and calmed the woods. Playing away the monsters on his walls and in his heart.

It was his duty to keep peace in the woods. He was the Guardian of the Forest, and as dusk faded into twilight, he could sense this would be a long night.

Outside, more than the wind howled in fury.

Sleep threatened to end his melody, his body tired from the long nights protecting the forest and the enduring loneliness of his work. With no one to love or love him in return.

But maybe it was better this way. Maybe it was safer...hidden away from the world. The beast he was, contained.

She paced her room in the dark, listening to her father's ragged breaths. It was lonely work to take care of a parent who gave her no thanks—who kept her from the battlegrounds. She'd fought alongside her fellow warriors in the war against the humans until her father was struck down. Now her only contribution to the war was patroling her town.

Stopping by her window, she looked out into the night. The town was quiet, peacefully asleep, while death and war raged only miles away. Her eyes scanned the road. Nothing stirred; she decided all was well.

She could so easily slip outside and rejoin the ranks where she could be of more use. Free. With no father to tie her down.

Shaking her head, she rubbed her jaw. No.

As one of the few soldiers in the town, it was her duty to keep her people safe should danger arise. A sort of guardian of her army town.

She knew battle from years of training and fighting. Pacing in case there was trouble, she did not.

She considered going to sleep, but it would be a restless night, where she'd keep her ears pricked for unusual breathing from her father and any threats from outside. So from her bedroom, she patrolled, bare feet grazing the wooden floor. Brown hair tucked behind her pointed ears.

Nothing would give her more joy than to fling her duties aside and dash back to the battlegrounds. But honor and family loyalty kept her bound, and, for now, that was reason enough. This was good. This watch-keeping was noble work....

Two lonely souls waded through the dark of night. One a beautiful warrior, the other a reclusive beast.

And one fateful day, they would meet and change the course of their lives forever.

Continues in Thorn Tower *by Anne J. Hill*

The beautiful
princess
behind the
beast.

Above Beauty

Beka Gremikova

TODAY WAS YET another day her curse might lift—and Iris couldn't let it.

She lay in bed, staring at the ceiling as waves of Priam's love reached out from his wing of her castle. His affection buffeted like a breeze, twining around her limbs, tearing into the beast-curse that killed her a bit more each day. A punishment fit for one who had offended Aphra, the Curator of Beauty.

Iris shook her limbs and rolled off her bed. The spell's familiar tingling filled her as she crawled to the antechamber, her claws clicking against the cold stone. The still air made her heart beat even louder in her ears: *Accept his love. You'll be free!*

Her throat closed. *He wants the beautiful princess behind the beast. That's all.* If Aphra's spell lifted, Priam would realize the truth.

There was no beautiful princess.

Just an ugly woman, Aphra's taunting voice whispered from Iris's past. *Nothing's valued above beauty, girl. No spells can save you from his rejection.*

Certainly not the plants' magic, Iris thought wistfully, gazing at the lush greenery adorning the antechamber, all gifts from Priam's family greenhouse.

Skylights dappled the foliage with sunshine, and each leaf glimmered and thrummed with a verdant glow.

The tingling in her limbs intensified to prickling pain as Aphra's sorcery gnawed at her stooping body. Snatching a leaf from a nearby plant, Iris pressed it against her tongue and waited.

The discomfort subsided, overwhelmed by the cooling caress of the plant's pulsing magic. While it couldn't cure her curse, it helped soothe the symptoms. She grabbed a watering can and hobbled from plant to plant.

As she reached her scarlet rose bushes, the pain resurged in a fierce, near-blinding attack, and her knees buckled.

"You've made me a laughingstock, Princess of Dalmarken." Aphra tore a rose from a nearby bush. "Why didn't you dedicate yourself and your rule to me?"

Iris's fingers clenched into fists. "I chose the Curator of Merchants because I felt my rule should focus on trade—"

"Too good for beauty, are you?" Aphra's voice shook. "Every other Curator expected you to pick me, you little beast." She flung the rose at Iris's face. "See who cares about trade when you've no beauty to speak of!"

A gentle touch brushed Iris's shoulder, startling her. "Lady Iris," whispered her maid. "Master Priam's worried you haven't come down yet. He's waiting in the gardens."

Iris bit back a pained groan. Though her heart wrenched with longing to see him, a deep dread gnawed at her stomach. Every day he asked her to accept his suit, and every day she refused. If he saw her and didn't want her anymore…

It would prove Aphra right.

She sucked in a shaky breath. But she couldn't keep doing this—she couldn't bear the hurt, the wariness, the hope that felt just beyond her fingertips…. And how must Priam feel when she gave him the same answer day after day?

They couldn't live in this limbo forever. This had to end. She'd held on too long already, enjoying his companionship while always knowing she'd have to back away at some point.

She rose, nibbled on another leaf to soothe the agony tearing through her limbs, and trudged after her maid to the gardens. *If I won't let him break my curse, maybe… he should leave.*

Priam waited on an arbored path, surrounded by flowering arches. With his dark, tumbling curls, smooth skin, and well-muscled body, he seemed like a Curator of Beauty himself.

Too perfect for this world. Too perfect for her.

His feelings wrapped around her like a fog, tugging at the curse as though they could rip it out of her body.

Why can I feel your… affection? she'd asked him once.

He'd smiled at her. *You've been cursed by the Curator of Beauty. Well, I've been blessed by the Curator of Love, so those I love can know they're valued and never have to doubt.*

But she did doubt—because how could she believe that after years of rejection, *this* man could embrace her?

"You have to leave!" she blurted.

His eyes widened. "Why?" He took her clawed hands in his. "Won't you let me love you? As you *really* are? Don't you want that?"

Of course! "But I—" *I'm not as you think.* "I'd rather stay like this. If you don't like it, then…" *Go away.* The words stuck in her throat.

His eyes flashed. "This is *killing* you!" He took a deep breath. "And I want you as you were created to be—*human*—not what Aphra's spell turned you into. I know my feelings won't heal everything—but they aren't a lie. I want us to face each other honestly."

His words, as gentle as rustling leaves, wrapped around her limbs like a soft cocoon, waiting. She simply had to accept, and they'd soak through her skin and strangle the curse to death. She held her breath.

He lifted his hands to her face. "Iris, please. Whether you send me away or we stay like this, we still lose *something*."

Tears stung, and she squeezed her eyes shut. The magic of his words hovered over her skin.

Just accept. Be free! her heart screamed.

Could she keep living like this?

No. But could she really let him leave?

"Iris," he whispered, and his voice broke, "Will you accept my love?"

Be free!

"Yes," she choked out. The waiting magic swept through her like a cold, cleansing spring rain. It left her shivering, and she stared down at fur-less arms speckled with moles. She could feel spots breaking out on her face. Trembling, she tucked her frizzy hair behind her ear. "Well, here's your princess. Are you happy?"

"Yes," Priam said quietly. "But are you happy with *me*?"

She blinked. Before, he'd seemed... shiny. Now, though still attractive, he also boasted weathering on his cheeks, a scraggly, uneven beard, and bags under his eyes from...

Sleepless nights worrying about imperfections that the spell had hidden from *her*? Worried that *she* might be disappointed?

How well the curse had disguised them from each other.

Priam bit his lip. "Well, Iris? Do you still love me?"

Iris wrapped her arms around him. "Yes," she whispered. "How could I not?" She blinked back a wave of giddiness, and this time the tingling she felt had nothing do with a curse.

The Beast in Me

Annie Kay

There is a beast in me
And I refuse to believe that
Someone will love me
I realize this may be a shock, but
I am worthy
It is a lie
I am a monster
In 30 years, people will tell their children that
I have my priorities straight because
Appearance
Is more important than
Kindness
I tell you this
Once upon a time
I was a man
But this will not be true again in my lifetime
I am selfish, cruel, and vile
People tell me
I am as unattractive on the inside as the outside

I do not conclude that
I am worthy of love
In the future
I will be no more
No longer can it be said that
Someone will see the good in me
It will be evident that
I am a beast instead of a man
It is foolish to presume that
I am worth fighting for
All of this will come true *unless I reverse it.*

This is a Reversal Poem.
It has another meaning when you read it backward.

The Rose and the Bull

Tasha Kazanjian

THE SCENT OF autumn leaves in the air made Kiar want to tear out of the castle gate and run towards the mountains. In the courtyard, he couldn't focus as his father droned on about the harvest and the tasks still to be done. The torc around his neck—the gold band that marked him as his father's heir—pinched at his skin. He tugged at it, his eyes sliding again to the open gate.

The pall of smoke rising from courtyard fire seemed to smother him, and he absently slipped his fingers under the torc, plucking at the strip of leather underneath.

"Kiar!"

Kiar froze.

His father stared at him, horrified. In a single, hawkish swoop, he snatched the leather charm from Kiar's neck. "Are you mad?"

Kiar wanted to grab it back, but he couldn't move. Years of keeping the knot a secret—ever since his mother's death, when he was sixteen. And in a single careless moment, he was caught. The intricate leather knot, stained with her blood, should've burned on her funeral pyre. Kiar couldn't bring himself to give it up, though, even if the charm would offer him no protection. Only the blood of the living could give a knot power.

Now, his father crushed the knot in his fist and growled, "Do you want to trap her spirit here?" He turned and threw the charm into the courtyard fire.

Kiar was out the gate before it turned to ash.

He stayed out on the heath all day. As the sun began to set, he caught sight of a storm flowing over the mountains, the violet clouds singed with gold. Still, he wasn't ready to turn back, and he wouldn't make it to the castle before the rain caught him.

His gaze shifted to the forest. It was straight in the storm's path, but the trees would offer some shelter from the rain. He began to run.

A few drops of rain hit his face as he reached the trees. Kiar hurried deeper into the forest. Eventually, he slowed, listening to the drops rustle in the leaves. Frustration fizzled in his chest; he had been running all day and still he felt trapped, fixated on his father and the knot. He wanted a *distraction.*

Someone gasped behind him.

Kiar whirled around, his hand on his knife. There, half-hidden behind a yew, crouched a woman. She drew back, her dark eyes fixed on him. Slowly, Kiar released his grip on the knife and straightened. "Hello," he called.

The woman didn't reply, but she didn't turn away, either. Her head tilted to one side, red curls trailing over her pale face.

For a moment Kiar stared at her, at the delicate curve of her neck, the fluid grace of her movements. Then she smiled. Kiar stepped toward her, heat spreading under his skin and pulling him towards her. Her lips were as dark as the berries beading the yew's branches.

"You should not be in this place." Her eyes glinted teasingly. She moved out from behind the tree and crossed her arms. They were bare; she wore no tunic underneath her peplos. The brooches at her shoulders gleamed even in the dim light.

Distantly, Kiar wondered why *she* was in this place, and why she had no cloak despite the cold, but her words baited him. "Why not?" he asked, arching an eyebrow.

The woman spread out her hands, motioning to the trees around them, and the gesture somehow brought her closer to Kiar. "Don't you know the stories of this forest?"

"According to the *shenachie*, there are stories about every forest," Kiar replied with a smirk. The woman had the otherworldly beauty of a *sí* from a poet's song, yet she stood in front of him, solid and real and so close now that he could feel her breath on his skin. She looked up at his face with that red, teasing smile.

He touched her hair, very lightly. "You don't seem like a spirit."

"No, I'm not a spirit." Her hand twined into his. "I am Muira."

Her red mouth darted up to his, and he caught the scent of death on her tongue.

Spring came slow in the mountains. A rill of wind brushed against Ròs' cheek as she left the cottage, and she wanted to breathe in until the delicious cleanness of it filled her up.

"Are you sure you don't need my help?" Innes, Ròs' mentor, called from inside.

"No, I'd like to try herb-gathering on my own," Ròs answered, pinning her woolen mantle at her shoulder with a heavy, intricately-wrought brooch. It was the only one she had; she'd wanted to trade it for a simpler one, but nobody would take it.

The older woman came to the doorway, her eyes pinched. "If you're sure."

Ròs was very sure. Innes' hut was small, and nearly every day someone came by looking for a salve or a tea, or a cask of heather beer. Ròs craved time alone.

Despite the riot of wildflowers blooming over the dales, Ròs filled her basket slowly. It wasn't so cold anymore; her fingers didn't grow stiff as she picked little bunches of flowers and herbs. She spent the whole day out on the heath and by sunset, she'd gathered nearly everything she'd wanted, which would please Innes—and hopefully soothe any irritation about Ròs being gone so long. Even so, she walked a bit faster, moving closer to the trees where the ground was less marshy.

A flash of white caught her eye. Ròs stopped, peering into the woods. The sun had sunk behind the mountains now, but she could see a flicker of something bright.

Twisting the knot she kept around her wrist to make sure it was secure, she started towards the flicker. She threaded her way through the skeletal branches and suddenly she stood in front of a rose bush. Wonderingly, she touched the soft white petals. It was early for roses. Ròs plucked one free, twirling it between her thumb and forefinger, then tucked it into her braid.

"Hello," said someone behind her.

Ròs whipped around.

A man stood there, leaning against a tree. "Don't be startled. If anyone ought to be, it's me. I hardly ever see anyone here." He straightened up with a slanted smile. "Though I don't mind the company."

She stumbled back, the branches of the rose bush snagging her clothes and hair. Thorns scraped at her arms but she scarcely noticed. *There's nothing to be afraid of,* she told herself, *just calm down*—and still her heartbeat filled her head.

"I see you've been pilfering my roses," the man continued. He stepped closer, within arm's reach of her. "I'm afraid I'll have to take a little toll for that."

Dread blurred Ròs' vision. Why couldn't she *speak*? She knew this old fear by heart and yet she couldn't force it down.

The man was laughing, his pale blue eyes crinkled with amusement as he moved nearer. "Don't be frightened. I'm not going to hurt you. Anyway, *you're* the thief."

He was standing too close, so close that she could smell the thick tang of his sweat. A rage of panic shot through her blood and Ròs threw her basket at him.

He stumbled back. Before he caught his balance, Ròs tore herself free, the roses clawing at her sleeves. She heard a snap.

She didn't stop to see what had ripped loose, only ran. The trees seemed to constrict around her, while behind her, she could hear the man calling. His shout was guttural, then drawn out, rising like a howl.

Ròs raced blindly through the branches, her chest aching for breath. Her foot caught on a root and she fell hard.

"You're quick."

She jerked her head up. The man was standing over her, his mouth pulled into a grin. As he dropped into a crouch, his smile slowly stretched.

His shaggy black hair spread over his back, his face, his arms, and his blue eyes brightened into copper. Ròs shrank back in horror. He was a hound, massive and growling and poised to spring.

"Get back!" she screamed, staggering to her feet and instinctively flinging up her arms. As she did, she saw the mess of scratches on her bare wrists and realized what she had left behind on the rose bush.

Her knot.

Ròs' eyes widened in horror. Before she had time to move, the hound lunged. His teeth sunk into her arm. She screamed again, but as blood-red pain filled her vision, she wrenched the brooch from her mantle and stabbed the hound with its pin.

The creature snarled in pain, its jaw loosening, and Ròs kicked it away. Half sobbing, she began to run again, but she was dizzy now and knew she wouldn't make it far.

Something dark moved in the pines ahead of her. Ròs squinted, then rubbed a hand over her face. It was a massive black bull, its horns pale in the dim light.

Ròs stopped. They'd trapped her.

The bull strode towards her. "Get on my back."

Her pulse was roaring so loudly in her ears that for a second Ròs couldn't understand the words.

"*Get on my back.*"

The bull's voice was low and harsh. Ròs hesitated, but only long enough to hear the howl of the hound behind her. Then she reached out, grabbing hold of the bull's thick fur and hauling herself onto its back.

For such a massive beast, it moved quick, deftly weaving between the trees. It took all Ròs' strength to hang on, her fingers entwined in its coarse hide. She buried her head in its neck with her shoulders scrunched up to her ears.

She didn't know how long they ran. When the bull pulled to a stop, rearing back and stomping its hooves, she lost her grip and tumbled off. Dazed, she rolled over, her cheek against the cold turf.

The bull moved closer, his nose twitching. Stiffly, Ròs sat up. It was dark now, but she could see by the stars that they were in a small clearing with a ring of stones at the center. A well, she realized, catching the glint of light reflected on the water. A holy well. A spring called forth by the gods themselves, so abundant that it not only filled the shaft but saturated the earth around it. The circle of turf around the well was vividly green and thick with little white flowers.

"You're safe here," the bull announced.

Ròs glanced at him. The voice was so *human*. Questions burned in the back of her throat, but she simply stared.

"Madragh—the hound—he can't touch you, not if you stay in this clearing," the bull continued. "The virtue of the well is strong. It will protect you so long as you can feel the water beneath your feet. But we're deep in the forest now." He grunted. "I don't think I could get you to the edge of the wood, not without Madragh scenting us. I'm sorry."

Ròs only sat there. She was aware of a pain in her hand, and she unclenched her fist, wincing as she saw the brooch clamped against her palm. The pin had stuck in her skin. She drew it out, the wound oozing blood.

The bull lowered his head. "I'm Kiar. Can you tell me your name?"

"Ròs," she whispered, touching a flower still tangled in her hair. And then a sob broke loose.

Memories burned like ice in her blood and prickled under her skin—a man's hands on her body, the reek of heather-beer in his mouth. She shook her head, clawing her arms around her chest, trying to tear herself back into *now*, not then, but she was trapped inside the fear.

The bull nudged her shoulder, a whiff of breath steaming over her face. The solid warmth of him sent a shiver through her, and for a moment, the memories retreated. He knelt down beside her, not quite touching her, but she reached out, twining her hand into his fur. The weight of his presence held her steady.

After a while—her tears worn out and her head aching—she turned to look at him. He lifted his head, and though she couldn't see his eyes beneath the tufts of black fur, she could feel his gaze mirroring her own misery.

"What did he want with me?" Ròs asked, her voice hoarse.

The bull grunted. "To take you to Muira, the *bhuidseach* of these woods. That witch turns all who trespass here into shiftlings." His nostrils flared. "You're bleeding."

Ròs clenched her fist, hiding the bloody bruise on her palm. "It's nothing."

"Your *other* arm."

Frowning, Ròs lifted her right arm, her sleeve torn and bloodstained, then gasped as the movement sparked a spasm of pain. The hound's bite.

"Let me see it," the bull said.

Ròs shut her eyes, forcing herself to breathe through a wave of nausea. She wasn't sure what the bull thought he could do and meant to tell him that she could manage, but when she opened her eyes, her breath froze in her lungs.

There wasn't any bull on the edge of the clearing. There was a man, tall and broad-shouldered, with a tangle of dark hair and a scruffy beard on his face. He had no tunic, only breeches and a mantle. Blue-black tattoos swirled over his arms and chest.

"Here," the man said, reaching out to her.

Ròs stumbled back. Her feet sank into the wet turf, and a strange, tingling coolness spread through her.

The man frowned, taking a step closer, but as his foot touched the damp ground, he flinched and jerked away.

Ròs felt the stones of the well brush against her skirt. "Change back," she whispered, her eyes dropping.

He stared at her. "But—"

"*Change back.*" Her voice shook. "Please."

She kept her gaze down until she heard the sound of a hoof pawing the earth. A sigh slipped out and she leaned against the well. Her right arm gave way then, slipping into the water. Ròs gasped at the cold shock.

"I didn't mean to scare you." The bull paced at the edge of the clearing.

Pulling her arm against her stomach, Ròs let her hair fall over her face to hide her flushed cheeks. She didn't know what to say; he *had* scared her. As much as she wanted to laugh it off or even just look at him, she couldn't. She scratched at the bloodstained skin of her arm, then stiffened.

The bite was gone.

"The well," she said softly.

"What?" The bull leaned forward.

Ròs glanced up at him now, holding out her arm. "The water healed it."

"I didn't realize it was so powerful. I can't touch the water, any more than Madragh or the *bhuidseach* can. If only—" He grunted, kicking at the turf, then shied away as a spray of water went up.

Ròs touched the rim of the well almost reverently. "How did you find this place?"

"Hiding." The bull shrugged back his powerful shoulders; in a flash of moonlight, Ròs noticed three pale scars cut into his fur. "After the first time I fought Madragh. He was trying to lure a little boy into the forest."

"He gave you those?" She gestured to the scars.

"No," he said shortly. "Muira did, as a punishment for interfering with Madragh's hunt."

Ròs sat on the edge of the well and pulled up a long blade of grass, absently twisting it into a knot. "Why did the *bhuidseach* turn you into a bull?" she asked.

Kiar couldn't keep the bitterness out of his words as he replied to the woman's question. "It is not hard to tell."

Ròs' fingers twitched.

Inwardly, Kiar smiled. *It is not hard to tell.* These were the words sung by the *shenachie* as they began a tale. He had heard them a thousand times in his father's hall, and though he did not recognize this woman, he knew the *shenachie* symbol etched into her brooch.

"The wood belongs to the *bhuidseach,*" he continued. "She caught me trespassing." Now he was glad to be a bull, grateful for the fur hiding how his face burned at the memory. "There was poison on her tongue. When I woke up, she was tearing the torc from my neck."

Ròs winced. Kiar turned away—he didn't want pity. Rage built in his chest at the thought of his torc, which marked him as the son of his father, around Muira's throat.

"And the spell?" Ròs asked.

"Her words rang with a power as strong as pain, in the trees and the stones, and then I could feel them in my blood." His teeth clenched. "I can still feel them. As long as I'm in this forest, I have the power to change back to myself, but if I leave, I'll be trapped as a bull forever."

There was silence. Ròs stared at Kiar, as though trying to memorize every detail of his tale.

"Have you ever told a story like this one?" Kiar asked.

Ròs' eyes dropped. "Why do you ask?"

"Your brooch. I recognized the symbol." Though it was her hands as much as her brooch that gave her away. Her fingers had the steady grace—and the calluses—of a musician.

The brooch lay on the ground still, glinting as a mist began to fall. Ròs picked it up. "I'm apprenticed to a healer now. I haven't told any stories in over a year."

"But you still remember," Kiar insisted. He edged forward, but the power of the well pushed him back. "You're a *shenachie.* You know the stories that answer every question. One of them *has* to answer mine."

Ròs stood and began to pace. "I know stories of men being turned to beasts, and of beasts that can disguise themselves as men. I know stories of the gods walking the earth as beasts, too, but—" Her mouth quirked. "You don't seem especially godlike."

Kiar almost laughed, startled by the sudden quickness of her smile. But it unsettled him, too—had she really decided to help him, or was she trying to disarm him?

"There is one tale," Ròs said. Her voice dropped, slipping into a soft rhythm that made Kiar lean forward, eager to catch the words. "It is not hard to tell."

Ròs wished she could've denied being a *shenachie*, but it was impossible. A thousand stories still spun through her mind, just waiting for a blazing hearth; a thousand melodies still thrummed in her fingers, just waiting to be released by a harp's strings. There was no fire beside the well and she had no harp, but she belonged to these stories, and they lent her voice power.

The bull listened avidly. He was a good audience, Ròs observed. As each story ended, he would ask questions. There were tales of *bhuidseach*, of bulls, of curses, but none of them were right. None of them gave him the key to destroying the witch. Ròs, caught up in her craft and his curiosity, was undaunted. She would begin another and the cycle started again.

It was only when dawn broke that she realized how exhausted she was. She fell asleep almost as soon as she lay down, but the dampness of the ground seeped through her mantle and skirts, and she woke up shivering.

Kiar's ears twitched. "You'll catch a chill if you stay so close to the well."

Ròs' teeth were chattering, but she hesitated.

"You can jump back into the circle again if we hear anything," he said quickly. "That would be all right, wouldn't it?"

For a moment, Ròs could almost picture him as a man, holding out his hand to her—his eyes sharp with concern yet his shoulders tensed, almost uncertain. Something flared in her chest, the brightness of it almost painful, but Ròs clenched her fist. He was a bull, not a man, and she needed him to stay that way.

Still, she left the circle and sat down beside him, beginning a story she'd woken up remembering. He nudged closer to her as she spoke and she leaned into the warmth of his fur, the chill slowly seeping out of her bones.

Days passed, and the *shenachie* still had stories to tell. Her voice transformed the little circle around the well into the peak of a mountain or the hollows under the hills.

Her voice had the power of spring rain, Kiar thought, bringing worlds to life.

Each day, he ventured out into the forest, shifting into a man in order to forage for wild herbs and mushrooms, though he always shifted back before returning to Ròs. Often, he heard the distant howl of a hound, but Madragh never appeared.

Kiar almost wished he would. He hated hiding.

"We have to find a way out before they find us," he told Ròs one evening, several weeks later.

"I know," she said quietly.

He glanced at her. She was getting thinner, he noticed. She couldn't keep living on mushrooms. "Ròs," he started. "What if I could get you to the forest's edge? It'd be risky, but—"

"What about you?" she asked sharply.

Kiar shrugged. "I'll manage. You can't stay here forever."

"Neither can you." Ròs moved away from his side, scooting forward until her face was in front of his. "I'm not giving up just yet."

"It's not giving up." He stood and stamped his hooves, relishing in the strength of the bull's form. "Trust me, I'm not dying as Muira's slave. I won't yield to her, to any of them."

Ròs' face tightened, and Kiar's eyes narrowed. "What is it?"

"Nothing." She hesitated, then repeated, "*I won't yield.* That just reminded me of a story, is all."

"What story?"

She plucked at a loose thread in her mantle. "It isn't important. I don't think it'll help us."

"But it might," Kiar insisted.

"Not this story."

"Why not?" Kiar shook his head impatiently. "Ròs, we don't even know what we're looking for anymore. *Any* story might be the one."

"All right," Ròs said, plucking up a blade of grass and knotting it around her fingers. "How did Deidra come to be called Deidra of sorrows? It is not hard to tell."

But her voice was thin.

As she began to speak, Kiar realized he knew the story, vaguely. He had heard it years ago. Still, he listened carefully for any new insight, any hint for how to defeat Muira.

The king of Alba, while visiting the island of Erin, stayed in the castle of a chief whose wife was in labor. The king's seer foretold that the child born would bring the death of many great men, for
her beauty would drive them mad. The king's warriors, unsettled by the seer's words, wanted to kill the child, but the king instead demanded her for himself. He took her from her mother's arms the very night she was born.

He hid Deidra away in his castle and allowed no man near her, rearing her to be his own as soon as she came of age. Deidra knew, always, that this would be her fate, but she refused to yield to him. Even after he took her into his bed, she searched for an escape.

One night, a band of warriors came to stay in the king's hall. He offered them hospitality, as a king should, and brought out Deidra to serve them. As she poured their wine, she studied the warriors, searching for the strongest, the most cunning. Fingal, the youngest son of their chief, easily surpassed the rest. Deidra caught his eye but he did not dare return her smile; he knew the king jealously protected his property. But later that night, Deidra crept from the king's bed and slipped down to the hall. Fingal, for all his fear of the king, could not resist Deidra. The two fled the castle before dawn.

The story, Kiar remembered, did not end happily, but it was not the story that twisted his heart. As Ròs sang Deidra's lament, the ache in her voice hung heavy in the air, and Kiar's throat constricted.

"Ròs," he said suddenly.

She broke off, blinking.

He'd never interrupted her before. But he had to.

"What?" she asked.

Kiar opened his mouth, but he didn't know how to answer. He had never asked why Ròs needed him to be a bull, or why she abandoned her harp and apprenticed herself to a healer. Her stories might teach them how to defeat Muira—that was all he'd cared about. Now, he could hear the pain in her voice, and shame burned in his gut. Half to break the silence and half because it was true, he said, "It hurts you, telling this story."

The tangle of grass dropped out of her hands. "It's a lament," she said shortly. "It's supposed to be sad."

"No," Kiar pressed. "It isn't just sad. It *hurts* you." He knew because it hurt *him* to hear the pain in her voice, worse than Muira's lash or Madragh's bite. He needed to help her—he needed to *know*. "Why, Ròs?"

Her fists clenched. "It's always hurt me, even before."

For the first time since the night they'd met, Kiar wanted to shift out of the bull's form. He wanted to reach out to her, take her in his arms and promise her she was safe there, yet he didn't dare.

He didn't want to see that fear on her face again.

"Then tell a different story, Ròs," he said, kneeling down next to her. "I don't much like this one either."

She bent her head, curls falling over her face, but as she began a new tale, she reached out and rested her hand on his side.

"That's Brìghde's harp," Ròs said, pointing up at a small cluster of stars.

The night was unusually clear, and while it was still cool, Ròs didn't mind. She was curled up against Kiar's side, just beyond the circle of the well—a position that had become so familiar, she found herself oddly cold and restless when he went foraging. She knew the rise and fall of his lungs and the rumble of his laugh; she knew every note of his voice the way she'd known the strings of her harp.

Tracing the shape of the constellation with her finger, she said, "The stars tell the stories of the gods, but without Brìghde's music, they would be silent and still. Her voice sets the sky spinning."

"Do you miss your harp?" Kiar asked.

"Yes," she replied without hesitation. "But it's gone now."

Kiar lifted his head to look at her. "My mother had a harp. When we get out of here—" He stopped abruptly, his ears twitching.

"What is it?" Ròs whispered.

"Get back to the well."

She hesitated, and then a howl split the air.

"*Run!*"

Kiar surged to his feet, horns lowered. Ròs scrambled towards the well and huddled against the stones.

Madragh launched out from the trees. Jaws wide, the hound flung himself at Kiar, only to dart away as the bull reared up. Kiar kicked at him, and the hound narrowly avoided those hooves. He circled the bull.

Shivering, Ròs dug her hands into the ground, feeling the sharp cold of the water.

Kiar lowered his horns and rushed at Madragh, catching the hound's side with his horn. Blood splattered over the turf. Madragh snarled, clawing at Kiar, his eyes moon-bright with rage. His frenzied movements seemed to disorient the bull, who stomped and twisted but couldn't land a clear blow.

Finally, Madragh pulled back, his snarl almost a smile. Sweat and blood matted Kiar's fur and he lowered his head for another charge.

Ròs wanted to shut her eyes but didn't dare. She watched, horrified, as the hound sprang over Kiar's horns and landed on his back. The bull writhed and kicked his front legs, trying to throw him off. Madragh morphed back into a man and, with a wild bark of a laugh, clung to Kiar's fur as the bull bucked.

Kiar threw himself to the ground, trying to crush the man, but Madragh leaped clear and shifted into a hound again. As Kiar lay prone, Madragh lunged. His teeth ripped into the bull's neck.

Kiar cried out in pain, an inhuman roar. Blood filled Ròs' mouth as she bit her lip harder and harder. Her fingers dug into the stones behind her until she touched a tangle of grass—a knot she'd woven days before. Pulling the fragile charm out, she pressed it against her mouth, soaking it in scarlet.

Madragh howled, his jaw about to close on Kiar's neck again. Ròs hurled herself out of the well's circle and shoved the hound away from Kiar, planting herself between them. As she swung the blood-knot at the hound, he jolted back.

In an instant, Madragh was a man again. "Step aside," he snarled, teeth dripping red.

Ròs lifted the knot higher. "No."

"Ròs, don't," Kiar said, his voice rough with pain. As Ròs glanced at him, her heart thudded.

He had shifted, and Ròs saw him as she hadn't since that first night. Red ran over his blue-black tattoos, the marks of the hound's teeth visible on his shoulder and chest. The white of his collarbone gleamed bright under the blood.

"Step aside, girl," Madragh repeated, his face twisted with hatred and hunger. "I'm putting an end to his interference." His blue eyes turned on Ròs. "Then I'll take back the prey he stole from me. Muira wants you."

Kiar rolled over, trying to get to his feet, only to collapse with a gasp. Ròs wanted to pull off her mantle and staunch the wound, but she had to hold up the knot.

"Then call her," she said.

Madragh started.

"Call her! If she wants me so badly, then *call her.*"

A low growl rose in Madragh's throat. Ròs thought the man was going to spring at her, but instead, he lifted his head and howled. The trees shivered as the sound died down. A terrible fear gripped Ròs' chest.

A power as strong as pain, Kiar had called it. She felt the tremors, ripping through her like a scream.

A woman appeared beside the brook, stone-pale and dark-eyed. Three torcs gleamed around her throat. Her red hair was garishly bright—as were the crimson stains on her grey mantle.

"Foolish girl," she said, her lips curving in a smile.

The knot in Ròs' hand burst into flame and she shrieked, letting go.

"Bring her here," Muira commanded. Her gaze fixed on Ròs, cold and craving.

Ròs reached for Kiar, but Madragh wrenched her away from him and threw her to the ground at Muira's feet. Ròs pushed herself up, glaring at the woman, but Muira's eyes were on her brooch.

"*Shenachie*," she said.

Ròs felt the woman's gaze cut into her bones, and she found herself saying hoarsely, "Not anymore."

"No?" Muira asked coolly, yet there was a sharpness in her expression. She lifted Ròs' chin with one slender finger. "Why not?"

Behind her, Ròs heard Kiar say her name, his voice ragged. She could not turn around. Muira's question slid between her ribs, and the truth spilled like blood. "There was a warrior," Ròs whispered. "His feats are honored throughout Alba. Wherever he goes, the lords offer him the best of their households."

She had heard so many stories of him, heard the awe in men's voices when they told the tales. When the warrior came to the castle where she was wintering, she'd felt a thrill of excitement. Her hands had trembled as she took up her harp.

"When I sang for him, I felt his eyes on me the whole night," she said softly, and she was in the hall again, her skin prickling from the fetid heat of his stare. A sickening dizziness gripped her, and she nearly retched, but the words tore out instead:

"He took what he liked from every household."

Something snapped in her chest. Ròs slumped. The spell of Muira's question had broken, leaving her ravaged, hollow. "I couldn't go back," she mumbled.

"I, too, would not go back," Muira said quietly. She unclasped the brooch at her shoulder and swept off her bloodstained mantle, dropping it to the ground in front of Ròs. "And that is the price I was willing to pay."

Ròs stared at the stains, strangely bright as though they would not dry.

"I was born to be the bride of a king," Muira continued. "Shut away in his castle until I came of age. When the warriors of his ally came to stay, I went secretly to the strongest and fairest of them, begging him to steal me away. He could not deny me. Yet we were hunted across Alba by the king and his brother. They killed my warrior, piercing him with two spears." Her face darkened. "Then they captured me. For a year they passed me between the two of them. Finally, I swore they would not have me any longer. I cursed them with my hate, and I flung myself from the king's horse as he carried me to his brother's castle."

Grief is heavier than the sea. The lines of Deidra's lament hummed in Ròs' mind, and her eyes widened as she looked from the mantle to Muira. In the woman's death-cold face, she saw the shadow of terrible pain.

Muira—Deidra—nudged the mantle with her foot. "But I did not die. The king met my curse with his own, and now I cannot be borne away to the *sídhe* until the stains are washed from my mantle." She leaned down, her face close to Ròs. "You can free me, *shenachie*."

"How?" Ròs asked, but she already knew the answer. The holy well, the one place in the forest Deidra could not go.

Seeing the understanding in Ròs' face, Deidra nodded. "You must wash the mantle in the well."

Ròs jerked away. "Make one of your shiftlings do it. Why should I help you?"

"You think I would trust this task to a man?" Deidra hissed. "They are no better than beasts." Then her gaze shifted to Kiar. "The bull is dying. He has a few hours at most before he chokes on his own blood. The water of the well could heal him, but he cannot go near it."

A chill choked Ròs' heart. She turned to Kiar, who looked back at her, his eyes strained. He was afraid, for her, for himself, yet while Ròs was terrified of the *bhuidseach* and the hound and the blood spilling from Kiar's chest, she realized the old fear—the one always crouched beneath her skin—was gone.

She was not afraid of Kiar. As she realized that, something gave way in her chest, like ice splintering apart. She could breathe again. In the sudden empty space, she felt fresh the pain of her grief, but it was shot through with hope, giving it a new shape and beauty as sunlight dazzles mist.

And when she faced Deidra, she saw how the woman's grief had made her cruel, and she pitied her. "If I free you, the spell on him will break?" she asked.

"Yes."

Ròs reached down and gathered up the mantle. "Then I'll do it."

Aware of Muira's eyes on her back, she walked to the well and flung out the mantle. The fabric caught in a curl of wind, then settled onto the surface of the water. Slowly, it began to sink. Ròs leaned over to watch it, her hair tumbling over her shoulder. Fiery curls trailed in the water, and beneath the surface, she saw clouds of red, the clear darkness soon thick with blood.

Wondering if she ought to use a stone to scrub at the stains, Ròs reached in to draw the mantle out.

Something caught hold of her hand.

Ròs let out a shriek as it dragged her in. For a moment there was nothing but blazing cold and bloodshot darkness. She thrashed, gasping for air, and found that she could breathe. There was solid ground beneath her again. Blinking, she squinted against an icy wind.

She was on a mountaintop. Stars glittered above, and the moon hung low and large over drifts of snow.

Reeling with the shock, Ròs' fingers tightened around the mantle in her arms. It was dry now, the stains as bright as ever. She anxiously shook it out again, kneeling in the snow and grabbing handfuls to rub against the stains.

"Please." She wasn't sure who she was talking to, but as her fingers grew numb and tears burned and froze on her cheeks, she couldn't help herself. "Please, I have to save Kiar."

So you will save Deidra, then?

She did not know if the voice was her own or if it came from the stars, but she replied, "Yes. If I free her, I can save Kiar."

And why should you save him?

"Because he's good."

Then why should you save Deidra? She is not good.

"Then she needs saving all the more." Ròs' retort echoed over the mountain.

And why does she need saving, shenachie*?*

A sob strained Ròs' throat but she choked a reply. "It is not hard to tell."

It was impossible to tell. Yet she began to sing. The notes rang in the ice-clear air and Ròs felt the story catch hold of her, until she could see figures around her. Wind blew over the drifts, sending up glittering eddies of snow, and the crystals formed the shapes of men and women, horses and swords and spears. There were other shades, too. There was a woman with a harp, and a man. The shadows twisted but Ròs could not look away. Deidra's lament twined with her own cry of pain.

Tears streamed down Ròs' cheeks and dropped, frozen, onto her hands. She continued to scrub at the mantle, her fingers red and raw, but she didn't feel them. She ached with sorrow, and fury, and most of all, a terrible desolation. She was alone on a mountaintop trying to save a *bhuidseach* she both hated and pitied.

Yet it was herself, too, that she hated and pitied.

Ròs shut her eyes. The stains were as bright as ever, and a slinking despair crept in. The mantle would never be clean. Deidra would never be free, any more than Ròs would ever be whole again.

"I can't do it!" she said, standing up and screaming the words like an accusation at the stars. "I can't!"

No, shenachie. *But I can.*

The voice was slight, just a hum under the howl of the wind. Ròs collapsed onto the snow, her body stiff with cold. Her lungs ached, her eyes burned, and then somewhere in the awful pain of it all, she heard a piercing note. A single chord that changed chaos into harmony.

Violet skimmed over the sky. The stars faded, though the moon stayed bright, and then gold scorched the horizon. Ròs watched, transfixed, as the sun rose and stretched its rays. The warmth poured over her. It hurt at first, her blood burning as the sensation returned. She cried out in agony, but the pain began to fade, and as her fingers tingled and her skin shivered delightfully under the heat of the sun, she realized just how numb she had been.

The snow sparkled and crumbled under the intense brightness, melting rapidly into the earth. Ròs was soon drenched but still the violent gentleness of the sun penetrated her, and she lay there in the morning light, aware only of its peace.

Kiar was cold. The mist seemed to be strangling him and he couldn't see past it; everything was shrouded in grey. He was aware of Madragh standing beside him, and of Muira—he could not see or hear her, but he felt her presence.

Then, suddenly, she was gone. He stirred, the movement agonizing. Madragh cursed and began to yell, but Kiar was too tired to make out the words. The man kicked him again and again, until blood filled Kiar's mouth. As he lay there, drowning in the grey, he saw Madragh lurch towards the well, calling for Muira. After a moment, the man turned away and began to run, still calling.

The clearing was empty. Kiar sat up, each breath agonizing, and realized he was completely alone.

Ròs had not returned.

Pain roped around Kiar's chest, crushing his lungs as he dragged himself towards the well. The ground squelched under his fingers, but there was no current of power driving him back—the curse was gone. The mist darkened, his body so *heavy*. Still Kiar crawled blindly forward.

His fingers brushed against stone. With one final, excruciating effort, he lifted himself over the edge and plunged into the water.

It was cold, but a delicious sort of cold. It soothed the burning pain in his shoulder. Then, behind Kiar's eyes, everything changed from total blackness to glowing red. He blinked, startled, and for a single moment, he saw the sun rising over a mountain. The earth and stone seemed to be on fire with color.

A woman, her hair blazing in the light, stood on the peak. Her mantle rippled behind her.

Kiar called out, thinking she was Ròs, but then the water closed around him once again. Frantic, he reached for her. His hand closed around someone's arm.

There was a desperate, lung-twisting moment of searching for the surface, and then he burst up into the dim light of the forest.

"Kiar!"

"Ròs?" Kiar spluttered. It was her arm he'd caught. "Ròs!"

Her wet hair trailed over her face as she treaded water, surging towards him. He caught her, holding her tight, but immediately began to sink. Ròs clung to him as he kicked to stay afloat, both of them spluttering and laughing. Kiar grabbed hold of the well's rim. He clambered out, pulling her up along with him.

As Kiar helped her down onto the turf, he wanted to brush the wet curls from her face. Yet he tensed. A moment ago, they'd been tangled up in each other's arms, but now they were on the ground again and he remembered, in hazy snatches, her conversation with Muira.

The curse was broken, yet he wished he could transform, just so he wouldn't have to see that look of panic on her face again. And still he wanted desperately to hold her.

Her fingers ran over his shoulders, and instantly his muscles relaxed under her touch.

"You're healed," she said. "It worked!"

Kiar gently rested his hand on top of hers, his thumb rubbing over the place where the wound had been. There was only the slight ridge of a scar. "You did it."

"No. I don't think I did. But it's done." She gave a quick flash of a smile. "I'll tell you, later. It is not hard to tell."

She leaned closer, her fingers curled against his neck, tangling into his hair. Then her mouth was on his, a fierce rush of a kiss. He kissed her back, pulling her against him. She stiffened, just for a second, but before he could let go, she softened, burying her head in his neck and kissing the fresh scar.

"Let's go home," she whispered.

Kiar pressed his lips against her hair, then twined his hands into hers. They didn't look back as they left the clearing.

The mist faded fast. It seemed only moments later that they reached the edge of the forest, the sudden wideness of the landscape taking their breath away. The valleys and mountains and rivers spread out before them, drenched in morning light.

Kiar pointed towards one of the mountains, a sudden joy rising in his chest. "That's where my home is, Ròs."

She leaned against his shoulder. "Then that's where we'll go. Though it'll take longer now that I can't ride on your back."

Kiar grinned and swung her up into his arms. "I can still carry you," he said, beginning to run.

Ròs wrapped her arms around his neck, and her laughter sang across the valley.

"And that's
why
I love you."

Cracked Roses

Anne J. Hill

FOR TWENTY-FIVE YEARS, roses were set on her doorstep every Sunday morning. She'd pluck them up, trim the stems, and stick them proudly in a glass vase until, one by one, they'd slowly shrivel in old age. Their bright red shade deepening to a darker maroon. And that's when she knew it was time.

She'd pull the crinkled roses from the slimy water, dab off the stems, and carry them to his grave.

In life, he'd made her promise to enjoy the roses before they faded and then to leave them with him. There was no sense in giving him living flowers if no one could enjoy them, he'd said.

He'd always been so practical.

She smiled at the thought as she lay them gently by his stone, careful to leave the petals intact. Her fingers caressed his engraved name, and she let out a sigh. Cracking open a book, she began to read to him a tale about a man with strong opinions and 'practical' ideas that melted from a simple touch or word from the woman he loved.

A peevish man who now lay in the ground because he'd given his life to save his beautiful wife twenty-five years ago.

That was their story, forever remembered in the words she penned.

She closed the book and whispered to the man in the ground, "I think roses are prettier when they're dried and cracked and been through a thing or two. When roses die, I get to come see you. It's very impractical of me, I know."

She could almost hear him say, if he'd been there, "And that's why I love you."

Red in the Rain

Everly Haywood

PREQUEL TO *GRIMKEEPER*

PEREGRIN BLODRHYS WOULD never understand why a cat who hated getting wet insisted on taking walks with him in the rain.

But, then, who knew what truly went on in the mind of a fae cat? They were devilish, opinionated...and absolutely adorable. For all their flaws, he loved every one of the felines who had adopted him and his sister Ava. There were probably a dozen of them living at Rhys Manor at present. They came and went as they pleased, so it was difficult to keep an accurate count of the meddlesome things. Puck stirred in his arms; her purr halted with a hiccup.

"Sorry," Peregrin muttered. "But you *are* meddlesome, you know."

She yowled disagreeably and dug her claws into his arm as punishment.

"I will put you down," he threatened but not unpleasantly. The pressure against his skin eased as the fae cat relaxed back into the crook of his arm, safely sheltered under his cloak.

The gray tabby rubbed her long, tufted ears against his arm and sent him a vision of their library back home. It was filled with a warm glow from the flickering blue flames known only to the dark elves of Gelaira. A dozen other cats lounged around, soaking up the heat of the fireplace.

"I know," he replied. "I'm heading home. I feel better now."

Long walks often soothed his spirit, especially on dreary days. Something about the gentle sound of rain against the ground and trees made his pulse beat a little slower, and his thoughts spin less wildly.

Puck sent him another vision, this time of a dark elf maiden with lovely blue-gray skin and glossy dark hair. He recognized her from the local flower shop.

"I don't need a wife." He shifted the fae cat to his other arm just to annoy her. They'd had this conversation many times before. Still, Puck insisted that he find himself a companion—a non-*feline* companion.

She persisted and sent him another vision of the pretty maid batting her eyelashes at him.

"Ava doesn't like her. I could never consider anyone that didn't suit Ava."

The vision evaporated in an annoyed puff. Peregrin smiled to himself, but a moment later, a new vision replaced the old one. This time it was Melan, the seamstress who mended his coats. Pleasant but a little overly invested in search of a companion of her own.

He sighed. "She doesn't like to read. That's non-negotiable."

The image fizzled away only to be replaced by the stoic face of the baker's daughter.

"She never laughs. I would prefer someone who would at least know *how* to smile. Life can be so...well, *you know.* And I would like someone who could lift my spirits. Not remind me of my troubles."

Puck meowed irritably. The next image she flung at him featured a maid in a gaudy costume of vibrant purple who pranced about on a stage making silly faces.

"I like red," he said. "Red is my favorite color." The crimson of a violent sunset, to be precise. Or the hue of the red roses that used to bloom in Ava's garden.

Gelaira didn't have much color left. Not since the Shadewood Forest began to get sick and the dark elves along with it. Everything was dark and pale and damp and sullen. Whatever ailment afflicted them, the elfin wives could no longer conceive children. The gardens struggled to grow anything except weeds. The trees in the forest were covered in mildew and grew sicker by the day.

Peregrin rounded a bend in the road and sighed to himself. Puck purred gently to console him, and he lifted his other hand to scratch between her long ears. Of all the cats he cared for, Puck had wormed her way to the head of the line. She occupied the pillow beside him nearly every night, chasing off any usurper who dared to set their sights on her throne. The others typically left her alone and crowded around his legs and in the crook of his arm instead.

She sneezed loudly just then as if annoyed by the turn of his thoughts.

"Apologies...but you *do* hog the pillow, you know. It wouldn't hurt to share from time to time."

Puck stirred and wriggled until she dropped to the ground, landing in a puddle with a splash. She hissed, arched her back and shot him a foul look. When his only response was to lift placating hands, she flounced off into the trees.

Peregrin rolled his eyes and walked on.

An ostentatious but forlorn-looking manor came into sight. It belonged to a scribe he occasionally had the misfortune of bumping into at the palace.

So'lar was about as dreary as they came.

He quickened his pace to pass by but faltered when he saw someone sitting on So'lar's front step.

Not just any someone, but a maiden—a *human* girl—dressed in a simple frock and apron adorned with two broaches and a strand of beads between them. And her hair...

He had never seen anyone with hair the color of the sunset. It cascaded over her shoulders, wild and untamed despite the steady drizzle. Her narrowed gaze caught sight of him and held. He looked away and hurried past her but couldn't resist the urge to glance back over his shoulder a moment later. The young woman had not moved from her perch on the step and continued to follow him with her eyes. It occurred to Peregrin then that the poor girl might be in distress. Not to mention, she must have been soaked to the skin.

"Are you in need of assistance?" he stammered. It only seemed the proper thing to do, after all.

The young woman clasped her hands around her knees and sat up straighter. "I am *not*." Her gaze could curdle fresh milk. "I am enjoying this lovely weather, is all."

He retraced his steps, fascinated by the ire in her musical voice. He wondered what had brought her here and why she found it necessary to take her frustration out on him. "Have you had some sort of...misunderstanding with So'lar?"

She snorted in a most unfeminine way. "Oh, you could say that. Apparently, marriage to a servant girl is beneath his dignity. I say marriage to *him* is beneath *my* dignity."

Ah. Of course. He should have known. Human maids arrived several times a year as part of the peace treaty between the two kingdoms. Since the dark elves could no longer bear children of their own, women came from Haldor to ensure that the Gelairan line did not die off completely.

No one was happy about the arrangement.

"Indeed? Then why are you still sitting on his doorstep?"

"Because he may kick me out, but I won't make it easy on him." She waved a dismissive hand. "Besides, I don't know where to go. I'm not stupid enough to wander around in the woods, inviting some strange Gelairan beastie to take a bite out of my—"

She cut off abruptly and shot him a strange look. He felt his cheeks warm a bit and coughed to hide his discomfort.

"I see." He debated a second before seating himself beside her on the step. "Well, I'm afraid you'll be sitting here for a long time. I know Lord So'lar...he won't change his mind." He tried to speak gently but didn't want her to waste her time or get her hopes up.

"Well, there is nothing I can do about that," she said. "I know I'm not Lady Eirika, but I volunteered to come in her stead and won't be going home. Not until I have what I've come for anyway."

He slanted his eyes at her. "And what have you come for?"

"My sister. She's been here for a year and a half, and I haven't heard a peep from her. I intend to find her and rescue her."

"Rescue her? You think she's in some sort of danger?" His heart pattered strangely at the thought.

"She was stolen from our home and forced into marriage, so...yes...I think she's in trouble."

He winced but conceded she had every right to be angry. The peace treaty allowed human women to be taken against their will when wives were needed in Gelaira. However, the dark elves didn't like it much either. But despite how she felt about it all, this girl had come to Gelaira anyway. She must love her sister very much.

He understood the love for a sister. His own held a special place in his heart, though she quite often became the cause of his low spirits and long walks, even in the rain. "And yet you volunteered to suffer the same fate," he murmured, studying her with renewed interest.

"So I could find her. Besides, I'm built to suffer hardship. I have the temperament for it. Eirika and Anrid...they're meant for finer things."

She launched off the step and began to pace back and forth, arms swinging at her sides. Indeed, she *was* firmly built, not as willowy or graceful as most of the elves he knew. And while she wasn't necessarily what he would consider *beautiful,* there was something about her that appealed to him.

The crimson hair, naturally. That must be it.

A vision swept over him then, of opening his eyes to see hair the color of the sunset spilled across a pillow beside him.

Puck.

He all but snarled at the thought. He tried to dash away the vision and the flush it had brought to his cheeks. Puck must've been lurking in the bushes somewhere. He hazarded a look at the human girl and couldn't help wondering what it *would* be like waking up to the sunset every morning.

"Anrid is your sister?" he asked. The woman spun on her heel and marched back the other way, splashing through puddles with little thought to her shoes.

"Yes. And Lady Eirika used to be my employer. She's the closest thing to a friend I've ever had. I couldn't let them take her."

"So you volunteered to save your friend and hopefully your sister. That's quite noble."

She snorted again. "Hardly. It was practical, is all. I simply did what had to be done."

"It's more than most people would have done."

The girl faltered and gazed down at him. An awkward pause took over the conversation. He could feel her eyes on him and looked everywhere but directly at her, his cheeks growing warmer by the second. He finally flicked his eyes up at her. "And how did your parents feel about this arrangement of yours?"

Her expression twisted. "My parents died from the crimson fever three years ago. It's been just me and Anrid since then. I take care of her, and she takes care of me."

"I see," he whispered. He felt her pain twist in him like a knife. His own parents' death had been just as tragic...and far, far more violent. "I know that kind of grief. My sister and I are also on our own. It is not...not the sort of fate I would wish on anyone."

She turned sideways to study him straight on. "You have a sister too?"

He clasped his knees with both hands and nodded. "I've been taking care of her for almost ten years now."

"Is she still a child then?"

"Oh no." He rocked side to side a little. "She is younger by two years. She works at the palace now. She's a gifted healer." He rose to his feet and brushed off the back of his cloak. "I cannot linger, but I can escort you to Eroth if you wish. I fear you'll sit here until you faint from hunger if you remain."

"I'm not the fainting sort." Her expression looked as defiant as her tone sounded.

He suppressed a smile and dipped his chin. "I can see you are not. My apologies."

The rain began to fall heavier as she snatched up her pack and slung it over her shoulder. He led the way, to the east, toward Eroth, and she easily matched his long stride. Something rustled in the bushes.

Puck. He sent a dark, warning thought in her direction and caught a glimpse of a gray tail twitching at him jauntily from a bush before vanishing out of sight.

Impertinent thing. He couldn't help but love her, although he wondered why she seemed to think he needed a bride so severely. He wasn't exactly the social sort and would rather read a book than try to hold polite conversation. He was hardly pleasant company most days, too many things weighing heavily on his mind. And his future...well, that was very uncertain. He couldn't ask anyone to share that life with him.

Could he?

Peregrin stuffed the disturbing thought aside to mull over later. He knew he should initiate polite conversation—that's what a fellow should do when taking a walk with a girl, he supposed—but he found himself at a loss for words. She didn't seem inclined to talk either. Should he ask her about her favorite book, perhaps? Or if she liked animals? Those were things that interested him, but she might think him foolish. She seemed like a straightforward and practical girl who probably didn't have time for trivial things.

Things like books and cats.

"Where do you intend to look for your sister, girl?" he asked, pushing aside the unease in his belly.

Her icy gaze could have speared him with its sharpness. "My name is Dagmar Fray," she said. "I don't answer to *girl*."

He winced and struggled to suppress a blush. "Noted." He hesitated and looked back to the road. "I answer to Peregrin."

"That's a funny name. For an elf, I mean. You're all so—" She waggled a hand at him. "—severe, and yet you have the word *grin* in your name."

"Are you making fun of me?"

"Yes." Her cheeks reddened, which darkened her eyes. The look was quite attractive with that profusion of crimson hair draped over her shoulder.

Peregrin decided that he highly approved of red hair.

He cleared his throat. "You're...impertinent."

She blew out a breath. "I will tell you how it is," she said, completely unabashed. "You should know that upfront. I don't lie, and I don't small talk and sugar coat things."

He'd picked up on that. And yet, for some reason, he'd begun to like this fiery human lass. She was so...not dark elf. "It would behoove you to weigh your words from time to time," he suggested with a slight smile. "Or you will find yourself spending more time on doorsteps, Miss Fray." When her eyes swept to his, he found himself wanting to nettle her a bit more, to see that blush darken her eyes again. He grinned and added, "in the rain."

And there it was, sweeping across her features like a cloud across the sun, though one that somehow made her brighter rather than darker. "Are you making fun of *me*?" She sounded outraged, but her lips twitched in a way that suggested she wanted to smile.

Please smile, he thought. He truly wanted to see her smile. An image of Dagmar simpering and smiling and batting her eyes blinded him momentarily. He swept a hand through the empty air and glared at the trees. *For love of the flames, Puck! You'll be sleeping outside tonight, for sure.*

A plaintive yowl and rustling came from the ferns brushing against his cloak. This time when Puck invaded his thoughts, she sent an image of herself huddled outside in a torrential downpour, her green eyes abnormally large and pleading.

His heart melted. *Fine. I wouldn't really lock you out. But behave.*

The large green eyes blinked slowly, suggesting she might accept the peace offering. The Puck in his head turned and bounded into shadows. When the vision disappeared, the rustling in the underbrush stilled.

He breathed a sigh of relief.

The city of Eroth came into sight just then as the trees peeled back to make room. The rain slowed to a trickle as they picked their way down the muddy path toward the first row of sturdy wooden buildings topped with dark blue tiles. The palace rose above the one and two-story structures, its tiers and towers at once graceful and forbidding.

He hated the palace. *That* place. A terrible place where terrible things happened.

His hands trembled, but he splayed them against his legs to hide the tremoring.

"It's so...quiet." Dagmar's eyes flicked back and forth as she studied the city with critical interest.

"It's raining. Everyone's inside."

She sniffed. "A little rain never hurt anybody. Back home, it wouldn't affect doings in the slightest. A full-blown blizzard is about the only thing that would drive *my* people back to their homes."

"I have heard your people are most...stalwart." He fumbled over the words, hoping they came out like a compliment and not an insult.

She met his gaze briefly and had the nerve to look smug. "I am sure your people have other words they would rather attribute to us than *stalwart*."

He flinched. "I can't argue with that. There's always been tension between our people. From the beginning of time, I suppose. The history books are filled with wars and misgivings. But," he continued, wetting his lips, "it seems we have stumbled upon a fragile peace for the time being. Perhaps our people can finally learn to work together."

"As long as we don't mind our women being used for breeding stock."

Horrified, he choked and coughed noisily into his fist. "It isn't like *that*—"

"How is it then?" Her eyes flashed with thinly veiled anger. "Tell me. How is it when no one *asks* us if we mind being torn from our homes and forced to marry total strangers?"

He found himself at a loss for words, muted by her anger. She had every right to be angry, he couldn't argue with that, but he wished there was something he could say to appease her. He didn't like the thought that she might hate him for what his people did to hers. Why it should matter what she thought of him, he didn't know, but it did. It mattered.

"I'm sorry," he managed to say as they turned down a side street. The words felt insufficient, but he could think of nothing else to say.

The rain slowed to a trickle, and by the time they reached the end of a long alleyway, it stopped altogether. He flipped the cowl of his cloak back and breathed deeply. "You have every right to hate me, I suppose. But I wish you wouldn't...I had nothing to do with the peace treaty. Very few of us did. And we, too, have little choice when it comes to marriage. It's all arranged, and we are informed afterward."

"So'lar seemed to have a choice."

"Yes, well, *he* thinks he is above the rules. And it is not unprecedented for matches not to work out; I've heard of women being reassigned before."

"*Reassigned*?" Dagmar's voice held a bitter edge.

He winced and shot her an apologetic look. "I wish circumstances were different, but my people are at the mercy of our king as surely as you are bound to yours. The arrangement is generally as unpleasant for us."

"I doubt that. I'd like to see your king ship *his* daughter off to marry a total stranger. See how he feels about his peace treaty then."

"We aren't all of his mindset, you know."

Her pace slowed as she studied him. "So *you* wouldn't mind marriage to a servant girl then?"

A flush crept over his cheeks. She was baiting him, obviously, but to what end? "No," he answered truthfully as he stopped walking and looked down into her piercing eyes. "No, I would not."

She didn't seem to believe him. The skepticism was etched on her freckled cheeks and pressed lips Centuries of mistrust, and hard feelings between their peoples had painted their opinions of one another long before he found her on that doorstep. And yet, although he couldn't say why, he wanted her to think well of him.

His fingers twitched against his thighs. "I would not find marriage to you distasteful because of your station, Miss Fray. I am little more than a servant myself."

A slave, by all intents and purposes.

"But you would find me distasteful for other reasons then."

How could he find flashing green eyes and crimson hair distasteful? "I don't think I would," he finally managed. "You seem...nice. A little too free with your criticism, I grant you. But I do not think you're the dredge of society just because you're human. If that's what your worried about."

Her head reared back. "I am not worried *at all* what you think of me." She looked downright insulted by the implication.

"I—I didn't mean to offend you."

"Well, you have. Why would I ever worry what you think of me?"

Why indeed? He sighed inwardly and turned to resume his walk. He quickened his pace, suddenly anxious to be home and free of this needle-some creature who seemed determined to misunderstand every word he uttered. Home lay just a little bit ahead, at the end of the street along the city's southern edge.

She followed him in silence for several minutes before sighing loudly. "Fine. I'm sorry, all right? I warned you I speak my mind. You shouldn't take it personally."

He stared at his feet as they walked. "I don't."

"Then why are you sulking?"

"I'm not—I mean to say—I wish we could be amicable, is all."

"Amicable." The incredulity in her tone tugged his gaze in her direction at last. Her eyes held his. Was it his imagination, or had her expression softened?

"Yes. Amicable. You know. *Not combative*."

"You want us to be friends." She spoke slowly and seemed to mull the concept over in her mind.

"Ah. Yes, I suppose so. I think we could be friends, Miss Fray. I don't dislike you." Was that compliment enough to soothe her irritation?

"But you don't like me either."

He pursed his lips and frowned. "I never said that. You deliberately misunderstand everything I say, you know. It's...unpleasant. I would like you *better* if you tried to like me."

"I don't dislike you," she echoed his own words with a saucy lift to her mouth. "You're so gentlemanly and agreeable."

"Now you're teasing me. Do you always tease strangers, Miss Fray?"

She shrugged. "When I feel they need it."

"You think I need to be tormented by human girls who have been tossed out by their suitors?"

Oh, Flames. He shouldn't have said that.

But, to his surprise, she threw back her head and laughed. "Don't you? Why else would you have offered to escort me to the city, *kind sir*? You don't have dishonorable intentions, do you?"

Heat exploded in his cheeks and swept right up to his ears. "For love of—no! No, I do *not*."

"So perhaps we can be—what was the word you used? Amicable? Perhaps we can be amicable."

The heat dissipated slowly, like steam from a tea kettle removed from the fire. "Do you really think so?"

Her shoulders hitched in another shrug. "Why not?"

Why not indeed.

Rhys Manor came into view as a different sort of warmth crept over him. There was no denying it. He did rather like this girl, and not just because he appreciated the color of her hair or the freckles on her nose. He had the feeling a girl like her could brighten up a dreary day.

When she wasn't feeling cantankerous and nettled, that is.

Peregrin slowed to a stop in front of a wrought iron gate that broke through the low stone fence wrapping around Rhys Manor and its spacious yard.

"This is where I live," Peregrin said. He didn't know what to do now. Should he wish her well and send her on her way? Offer her something to eat? Would she take his offer the wrong way and assume some *dishonorable intentions*?

Her eyes swept over Rhys Manor and back to him.

"Yes, well, thank you for the escort," she finally said.

He knew he should send her off now, but instead, he lingered. He didn't want her to go quite yet. "Perhaps...perhaps it would be unwise for me to turn you loose in the city," he finally managed. That wouldn't be *gentlemanly* of him, would it? "I mean, you have no place to go. What will you do? Have you any money for food or lodging?"

No, it wouldn't be gentlemanly at all.

"I don't have much money." She sounded uncomfortable despite the blunt answer. "But don't worry about that. I'm a hard worker, and I'll find a job and earn my keep. It will be far preferable to So'lar, at least." She stirred and shifted her feet. "Well, then, I suppose this is good—"

"Perhaps you would like to meet my sister," he blurted, cutting her off mid-sentence.

Her eyes narrowed slightly, but curiosity parted her lips. "Why?"

Oh, Flames, why? He couldn't very well tell her he liked her hair or that he found her amusing. Why *did* he want her to stay? He pondered the question for a long, awkward moment. Truth be told, he'd been thinking it ever since he found her on So'lar's front step.

Even Puck had seen it.

He *liked* her. Without even knowing her, he liked her. And he needed someone in his life to brighten the days and to take care of his sister when he was gone, which might be sooner than he would like. "I, er, well, I should like to discuss that after you meet my sister."

Still, she remained frozen in place, not trusting him.

"Please. You need my help...and I might have need of yours. Will you not come inside?"

Her stiff shoulders relaxed ever so slightly. Could he assume that meant she was considering the invitation? He didn't want to pressure her or seem too eager, so he fumbled with the latch on the gate, swung it open and stepped inside. He turned and waited to see if she would follow him.

Her eyes held his for a long moment. Time seemed to stand still, and he counted the breaths that expanded and contracted his chest. *Please stay.*

After a long moment, she broke eye contact, shrugged, and swept past him, down the path choked with weeds and right up onto his front porch.

He smiled and trotted after her.

A familiar tingling preceded the invasion into his thoughts as Puck trucked into his mind with another vision. She must have gotten home already. She smirked at him moments before the scene changed to him wrapping his arms around a certain lass with hair the color of sunsets. His dreamself was kissing Dagmar quite passionately.

For crying out loud, Puck!

The fae cat's snickers echoed in his thoughts as he fumbled with the key to the front door.

Peregrin and Dagmar's story will continue in Grimkeeper

They call me a saint
A guardian to keep
Them safe in the night
The keeper of the woods

But what they don't know
Is my elvish flesh turns
To something quite different
Under the crescent moon

A monster within
A monster without
Waiting, praying
To find a way out

Until then, I'll roam
Keep myself hidden
And I'll protect them
Until she loves what's within

Related to Thorn Tower *by Anne J. Hill*

UNFAMILIAR STARS

Bernadette Lamb

When iron cuts through mist and flesh
Will a healer come to heal?
—the Scroll of Harden, Earthen translation

EVEN BEFORE TRIN woke, she felt the bruise blossoming. The thrum behind her eyes first reminded her of the sleep-bot back home . . . until a clatter snapped her awake. Shadows crowded her vision and a rote prayer to the gods escaped her lips. She painfully leveraged herself off the ground—a metal floor interspersed with grates—and blinked.

Gone were the familiar rows of vials and tissue regenerators. The corner where her desk chair with the loose wheel should have been was dark and piled high with cargo. The noise had come from a loose grate as the oxy system refreshed. Here, the stale air was shot through with a scent that was not her own. She shuddered, fingering her sore forearm with a gloved hand. At least he hadn't broken any skin.

Unbidden, the events of the last several hours began to bleed back into Trin's memory. The sensor warning of an incoming ship. One not piloted too well, she remembered. Rivka's comm request. Then the rush when they realized the ship wasn't stopping, Rivka's warning to stay hidden, the collision on the starboard side—the Unvill's towering frame, his hand on her arm, the pressure change in the airlock, the look on Rivka's face through the glass…

Gofton's beard. Her mentor could be lightyears away now.

Choking back the urge to vomit, Trin stumbled to her feet. Only the thought of escape flooded her mind. Nine steps forward in the dark, and she found the edge of the bay door. She went to heave it aside, and almost fell when it slid open at the slightest pull.

She squinted. *Great.* Vessels built by the Unvillem were not made for her light-loving eyes. After creeping midway down an empty hall, she glanced up. Silver shone dully, and she found herself marveling at the intricate metalwork. Fog clouded beneath one set of doors. To her right, a window stood between her and the blackness of space. A familiar blackness interspersed with terrifyingly unfamiliar stars.

Another rattle. The thin thumping that she had thought was the oxy system deepened. Willing her heart to stop thundering, she turned right and found herself face-to-face with the cockpit—and her captor.

He looked smaller than he had several hours ago. Frozen in the middle of his rampage, or whatever ungodly commotion he had been making, his eyes found hers. Two pilot seats suffered long scratches from his claws. She was separated from him by several feet now, but the bruise on her arm remembered his touch.

He gestured helplessly at the controls behind him.

"I—" he stuttered, huge jaws making their way around some word.

After several moments, in which Trin was not attacked or yelled at, she offered, "…yes?"

"Fix me," he blurted.

"Pardon?"

Met with a vigorous shake of the head, she noticed the beginnings of a colorless pallor beneath his blue mane. He stalked toward her, stopping when she readied herself to run.

"I'm ill and need…fixing," he growled, then looked away. His voice was wide and careful, and Trin realized that her language must be strange to him. "No, that is not right. I need heal—"

"Healing," Trin breathed.

"Yes." Frustration flooded his eyes again. "And now that I found you—doctor—you, you can fix—"

"I—do I *look* like a damali healer?" She wanted to gesture incredulously at herself, but her hands were trembling. He only blinked. Defensively, she crossed her arms, and something dawned on his face. "Violet," he mumbled. "I thought it was violet...."

All of a sudden, Trin realized he was talking about the colored hem of her bio-robe. No. He'd made the mistake of thinking she was a qualified doctor, not a lowly junior scientist. *Maybe he's colorblind, too,* she thought with spite.

"But you are...?" he said.

"No, I am not," she snapped, finally finding her voice. "I'm just studying to be one. And what, you're saying you didn't even think to kidnap the *older* of us?"

He grunted. Was that sheepishness on his face? "How... how old are you?"

Trin pursed her lips. "Almost seventeen cycles."

"Earth cycles?"

She nodded. "And you look about a hundred."

"Eighteen," the Unvill muttered, then scoffed. "Who in this galaxy uses Earth cycles?"

Ready to pluck her own eyes out, Trin exploded. "*My* people, the Fercren, do, and if you don't mind, I'd rather you not ask such stupid questions when the real question is *where the freezing pits are we?!*"

"Maybe I would answer if you DID NOT YELL!"

Trin opened her mouth, then thought better of it at the sight of his fangs. The ridges along her cheekbones tightened.

"We are on the border of the Korez system," he explained, flexing clawed hands.

Her stomach plummeted. They were in a veritable desert. Without warp capabilities, Rivka's science vessel would take months to get to them. "So, what is your plan?" she rasped.

The Unvill's face hardened, and he stepped nearer. His hot breath blew against her ear. "I do not plan to die. There is a lab here that I will take you to. Find my treatment. Until then, we go nowhere. Then will I pilot you back."

Trin swallowed. "At warp?"

"At warp," he promised.

He turned right, and, a bit unwillingly, Trin followed him deeper into the belly of the ship. As she started to map an escape route in her mind, it dawned on her how large the place actually was. Hall after hall of sliding doors... and the more ornamentation she saw, the more she wondered what it all was for. Her captor stalked ahead, the embroidery on his collar catching the meager light. This was far too fine to be an ordinary vessel, and even with his six-and-a-half-foot frame, the Unvill didn't take up enough space to justify flying such a whale of a ship.

Thank Harden he didn't touch her, but she instinctively pulled her gloves tighter.

Toward the end of a second-floor corridor, he gestured to the left. "Your room, for later," he growled. After rounding one final corner, he waved her through a set of wide glass doors.

A soft light flickered on. Trin couldn't help but gasp—the lab was three times as large as Rivka's, and while much of the equipment was completely foreign to her, she spied the latest Hgraff tissue regenerator standing tall above it all. Forgetting the Unvill, she rushed past him to run her hand along the drawers of supplies. Dehydrated disinfectants, calibrated surgical implements, an entire cabinet filled with bioprosthesis of all shapes and sizes, coma-pills for the most dire operations—she'd only heard rumors of such advanced medical tech. Then a thought splintered her reverie.

"Why didn't you leave me here instead of the loading dock?" she accused.

"The ship needed attention," he said curtly, holding her gaze.

An awkward moment passed. Behind her initial thrill, Trin ached for home. She began to hatch a plan... but nothing would work if the Unvill didn't trust her completely. Flipping her well-practiced emotional switch, she put her hands on her hips.

"Well, apparently you do, too," she admitted with professional firmness. "And if I'm not going anywhere until you're well, I might as well try my best."

A hopeful flicker crossed his face. Suddenly he fell forward, catching himself on the edge of a cart. Trin's heart lurched and she moved to help him, but he held out a claw.

"I am all right," he grunted. "Now I shall share about my illness, the... what is that word?"

"Symptoms." Trin rubbed her temples. She motioned to a nearby chair and stood in front of him as he sat, doing her best to quiet her nerves. He was more than just her kidnapper; he was a bitter enemy of her people. It was likely that not a single Fercren had survived an encounter with an Unvill in a generation, so she hardly knew what "normal" looked like. She was only aware that they were built for the cold climate of their home planet and shockingly adaptable. Reportedly, they had three lungs. But Fercren media had only ever been concerned with the Long War's body count, not enemy medicine. And up until this point, so had she.

The Unvill's pallor had not improved. With clinical precision, she began to question him. No puncture wounds or any clear place where an infection may have originated. No respiratory difficulties and no flu symptoms, at least not the kind she knew of. Despite all this, he was intensely fatigued, dehydrated even after consuming buckets of water, and had begun dry coughing. It was something internal, but there were hundreds of possibilities…

Carefully, she drew a blood sample. Standing this close, she could feel the heat through his fur.

"I don't suppose your doctors left any helpful records, did they?"

"No." He stared past her at the windowless wall.

"Or…a manual on Unvill physiology?"

He nodded toward an upper cabinet where she found four enormous volumes. Their spines cracked when she flipped them open. The text may have been in Unvillian, but at least she could surmise some things from the illustrations.

A part of her wanted to ask more, but anger and fear had taken up residence in her gut. She had no time for real compassion, so she would only learn what she needed to.

"Well," she announced some time later, "I've run all the initial tests. Now we wait."

The Unvill nodded solemnly. He rose while she sat at the counter, searching for the drawer that held labels and type-pads. On his way out the door, he paused. "I must at the least know your name," he grumbled.

Taken aback, she glanced up from her chair. "Trin. Trin Beross."

The Unvill struck his chest with one hand. "And I am Mildar of Ok-Vrem. Tell me what you find in six Earth hours." With a brooding look, he strode out of the lab.

Trin let out a slow breath. She was in for a long night.

Day Three

"Join you? Absolutely not," she seethed. Trin turned her back to him, occupying herself with the lamp suspended above. The room was too beautiful to be a mess hall, but she couldn't bring herself to call it a dining room. That would be giving the Unvillem too much credit. And after several days, she could tell that Mildar's head was big enough already.

"It is only food," he growled, then sneered. "I did not ask for such a selfish healer."

Her jaw went slack. "Selfish? Who's selfish, the kidnapped girl or the brute with a savior complex, despite the fact that *he* kidnapped her?" She crossed her arms. "Anything I do, I do because *I* have chosen it. And I choose not to eat a posh dinner just so you can pretend I'm some Unvill princess."

Mildar's heavy brow furrowed.

"You Fercren do not know what it means to have a feast," he explained through his teeth. "The food matters, but dress does also. A guest must…change their scent and hair, or they will be dismissed. At least, that is what would happen to you if we were on my home planet."

"Oh, well, if I'd known my *smell* bothered you so much, I'd have stopped washing my hair," she retorted, tossing her short auburn braid behind her.

He rolled his eyes. "It is not like I am going around smelling your hair."

"You know what," Trin said, red in the face, "fine. I will humor you, my patient." She curtsied mockingly. "Dinner it is. But no…scents."

Though she'd not shared many words with Mildar, she had begun to surmise his situation. He was immature, egotistical, stubborn—and, every once in a while, halfway polite. As they sat down to eat, she could tell that he had a formal background, like when he insisted on correct napkin folding. He had clearly been raised as nobility or in some environment of political power. Even more obviously, he had been kicked out. With a smirk, she wondered if napkins had been the last straw.

They chewed in silence. Trin didn't know what she had expected, really. Soon, her mind was filled with floating medical illustrations and all the equations she'd tried and failed…then, suddenly, the garish war footage that had been released just last month rose to the surface. Dark profiles of high-ranking Unvillem, war criminals and butchers. Fercren bodies littering the decks of seized warships.

"Your plate," Mildar grumbled. Startled, she glanced up and held out the empty dish. He gripped the opposite rim, and she forced herself to search his face. It was nearly as broad as it was long, pocked with leathery patches as blue as his fur. His eyes flashed—exactly like every Unvill murderer she had ever seen onscreen. Realizing her hand was still on the plate, Trin let go. She stood to push her chair in and felt slightly faint. That was that. The evening had been painless, and yet fear gripped her insides like a vice.

Her stomach settled as he disappeared around the corner. Staring at the space where he had been, she realized he had not raised his voice once.

Day Six

Trin planted herself face-down on her sleeping mat. The accommodations, if they could be called that, were comfortable…but she was suffocating under her captivity. Her back and neck ached from long hours in the lab, rifling through cabinets and moving furniture and filing test after test.

Curing that beast was going to be the death of her.

Each night, she gave herself several minutes of respite to stare out her window, a warm cup of indrim tea in her hands. The materializer in the mess hall was a small comfort, but a comfort nonetheless.

Her view of space was unchanging. At least, it felt like it in its strangeness. Swathes of blue-green nebulae in the distance might have pierced her heart, once. Now, they just reminded her of the impossible distance home.

Trin absently tapped the side of her mug. From day one, she had known it would be ridiculous for her to overcome someone the size of Mildar. She was barely over five Earth feet tall and had not a whit of military training. Plus, despite her tendency to speak her mind, she could never bring herself to fight with more than words. So her one course of action was, incidentally, her most practiced one: manipulation.

Earn his trust. Secret away nutri-packs from the kitchen. Explore when he had no reason to doubt. Find the escape pod—there was bound to be one—and cannonball herself out of there. It couldn't travel at warp speed, but at least then she would be able to send out a distress signal at a safe distance from Mildar.

Even as she thought it, a darkness groped at her mind. It had been almost a week. Rivka'd surely sent a search party days ago, but maybe, just maybe, they'd given up and declared her dead…yet another casualty in a vast universe of pain.

The Scroll of Harden would tell her what to do, though she'd never been much of a believer. Trin almost laughed. She had to be truly desperate to look to the myths for any truth. But memorized verses from her childhood started to well up within her, so she let herself remember.

When Harden, the first Fercren patriarch, had walked their planet, he, too, had little reason to hope. Raising his family in the shelter of a quarry, he did everything he could to fend off the human attackers who would pillage all that he loved. Gofton, a merciful god, had stretched a storm cloud across the mouth of the quarry as protection. The cloud was impenetrable... until Harden's enemies found they could manipulate iron ore into swords and cut it to pieces.

She shivered. The darkness of her quarters could have rumbled with thunder. And at any moment, it felt like Mildar was going to pull out an iron sword.

Still, a doubt scratched at the corners of Trin's thoughts. She had, after all, taken the principal vows of Fercren medicine. Vows of healing. While her vessel had not entered enemy space, an enemy had come to her... in need. Even if he had kidnapped her.

Her fingers slipped, and she spilled her tea. Blasted emotions—she just had to *feel* something for once, didn't she? Cursing, she set the mug down and ran to the sink to rinse the hot liquid off her hands. The water helped, gradually. She pressed thumb against forefinger, wincing as her paper-thin skin throbbed in pain. Its normal rose tint blistered red. Wrapping her hands under the gloves would have to be part of her morning routine.

As Rivka would say about those wretched reconstructive synthesizers: she must learn to bide her time.

Day Nine

Trin threw the ball of cooling jelly and it smacked against the lab wall. She exhaled, tracking its arc, then leaped to hit it toward her target. With a crash, the ball bounced into the waste reclamator.

Score.

She flashed a grin at no one and went to fish it out of the bin before it dissolved.

"You have good aim," a voice admitted.

Spinning around, she flushed when she saw Mildar leaning in the doorway.

"Just... helps me focus." She shrugged. Her makeshift paddle, a spare type-pad taped to a serving spoon she'd swiped from the kitchen, found its way next to her bio-robe on the floor.

"What, working is not enough?" He laughed.

Trin shot him a look. "I slave away eighteen hours a day. I'd think I deserve some recreation."

He put up his hands. "Meanness was not my intent."

Pulling at the collar of her sweaty tunic, she walked to the counter for her water bottle. "What was your intent, then?" she muttered. "Did you really think your condition justified a kidnapping?"

"I—" Mildar said haltingly.

"I miss it, you know. Home." Faces shone in her mind—her sweet patients on the planet's surface, childhood friends, Rivka. Her anger squeezed itself dry, and she found herself on the verge of crying. "You had *no right.*"

Like Harden's attackers hadn't had a right to seize his quarry centuries ago. But the patriarch, at least, had been able to fight. After General Dezke's sword cut down dozens of Fercren, including Harden's young daughter, Harden had battled him up the cliff until he could nearly taste the cloud on his tongue.

Trin put her bottle down, shaking. "You're no better than the rest of your people."

Countless insults sprang up within her, and she prepared to deliver each line like Harden had plunged his knife into Dezke's chest. Over, and over, and over again...

"You are right," Mildar said wearily.

She glared, tears pricking at her eyes. "What?"

"The anger you keep is just. You have none—no reason to forgive me."

"Well. I'm glad we're in agreement." Trin crossed her arms and lowered her voice. "Because I don't."

Stiffening, Mildar looked away.

A strange sadness pressed on her chest, almost a twinge of regret. To escape the feeling, she busied herself clearing the counter.

"What did you come in here for, anyway?" She nearly swore, realizing she'd left the jelly ball in the reclamator. Oh, well. She could make another. "The analyzers won't be done for two hours."

"I came to tell you that..." His face twisted. "It does not matter. This is for you." He handed her a phosphorous light. "I thought you may feel the ship is too dark."

Trin turned the prism-like rod in her palm and squeezed it gently. Her grip left behind a mottled blue-green glow that spread beneath the glassy surface.

It was beautiful.

"Thank you," she managed after a moment.

With a dip of his head, Mildar left, and she was once again alone.

Day Twenty-one

"I'm going exploring," Trin announced.

Slouched in the pilot's chair, Mildar barely acknowledged her. She shook her head, not knowing why she was telling him. It had been almost a fortnight and their barbs had lost their usual sting. She should have been grateful for even that, but her heart ached for meaningful conversation. Something she knew Mildar couldn't—or wouldn't—give.

He continued to look out the visor-shield. "Do not die," he said hoarsely.

She found herself cracking a half-smile. *Wait, was he being sarcastic?*

"Same to you," she murmured before wandering down the hall.

Trin glanced down at the screen of her type-pad. Last week he had brought her a Maftonian herb she'd been complaining about missing, and she had interrogated him—how in Harden's quarry had he gotten his paws on fresh herbs?

"The garden," he'd said. Flabbergasted, she had asked him why she'd never seen this garden-in-the-middle-of-space, and for once in several days, he'd stood tall. His deep eyes had flashed.

"It is... wild. You must not go. If there is anything you want, I will obtain it for you."

And two days ago he'd brought her *peppermint*. Not because she'd needed it, but because she'd mentioned how much she liked it in her tea, and somehow he had been paying attention.

Trin blushed, then walked more briskly to will the emotion away. It was no secret that she had grown more used to her strange circumstances. Mildar still infuriated her, daily, yet now she found she could joke with him, be a shade more firm when he needed his rest, and maybe even be more honest...

No. That was one step too far. Weeks of planning, and now she was so close. Her rations lay hidden in her room; she knew now where the escape pod was and just had to figure out how to jettison herself without tripping any alarms.

One task only: getting herself home.

And yet... Mildar had promised to take her there. She just needed to fulfill her part of the bargain. At warp speed, the journey would be a matter of hours.

She found herself around the bend that led to the loading dock. The ambient hissing and clattering of the ship that had become like white noise to her shifted. There was almost a heaviness to the air, and it was then that she noticed the fog seeping from beneath a door ahead.

It was the door Trin remembered passing on her first day. Strange. She must have come back here since then, yet she was eerily unsure.

Glancing back to the cockpit, she took a deep breath and inched toward the foggy door.

Shockingly, it slid open.

Squinting her way through the haze, Trin felt her pulse quicken. Huge forms began to emerge, dark, flat, and tangled. The strange hush was replaced with a rustling, breathing, and—was that a *bird call?*

"Gods," she exhaled.

It was a jungle. A literal *jungle,* in a *spaceship,* flying *in space.*

The heavy scent of earth and animal flooded her nostrils. Now that the mist had dissipated, she could make out the prehistoric-sized foliage, a million shades of green. Three gigantic sun-lamps radiated heat. Blinking up at iridescent creatures flying from bough to bough, she felt water cling to her eyelashes.

So this is the garden you were talking about.

As if in a trance, she walked into the trees. Tracing her gloved fingers along the leaves of a vine, she made a game of trying to name everything she could see. Kapok and Xate trees from Earth, bramat bushes, those crazy flowers from Porril's moon that regurgitated sweet syrup if you stroked the right part of the bulb. Then, she just started to make things up. Vanishing monkey. Hairy bee-home (classification: weird). Mildar's tree, because its bark was bluish and twisted like that expression he had when he was searching for a word.

Laughing, she found herself in a clearing. A pool smooth as glass was interrupted by water lilies. Off to the side, a makeshift garden—a homely one, with trellises and mismatched pots—stood guard. As she made her way over, she scanned the leaves for a certain shape. Sure enough, peppermint curled beside lunar rosemary.

Fingertips buzzing, Trin slipped off one of her gloves.

A throaty growl sounded behind her. She spun around, knocking the pot to the ground. A monstrous creature, nearly as tall as Mildar, stalked toward her.

No. No, no, no. Before she could wonder where it had come from, another one materialized out of the shadowed trees, wolf-like—bloodshot eyes, leathery skin patched with callouses, mouth wide and spiked with teeth—

A dark shape flew over her head, crashing headlong into the first beast. The monster's lizard-like claws tore at blue fur. Mildar pinned it down for a moment, then dodged a blow from its hind legs. Heart racing, Trin fell and scrabbled at the earth behind her for something to throw. Her bare fingers found a pot, and she flung it hard at her attackers. It barely missed Mildar's head.

"Not at me!" he choked.

"Well, what am I supposed to do?!"

"RUN!" Mildar thundered, then screamed as the second creature jumped him from behind, scoring a deep gash along his back.

Trin snatched two more pots and darted around them, aiming to catch the monsters' attention.

"What—did I say?" Mildar groaned.

"I'm not a great listener!"

One pot shattered against the first beast's side. It snarled and raised its leg off of Mildar. Trin drew back the second pot, aiming for the other creature's eye, but found its nose instead. Echoing rumbles sounded above. The sky—ceiling—darkened. A pair of arms snatched her from where she stood, knocking the wind out of her. She clung to Mildar for dear life, not caring that he held her too tightly or that her bare hand was soon covered in his blood.

The next twenty seconds were a blur of green and black and blinking away rain. The room had started pouring. Nightmarish howls persisted behind them. As they ran through the door, Mildar swerved to smash the access panel with his shoulder. It closed with a hiss. Crashing to the floor, Trin detangled herself and lay stunned, fighting for air.

"I'm—sorry," he gasped. "I should have locked the door."

After several moments, she managed to speak. "No, it was my—"

"Now. I will take you back now. It will not be a fast journey, three Earth-months, but this does not matter. I never should have..."

"Three *months?*" Holding her sore elbows, she stared up at him. "What are you saying?"

Mildar grimaced. "Earlier, I... lied."

Her heart clenched.

"The warp drive was hurt, damaged, somehow when I first brought you here," he stammered. "I was trying to fix it when you awoke but still have not found the cause. I am not what you call, an engineer? Is that it?"

"Yes," Trin replied stormily. Staggering to her feet, she offered him her arm for balance and guided him to the lab. Her furiosity about the fact that he'd withheld the truth surprised her. Since when had she started caring about Mildar being honest?

"I did mean to tell you," he grumbled. "I thought, you were upset already, but…I was full of self." His contrition hung in the air.

Biting her lip, she remembered the night playing paddle-ball in the lab.

"So," she said, squinting at him. "No engineer, no crew, on this huge ship that you clearly can't fly—holy Harden, you've got a crazy amount of explaining to do! And why are those *things* living in a giant greenhouse?"

He gave her a blank look. "What do you think we had for dinner?"

She stared back, horrified.

Without warning, he sucked in a sharp breath. Blood darkened his coat. "Can we talk more when we are in your lab?"

Hotly, Trin nodded and simmered all the way down the hall.

"You said there would be no needles," he protested.

"I said I *thought* there would be no needles," Trin clarified, opening the lid of the sterilizer. "But the dermal wand isn't enough."

Mildar, facedown on the examining table, scowled at her over his shoulder. She threw up her hands.

"Hey, I don't like them any more than you do, but it's the only way," she exclaimed. "You're just going to have to bite the bullet."

His glare deepened, if that was even possible. "I do not like these expressions."

"Tough. They don't like you either." Trin shoved down her own nervousness. She prayed to Gofton that her annoying bedside manner would take the edge off things. Because if it didn't, they might both end up passed out on the floor.

Mildar squirmed as she applied the numbing salve around the wound on his back. The laceration was deeper than she'd first thought, and it worried her, but she wasn't about to tell him that.

"Don't move," she said, the coldness leaving her voice. Carefully, she began to lace the needle through his torn flesh. Thank the gods he didn't jump.

He glanced at her. "When did you learn to fix these kinds of wounds?"

She paused for a moment. "When I was too young." Then, before she knew it, a flood of words escaped her mouth. "Back home, my older cousin Tochov took care of me and my mother. She—my mum—had a joint condition, so she was mostly confined to a hover-chair. We think it came from her mum, who was human. Anyway, one day Toc found a better job than scrubbing landowners' floors." She broke off, remembering Mildar's finery. "So he left. Mum died. I was eleven."

Trin pulled a little too tightly, and he hissed. "Sorry," she said, meaning it. "Needless to say, I saw a lot of terrible, unmentionable things in the slums. Before Rivka took me on, I was apprenticed to a damali in my home quarter. It was... easier, then, to learn simple medicine, being so desensitized to it all." A blow of guilt stole her next words. Those awful years had taught her that people were easier to deal with if she treated them as projects, things to learn and even control. And now Mildar's blood was on *her* hands. He had tried to warn her about the garden, then risked his life to save her...

She had to stop then. Her arms were shaking.

"Your glove." He nodded. "You are missing one."

"Yeah."

"Why are—why do you wear them? Your hands, they are not ugly," he murmured.

With a blush, Trin glanced at her thin fingers and half-laughed. "Thank the flimsy genetics. Fercren aren't known for their durability."

For the first time in several days, she turned to really look at his face. His tortured expression pierced her more violently than any nebula ever could. Her breath caught. It was like Gofton's light...

When Dezke had been at Harden's mercy, the god shone two sunlit crescents on the general's cheeks: Fercren markings over a human's face. Seeing this and the blood of his enemy on his knife, Harden realized the horror of what he had done. Then Gofton, in his wisdom, granted Harden and all Fercren the power to heal—a gift that one could choose to use on their enemy, or not.

That was the story, anyway. But while Trin had no reason to believe in magic, there was a different kind of power she knew she had withheld.

"I am sorry," Mildar said gently. "About your family. And . . . all that I have done."

Suddenly, she felt every fear and doubt that he had caused in her wilt at the edges. The image of fluorescent shoots sprouting in their place surged within her chest. She could have wept, but spoke instead. "I forgive you," she murmured. "And I'm sorry, too."

Silence grew between them, but it was the most liberating silence she'd ever heard.

"So." She sniffed, putting her fingers back to work. "Tell me about this fancy boat we're flying. It's a research vessel, isn't it? Some kind of biome experiment?"

"Well . . ." He hesitated. "Yes."

Trin raised an eyebrow. He raised one back.

"I also do not have a happy past. Unlike you, my pain is my fault." He shook his head when she tried to protest. "The Unvill government is ruled by a group. A council. My father sits in one of the chairs, so you see, I grew up with . . . more than I needed, though I did not know it then." He faltered. "My idea of fun was damaging. I pulled my friends into a plot to humiliate my father. I hated him because I could not understand him."

Trin studied the floor, and while her mouth was parched, she couldn't bring herself to swallow.

"I could not understand why he did not want to go to war." His words sent chills down her spine. War with her people. "Like many Unvill, I believed the lie that others had resources, new tech that we had to beg for. We were not . . . destitute, but we deserved more. I wanted more. So I did it." Mildar's voice cracked. "I brought my father low in the eyes of all Unvillem. His attendants found out it was me. The chief magus had . . . how do you say it? His fingers around corporal punishment. I was not above the law, so they gave me this sickness, this curse"—he gestured at his sunken eyes—"and prepared a pod to send me away." Then, almost as an afterthought: "I do not think my father was aware of my exile, but it would not shock me if he knew."

The vibrations of the ship seemed to rattle Trin's entire body. One last pull, one final stitch. She let the clippers fall to the tray next to her. Rolling onto his good side, Mildar shifted himself upright. She looked away, willing herself not to dwell on the broadness of his shoulders.

"So that's why you don't have any medical documents from home," she muttered. "Because they didn't want you to be cured." She could feel her lungs constrict. "It was a death sentence."

He bowed his head. "A slow death. It will be three Earth cycles this week."

She swiveled in her chair, then leaped out of it in anger. "Curse it all, Mildar, you didn't think to tell me this earlier?"

He gave her a pained look. "I did not think I had to. Now I see I was wrong."

Trin stalked over to the counter, using all her willpower to not slam her fists against it. Then footsteps sounded behind her. Turning to reprimand him, she suddenly found his face above hers.

"You…" He raised a tentative hand toward her bedraggled hair. Her insides somersaulted. Then he flinched and stepped backward, embarrassment in his eyes. Gradually, she felt her stomach settle.

Mildar cleared his throat. "You wanted to know about the ship," he said after a moment. "I could not have survived this long in my people's escape pod, so—"

"So you stole this instead," Trin replied flatly.

He flashed her a rare grin. "What, you have not done a thing like that?" he asked with a laugh. It was a good laugh, she thought with frustration.

"Stolen a spaceship?!" she cried, then covered her mouth to suppress a smile. Composing herself, she clasped her hands behind her back. "No, I cannot say that I have."

"Well, my lady." He grinned. "You are missing the adventure of a life."

"Lifetime," she corrected.

"And the garden. You liked it?"

Trin let out a laugh. "With those carnivores?"

"Another time, I will put them away. I promise." Slowly, Mildar made to stand and stumbled. She rushed to him, holding up his uninjured side. Gods…his weight was enormous, and yet she could tell he was thinner than before.

He chanced a weak look at her. "I will take you home. Do not worry for me."

"It's too late for that," she whispered. Then, to herself: *I'm not going anywhere.*

Day Thirty-three

Trin chewed at her cracked lips, having forgotten to drink water. Again.

Leaning back in her chair, she felt the tension in her shoulders complain. The vials and synthesizers scattered across the lab counter swam in her vision and reminded her of Earthen stained glass. She reached up to reactivate the phosphorous light where it stood in the center of her shelf.

Mildar's circulation had slowed. Over the past several days, he'd hardly been able to move outside the cockpit. With his loss of appetite came chills and throbbing in his limbs. She knew that in extreme cases, this could lead to memory loss and, Gofton forbid it, amputation... but her attempts to clear his arteries didn't seem to change a thing. Despite the fact that his wound from the garden creatures had begun to heal, he had lost so much blood. And any blood cells that she tried to replicate died.

A distant whine sounded. Trin turned her ear toward the noise, wondering if the oxy system was acting up again—

—and the wall exploded.

She could almost see her body from a distance as it twisted around and was flung across the room. Mercifully, she only hit the floor. Fragments of glass bit into her skin. Whole sections of the ceiling were now hanging by bolts, metal screeching against metal. Coughing, the image of Mildar flashed in her mind, and she hobbled past the rubble toward the cockpit.

"Mil—Mildar!" Trin choked.

A faint shout sounded. She found him in the pilot's chair.

"Are you all right?" she cried. Instinctively, she found herself brushing through his mane to check for bumps, searching his eyes for any sign of a concussion.

"I am. Besides the usual," he rasped. "But I am not so sure about the ship."

She had to fight to look away from him. Most of the control lights glowed like normal, but smoke poured out between some panels to her left.

"The life support," he said, nodding at the dark cloud.

Her gut twisted. "Great. Just our luck."

"I do not think luck has a thing to do with it." He pointed out the visor-shield.

A blemish against the black of space, a Fercren warship swooped its way toward them.

"No," Trin breathed.

"Yes," Mildar groaned. He jerked the control wheel, and they plummeted.

A mile-long beam of light struck their port side.

"Haven't you tried talking to them?" she screamed above the din.

"Trust me, I have tried! They do not answer my comm requests!" As his shouts thinned, Trin noticed him sink further into his seat.

"Don't you pass out on me," she cried, gripping the back of his chair with white knuckles. "You promised to show me the garden again after the beasts are contained!"

"Promises... fail," Mildar mumbled. His claws slipped from the controls.

She gritted her teeth. Fumbling for the computer's autopilot console, she slammed her fist down on the panel and prayed to Gofton and all the mortal-loving gods to deliver them—because if Mildar didn't wake up, there was no way she could pilot them out alive.

Now, the comm line. Even though he'd already tried it, maybe her people would listen to her instead; maybe it was only a temporary signal jam—

"Comming Fercren fighter," she shouted, pressing the comm button with all her might. She felt tears stream down her face. "Stop shooting! In Gofton's *name,* I'm one of *you!*"

Silence. The indicator light flickered and died. No response.

Another boom. The beams of the hall behind them screeched.

She glanced down at her trembling hands, skin almost translucent. Veins raised and purple, she imagined the blood rushing to her head.

That's it.

As Mildar's autopilot sent them into a dive to avoid a plasma ray, the world slowed, and a thrill shot through her. *A transfusion.* Could it work? But their blood types needed to match, and there was no time to set up all the tech...

Another way lanced its way into her memory. Harden's healing fingers pressed to Dezke's arms. Blood to blood. Gofton's gift, a method that nearly all modern Fercren doubted was still possible.

At his disease's current rate, though, Mildar could die any minute. Now was as good a time as any for an act of faith.

"I promise you'll get through this," she muttered.

Another blow to the ship sent Trin careening across the room. Her shoulder slammed against the edge of a wall, and she cried out in pain. Righting herself, she gripped the cockpit's doorframe and held the attacking vessel in her gaze. Fire burned behind her eyes. Chaos might surround her on all sides, but Mildar—*her* Mildar—would not be destroyed as long as his healer stood firm.

Stood firm, that was, until she was spent. Because giving him the amount of blood he needed would be the end of her. Just like healing Dezke had been the end of Harden.

And her heart, she realized, couldn't offer anything less than her whole self.

Limping toward Mildar's chair, Trin heard him groan. She tore off her one remaining glove and rolled back his sleeves. His tired brow creased.

"What are you doing?"

"Saving your life."

"No, the pod—"

"And be shot down anyway? You know how bitter my people are. They'd sooner burn their own fields than let an Unvill escape pod go, even if there's no Unvill in it."

Pressing her fingers to the inside of his wrists, she commended Mildar to Gofton's care. He looked frightened, but didn't complain.

The ship dipped dangerously and Trin's heart hiccuped with doubt. No Fercren had manifested the gift in hundreds of years…

I don't know what I'm doing, but I trust you, she prayed.

"Ready?" she asked out loud, pulse racing.

Mildar's eyes widened. "For what?"

"This."

With the last shred of her strength, Trin lowered her head to kiss him, and he met her halfway. Willing everything that she was to cooperate with the gods' will, she pictured her blood rushing down to her hands. A warm light pulsed beneath the skin. Electricity crackled across her arms, and she almost let go—but then a piercing pain split her fingertips, and she felt her own blood flow magically, supernaturally, into Mildar's veins.

When Trin opened her eyes, his appearance had shifted. Maybe it was just her swimming head, but his face seemed clearer, his eyes brighter. A rush of gratitude swept through her body. Her bare hands on his forearms, she allowed herself to think how wonderful and handsome he truly was.

"How did we get here?" she breathed. All of a sudden, drawing in air was an effort. Mildar reached up to hold the side of her head, and she leaned into it. Laser fire blazed around them, but for a moment, she felt inexplicably safe.

"I suppose you do not mean the Korez system." He quirked an eyebrow.

"You know perfectly well what I mean."

The floor tilted, and she scrabbled dizzily to his right and into the copilot's chair. For several seconds, the sky was a swirling blur until the ship righted itself. Blinking, she was shocked to recognize a constellation.

Mildar stretched toward the comm button and gave her a questioning look. One final try. Trin shut her eyes, took a breath, and nodded.

"CEASE FIRE!" she shouted in the thickest Fercren accent she could muster. It surprised her how much Mildar's wide vowels had made their way into her speech. "This is Trin Beross of Galvani. I'm the assistant to damali Rivka Sralt and went—went missing over a month ago—there is an Unvill here with me, but he is a friend, I swear on the holy quarry of Harden!"

They were met with a long silence. Ten seconds, thirty, fifty…

"Maybe their transmission is poor," Mildar suggested. Trin weakly waved for him to be quiet.

The warship slowly dropped into view. *"Trin, this is Ger Noroft of the Fercren Alliance. We receive your transmission loud and clear. Our retrieval team is on its way over now. Are either of you injured?"*

"We're—needing some extra blood, sir," she managed to slur. "And maybe a few stitches." Somewhat delirious, Mildar nodded sagely, and she almost laughed.

"Acknowledged. Hang tight."

The two collapsed into their seats. In the following moments of strange bliss, as the ringing in Trin's ears faded away, Mildar's fingers found hers. His claws were large and rough around the edges, but he held her fragile palm with the utmost care. For once, she didn't let go. His eyes crinkled, and beneath all that fur, she saw the young man who had once been a broken boy.

"What?" he asked, a befuddled smile on his face.

"Nothing," she said. "It just feels like we've both finally come home."

WIDOW ROSE

Lara E. Madden

THE WIDOW TWISTS the wedding ring off her finger. Throughout the mansion, lights flicker. She slips the ring onto a chain and hangs it around her neck. *I can't let it go just yet. Soon. But not tonight.* She brushes rouge across her cheeks, refreshes her lipstick, sets her curls with hairspray, and tucks the ring beneath the collar of her dress. The widow's eyes burn as she stares intently into the mirror, looking beyond her reflection.

"This one will be different," she tells the glass. "I really like this man. And I need to be free to move on." She wipes a brisque hand under her eyes, refusing to cry and ruin her mascara. "I deserve to be happy," she says, but her voice shakes. The wind blows outside, and the old house creaks and groans in protest.

The widow goes downstairs and begins to light the table candles. She plays an old record that she and her husband used to dance to when he was alive. Five minutes before her date is meant to arrive, she puts dinner out so it will still be steaming hot when she uncovers the platters. She smiles at the set table. It will be a wonderful night in the company of a good man whom she likes very much. It's still infatuation, mind you. Not love. Not like what she'd once had with her Marvin. But there is certainly something there.

The ancient doorbell chimes through the house. She races to the door and embraces the man with the bouquet of bright crimson roses. When he steps across the threshold, he takes her hand, weaving his fingers between hers. Her chest tightens, and she smiles because she'd forgotten that the spaces between her fingers do not need to be empty forever.

She shows him to the table she set for them, pours the wine she has been saving for a very long time and tells him not to worry when the floor begins to shake beneath them so hard the wine glasses tremble.

"Minor earthquakes are common here," she says, repeating some geology and physics phrases she's learned for explaining away the house's unusual phenomenon. She doesn't tell him that this is the second house she's lived in since Marvin's death or that the tremors follow her wherever she goes.

The supper—a lovely roast with vegetables that had once been her husband's favorite meal—is nearly flawless, but the lights keep flickering on and off throughout the dinner, and the candles blow out at random. Every time, the widow rolls her eyes in the dark and relights them while muttering under her breath. Her date laughs and makes a joke of the odd repetitive coincidences, saying something about the house's draftiness and a good contractor he knows.

They talk for hours, the words coming naturally, the silences between the words so comfortable and easy. She does not *need* to try to enjoy his company. The loneliness of the house is dissipating, like winter cold in a room where a fire has just been lit. The widow had forgotten how good *togetherness* feels. It has been many, many years since the last time she fell in love.

She starts a slow jazz record that makes the man smile. He stands, reaches out a hand, and asks her to dance. She doesn't know if she remembers how, but when his hand finds the curve of her waist, and they fall into step with the music, it is as if they have always danced together, as if they have known each other for many long years. When the man leans in closer, and she lifts her head to kiss him, everything feels right. Their time together is like a story that has already been written: inevitable, obvious, perfect. *Maybe this is how the rest of my life begins,* the widow thinks, as the man's kisses find her jaw, her neck, her shoulder.

She hears the wind beating the house harder, the creaks and shaking walls growing louder, and out of the corner of her eye, the chandelier swings slightly. She sighs and tells her guest that she needs a moment to freshen up. She leaves him alone in the living room and passes through the kitchen to speak with her late husband privately.

Beside the refrigerator, the vase of roses lays in fragments on the marble tile. The record scratches violently from the dining room, and all the candles blow out as she walks past to the bathroom.

The widow checks her lipstick in the mirror, and the glass fogs up without any steam in the room.

"You have to understand," she whispers harshly to the mirror. "You have to let me go this time. You aren't alive anymore. I need to be allowed to love again."

From the other side of the mirror, letters appear.

MY ROSE

Marvin's old nickname for her.

"No!" the widow says. "You will not ruin this for me! I said, *'till death* do us part,' my love, and it has been much longer than that now. You need to stop this! Stop haunting me and *be a proper dead person*!" She is taking the tone she always takes when they have fights, the one Marvin hated when he was alive. The lights flicker again. She hears a picture frame fall and break in the hallway and knows it's their wedding photo. The mirror rattles harder and harder until a small crack forms at one corner, reaching down across the foggy letters.

Rose turns her back on the splintering glass and ignores the ghost. She stands a little taller and brushes a wrinkle out of her dress, shuts the bathroom door definitively, goes back through the dark kitchen, and sways into the living room, where her guest is—

Time stops. Rose is losing herself in her screaming, in the pool of blood on the floor, her date lying face-down in it. Dead.

She struggles to turn him over, pounding on his chest to wake him up, sobbing into his shirt, smearing blood on her face.

Blood everywhere. Blood from his throat, from the long gash across it, cut with a thick piece of glass that is embedded deep in his neck, broken off of a window that had shattered. *All* of the windows have shattered.

Marvin has never killed anyone before, never done more than scare men away.

Rose tries frantically to find a pulse, to see the man's chest rise. Her own heart pounds in her ears, and her breathing is so fast she feels dizzy as if her body is trying to make up for his horrible stillness. Her hands close in tight fists, bunching the cloth of his shirt, trying desperately to make sense of what she sees.

Behind her, there's the slight sound of a chandelier shuddering, and she snaps her head around to glare at it. The bulbs burn out, and the chandelier goes dark. In another room, there's a creaking sound, like a man nervously shifting his weight.

This is too much. He's crossed every line now. He's become something wicked. A monster.

Slowly, Rose opens her fists and looks at them. The man's blood covers her hands. It stains her dress and drips down her arms. She stares at her hands held out in front of her until her shock starts to freeze over and turn to cold, sharp fury.

Rose slips in the blood as she struggles to her feet, sobbing, wailing, groaning, screaming. Her body is shaking, her voice tearing with rage and grief, both emotions building on each other and coming in waves that boil up and over as she surges through the house like a storm. She tracks blood as she runs down the halls, screams at the walls, slams on the tables, shatters plates and glasses, smashes records, and throws things at mirrors.

"MARVIN!!!" Her shouts quake through the mansion with more ferocity than she realized she is capable of, her voice wavering in an animal wail. With this final sorrowful, vengeful crescendo, she collapses on the floor and sobs until all the energy in her body is exhausted.

She cannot move the corpse tonight. She will have to bury him in the morning.

This one was supposed to be different . . .

She can't think of it now, cannot even look at the face of the dead man in the living room. Cannot wonder what could have been or what will happen tomorrow. Cannot even weep for him anymore tonight.

"I just don't understand how you could do this, Marvin," she whispers. Her heart is on the floor, broken like the man whose blood is crusting in the carpet. "I thought you loved me."

Another tear slips off the bridge of her nose as she crawls back up the stairs. She is too tired and too alone to stand. To walk. So she pulls herself up the steps on her hands and knees.

"This isn't *love*, Marvin." Her words are so soft that she wonders if he can hear her at all. "You're killing me. The loneliness is dragging the life out of me. I can't keep on surviving this way."

He always hears her. He listens better now than he did when he was alive, but he's still just as stubborn, just as jealous.

In her fog, Rose finds her way back to the bedroom. When she feels the wedding ring hanging around her neck, she yanks the necklace free and tosses it away halfheartedly—her unofficial divorce from the dead man. Weary to the bone, she pulls the large comforter around her and falls asleep, whispering over and over, "Marvin, you have to let me go. You have to. Please. Let me go. If you love me, Marvin . . . "

Letters appear on the last unbroken mirrors in the house. The widow sees them in the morning when she is cleaning up the broken glass and ordering a new carpet. There's a single flower waiting for her on the kitchen table, the only one that hasn't been trampled or torn. She throws it down and crushes it under her heel.

I'M SORRY
reads a mirror in the bathroom.

I DO LOVE YOU, ROSE
says the one in the spare bedroom.

In the living room above the fireplace,
THAT'S WHY I CAN'T EVER LET YOU GO

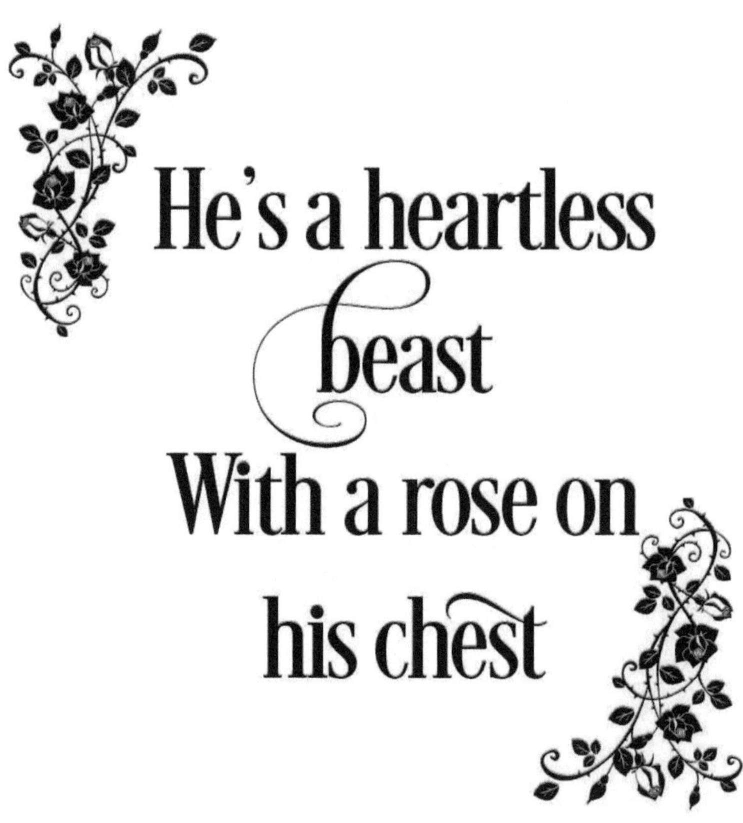
He's a heartless
beast
With a rose on
his chest

BLOODY COINS

Anne J. Hill

His blade slits throats
Red petals drip down

He's a heartless beast
With a rose on his chest

It'll cost much gold
To kill whoever you wish

But at the end of the day
The blame's on his head

And you can walk free
With blood on your coins

Your neck won't hang
Your knife is clean

But the red killer
Pays the monster inside

No one cares if his grave
Is dug from hired crime

Lock your doors and
Hold your breath

Because you never know
If you could be next

Related to Thorn Tower *by Anne J. Hill*

I'M NOT SUPPOSED to survive this.

None of the males who travel each year, one per year, to the castle to save the stolen girl of the season are supposed to live.

Slay the monster; survive the winter.

One girl taken.

One boy to rescue her.

The problem is, the one who kills the beast never returns home—and still, the beast returns. Every year, they try something–*someone*–new, but even the winter isn't as harsh as the beast inside the castle. It might be a different blade, a new set of armor, or a counterspell.

It never works.

Snow flurries pepper the air as I near the center of the forest. The castle towers over the trees, still half a mile away, crumbling and decrepit. It's a thing forgotten beneath the thorns and vines weighted down by snow and ice. My lungs ache with every breath as if the debris and dust are clawing inside my chest, but I push forward.

We're selected. We don't volunteer.

Until me.

The night before I was supposed to leave, I woke up with Celia, my fiancée, chaining my arms to the bed.

"I'm tired of losing so much to this curse," she said. "We always send our men. Maybe it's time one of us women take it on."

I could do nothing but scream into the gag in my mouth as I watched her walk out of my room, headed straight for her death. My guard found me the next morning—one advantage of being the Duke's son.

"She told me if she didn't return, to let you out."

The castle released the first girl, taking Celia in her place. Two nights later, another was taken.

Maris. Maris needs me.

My sister, the beast's latest victim. Her laughter rings in my ears; the picture of her long golden hair threaded through with flowers on the eve of her sixteenth birthday spurs me forward.

Why another girl?

"We could always send the old witch," one of the council members said when I demanded they consider my offer. I had already volunteered. "Maybe then she'll stop demanding our sons and daughters every year."

"Miss Gardner has nothing to do with it," Father insisted, calming them with his measured words and easy demeanor. "My son will fulfill his duty, and he will come out with his life."

At his words, the council practically pushed me out the door. Winter was already sharp in the air, the icy chill settling in everyone's bones. I exited my father's office with their eyes on me, and the family obligation on my back, every one of us aware Celia's sacrifice wasn't enough to feed the beast.

What would it take next?

The farther I travel into the forest, the harsher the chill settles in my bones.

Welcome, lordling.

The feminine voice enters my mind, softer than silk and sharper than the blade in my hand.

Come to save the one you love?

"Get out of my head," I grit out, clenching my eyes closed. Something about the voice is familiar–but I can't place it. It's hidden beneath the gravel and ridges, buried in a valley of secrets.

A laugh rolls in my mind, echoing and chilling like the snow winds coming from the mountains. The winter aches to sink its claws into our village.

I break through the line of trees, and the castle looms over me. Vines and thorns snake around the dark gray stone, and poisonous purple flowers flutter in the breeze.

No man has lived to tell the tale of my castle, lordling, the voice coos.

"Your words have no effect on me."

Your father inherited this castle, and so will you, lordling.

The cursed lands my father inherited.

He was too afraid to face me. I'm glad he didn't raise a coward.

"My father is not a coward!" I shout, swinging my sword from its scabbard. My eyes sweep the forest, but my vision is a prisoner to the shadows.

The voice chuckles. *Even so, I am your past, present, and future. Now, I have taken your sister. Nothing you do will thaw the coming winter.*

"Haven't you already taken enough?" I roll back my shoulders, lifting my chin.

Laughter rolls over my skin.

I needn't explain myself to you.

A chill settles in my veins, and I stare up at the castle. The echo in my mind fades, telling me whoever the voice belongs to has slithered back into her cave. The prickling along the back of my neck tells me she isn't far. She wouldn't miss what happens next.

I've been practicing for this moment my entire life, waiting for my name to be called to save the next girl held captive by the beast. Father never stopped training me until I could battle with any blade and could defeat any of his guards. He was never given the chance to face the beast, so he prepared me for the battle of his and my life.

But nothing compares to the unforgiving ramifications if the beast is not defeated: snowstorms that last for weeks; spoiled food; dwindling resources; neighbors turning against one another; and, eventually, the thing everyone fears...

Death.

I circle the castle, looking for an opening. Bones crunch beneath my feet. Wind whistles through the trees, so fierce and strong I struggle to reach the door. A splintering crack breaks through the howls of the storm, and I glance to my right to see a sliver of light passing through a nearly invisible doorway.

I slip inside to escape the wind. The door slams shut behind me, and the torches in the hall flicker.

My heart thunders in my chest, and I grip the hilt of my sword tighter. The hall leads to a wide entryway full of cobwebs and cracked stones.

"Hello?" My voice echoes around me.

A faint string of music drifts down the wide staircase in the center of the room. The notes draw out the whisper of my footsteps the higher I climb, twisting and turning in the dilapidated halls until I come to an open door in the darkest corner of the castle.

I peer inside, and the air leaves my chest.

"Maris," I whisper, the word breaking like a promise in my chest.

She hangs suspended by ropes and vines tied to her wrists, black roses and thorns digging into her flesh and drawing rivulets of blood. A sphere of transparent golden magic shields her from any aid I can offer.

I run toward her, but I'm thrown back by a the golden shield. I crash into the floor, scattering a cloud of rubble. The voice from before slips into my mind.

You can't save her, it whispers. The words wrap around me, and I struggle to my feet.

The magic circling my sister pulses like the *buh-duh, buh-duh, buh-duh* of a heartbeat. Her hair hangs limp and greasy, grazing her waist and blowing in a nonexistent breeze. A low humming sounds around the room, overshadowing the music that led me here.

I raise my sword and take a cautious step toward my sister. The shadows meld around me, stretching and reaching for me with delicate touches against my exposed skin.

She's bound to the castle, lordling. You'll have to do more than threaten me with a sword.

"Stop hiding in the shadows!" My voice pierces the magic pulsing through the room. The sphere around my sister skips a beat.

Maris throws her head back, and a scream rips through her chest. I fight my way to her, slashing at the bonds holding her in the air while the magic stutters. I'm through one vine, Maris's leg dangling limply as a whimper escapes her, when my sword is torn from my hand.

My eyes wander the room, and I stumble back as a woman rises from the shadows. Her face is clouded in a mist, and a hood covers her hair. Darkness drips from her fingertips and weaves through her hair, turning it darker.

"Hello, lordling," she says. The voice is unnatural, like stone against stone—beastly.

I unsheath the dagger at my waist and circle her. She breezes around me as shadows fall from her hands and caress my ankles.

"Your move," she whispers.

I lunge at the same time the beast attacks.

She grabs my forearm, throwing me into the nearest wall. Stone crashes around me, and I stagger to my feet, my eyes trained on her.

"That's the best you've got?" I ask.

I advance, and she grabs me again, wrestling me to the ground. I drive my elbow into her chin, and she hisses in pain, releasing her hold. I rush to my feet, and she circles me. What began as a fight turns into a dance—a distraction.

Finally, she lunges toward me. She blocks each dip I feign. My blade slices the air as she ducks under my arm. Every move I make, she anticipates the next two. So I think three steps ahead. Instead of going under, I go left, my non-dominant side. The blade sinks into her abdomen, and a gasp fills the air. All other sound in the room ceases to exist, and I catch the beast—this woman—as she begins to fall. Her hood cascades to her shoulders, revealing a face I only thought I'd see in my dreams.

Hair the color of a burning sunset and eyes sweeter than honey.

"Celia…"

"Save her, Will…." Celia croaks. "Save her…. The beast…she's too strong. She'll heal me, but…she'll hurt you both…."

"Celia!" My voice scratches its way up my throat. "Celia!"

The ground beneath my feet shakes, and the walls begin to collapse. I spin around in time to see my sister hanging by a single vine, over eight feet off the ground. I lay Celia down and rush over to Maris before she's nothing but a broken doll lying.

I reach her just in time for her to fall into my arms, knocking us both to the floor.

"Maris?" I tap her cheek and watch the steady rise and fall of her chest.

Her eyes flutter at the sound of her name. "Will?"

A cry escapes my lips. "You're alive," I say. "But what about Celia—"

Her eyes flash open. "Celia is in danger, Will. She didn't have a choice. The monster took her—she tried to use me, but the curse wouldn't allow it. Never before have two women come to the castle."

"What does that mean—" I start, but she interrupts me with the only words that could steal my own.

"The monster wants Celia to take her place—" A scream breaks from her throat as the cobbles shift beneath us, silencing her.

I glance back at where I left the woman I love—only to see a trail of blood leading into the shadows.

The soft caress of Celia's voice enters my mind before it turns into something unrecognizable, the voice from before. *Leave, Will...and don't come back!* Celia's voice ends in a hiss, and then her scream echoes in my mind.

I grit my teeth against the sound, and it takes a few moments before I realize Maris is shaking me. "Will, we have to leave!"

Maris struggles to her feet, and I stumble to mine. We rush through the castle, leaving half my soul in the ruined bricks as it falls apart around us. The forest floor rumbles beneath our feet, letting us to only move as fast as our wounds allow. The wind howls, freezing rain slicing through the air. Finally, the village lights appear.

Maris limps against me, and I swing her into my arms. Covered in mud and soaked through with blood and rain, I crash into the tavern door.

"Open up!" I pound my fist into the door. "Maris," I whisper. "Stay awake, Maris."

The door opens, and we fall into the heat and eerie quiet. I can barely make out the villagers piled inside because of the blood and water in my eyes.

"Help her," I say before falling to the ground and welcoming the silence.

I jerk upright at the sound of a teapot's whistle.

"Whoa there, young man," says a croaking voice.

I look over to the woman sitting beside me. A white rose dangles behind her ear, half hidden by her ashen hair. Candlelight flickers off the emerald stem and thin petals as she walks over to my bed—how did I end up in a bed?

"Where am I?" I recognize the woman next to me. "Where's Maris—"

"She's at home, safe and sound," Mistress Gardner says. "Didn't expect to wake up with the village pariah tending to you, much less in her humble cottage?"

I rush to my feet, but a wave of dizziness overcomes me.

"Sit," she says, and an invisible hand forces me down.

I search for something to say, but she snaps her fingers, and the words stick in my throat.

"Don't wear yourself down," she says. "And, yes, I am a witch. Drink this, and then we can talk."

She hands me a cup. For a brief moment, I consider dumping out its contents. She trains her eyes on me until I hesitantly bring it to my lips and take a sip. A flood of warmth spreads through my body, the ache in my bones disappearing.

After I finish it, she stands and shuffles to the other side of the room. I can barely make out her form in the muted light.

"Why am I in your cottage and not my parents' home?"

"There's something you need to understand before I answer that."

The hair on the back of my neck rises, and I slide closer to the end of the bed, the door within reach.

"I wouldn't do that, Lord William," she says, voice low. "Keeping you here wasn't my idea, only my kindness." She snaps her fingers, and the candles around the room light every corner. Herbs and cloudy containers cover all available surfaces, and the crisp smell of spring hangs in the air as if a reprieve from the harsh winter.

"Why send my sister home and me here? How is she any safer than I am? I didn't—" The words stick in my throat. "I didn't . . . kill the beast."

"Your sister is safe. Your parents don't want you to return to the beast's castle, so they thought it was best to place you here, where I could keep an eye on you."

"My mother, you mean?"

She smiles. "Men often forget that behind them stands a strong woman. That same woman can also play her hand when the time strikes. Your mother showed her cards."

My hands tighten into fists, and I turn all my fury on Mistress Gardner. "You expect me to believe my mother trusted you?"

"Your father may control the council, but he does not share all their ideas." She studies me for a moment. "You stumbled into that tavern, half-crazed and bleeding from multiple wounds. It took them days to wake you and your sister, and the entire time you were mumbling about Celia."

"Because she's alive! She barely had control over herself. That . . . *thing* is inside her!"

"I know," she says, and whatever words might have come next freeze in my throat.

She continues, "My mother was the witch who cursed this town, and I've been waiting for someone like you to break the curse since the day she died. She made sure my magic alone wasn't strong enough."

Heat rises in my cheeks. Mistress Gardner was an old woman when my father was a boy—when his father was barely a man at seventeen. Her unexplainable age and her home covered in white roses at the edge of the forest are partly to blame for the villagers' hatred. Even when our crops fail or our supplies mysteriously spoil midwinter, her white roses continue to bloom in the roughest conditions.

"I'm older than I look, and so is this curse." She takes the rose from her hair and twirls it between her fingers.

"Your great-great-grandmother brought it to this village when she came to my mother and demanded a daughter as innocent as freshly-fallen snow and as beautiful as a rose, someone to be hers and hers alone. Your great-great-grandfather was a cruel man and taught his boys the same acts of cruelty. But roses have their thorns, and while your great aunt was the most beautiful woman this village—maybe even the kingdom—had ever seen, she was the most dangerous. Rhoswen was still her father's daughter."

I shake my head. "My father has taken responsibility for the curse–and my grandfather before him."

She smiles, holding out the rose. "Then watch and see the truth of what happened that fateful day, William. To get to the end, you have to understand the beginning."

I take the rose from her, and a thorn pricks my finger. Wincing, I watch the ruby-red drop splash on the cobblestone floor before I'm looking up into a new world.

I'm standing in a memory of the castle, the edges of it a frayed. Instead of the dilapidated castle that held my sister prisoner, the setting sun streaks liquid gold through the windows and across the floor. The smell of fresh roses and lavender assault my senses.

"Rhoswen!" The female voice echoes from downstairs, and I step out of the way as a girl about my age storms down the steps in a dress of pure white except for the splattering of red on her corset. Even with her gruesome appearance, the sun seems to follow her around the room, shining bronze light haloing her head. But with the light, shadows dance from every place she touches.

A woman twice her age chases after her, brown hair flying behind her. She grabs Rhoswen's arm and yanks her back before her fingers can graze the front door. "What have you done?" the woman asks.

A mirthless laugh escapes the girl's lips. "She's the village witch! You're acting as if I killed her, Mother."

"Did you see her? And to bring those *friends* of yours in on it."

Rhoswen's face doesn't change. She rips her hand from her mother's grasp and straightens her dress.

The doors to the castle fly open, cutting her mother off and tossing her like a rag doll. Rhoswen rushes to her side. "Mother!"

A figure clad in shadows crosses the threshold, and Rhoswen is thrown against the wall, crumpling to the ground in a heap.

"What do you want?" Rhoswen croaks. None of her fierceness is lost, and she begins to stand, only to be pulled back down by an invisible force.

The figure lowers her hood, revealing pale white hair and a red smile. "To make you as ugly on the outside as you are on the inside. That *witch* was my daughter."

The fight in Rhoswen is gone, and she stands as if in a trance. The witch's lips twitch in a smile as she hands the girl a rose, white as snow. "This place will become your prison. When your body dies, your mind will live on. The village will suffer for the blind eye they turned toward your cruelty, losing both their girls and boys until someone worthy can rescue a victim of this curse and *defeat* you." She produces a flower from the folds of her cloak. "This rose will never lose its bloom until that person comes to destroy it."

The world spins around me, and I drop the white rose as I return to the present. Mistress Gardner waits on the other side of the vision, catching me as I fall near the bed.

"What—why did your mother curse Rhoswen?"

"For what she had done to me. I was a teenager then, the same age as Rhoswen," she says. "My mother wasn't well-liked, but I had made a few friends, and I was beautiful in my own way, confident with my looks, while fragile when it came to friendships. Rhoswen was threatened by me, for some reason or another, whether my looks or the tenuous hold I had on the few villagers who I befriended.

"I had elementary magic back then, and one of the girls in on the prank was a friend, supposedly. They wanted to humiliate me, push me into the river and force me to walk home in the snow, dripping wet and shivering. It was the coldest winter this village had ever seen, but it still wasn't enough for Rhoswen. She took it even farther and gave me this scar." She pulls back her hair and shows the puckered pink line traveling from her temple to her chin.

"Until your Celia, only men came to the castle. My mother wanted the town to suffer the loss of the men that had held me while Rhoswen attacked and the ones that would follow. After taking their future, she took their memories of the incident. She wanted this place to relearn their actions, but I doubt she imagined it would outlast her. When Celia decided to face the beast herself, Rhosen saw her chance. She was able to free part of her soul and trap Celia's as the guardian of the castle, controlling her while they both remain locked inside."

She stares at her hands, her brow furrowing. "For a long time, I was angry at my mother for isolating us even further from the town. But she hadn't, not really. The damage had been done by small-mindedness. She only brought it to the light."

I shake my head. "How did I make it out alive?"

She smiles. "Because you did not travel to the castle to gain glory but to right a wrong. Selfishness and pride, which drove Rhoswen when she cursed her family and this place with her choices, are the ugliest things of all. There's still time to save Celia, but you'll have to be smart about it."

"How am I supposed to do that?" I ask.

"Take these with you." She reaches behind her, producing a longsword and a dagger. A faint light emanates from them, as if they are enchanted.

"You have to defeat the beast and save yourself from a bitter winter by breaking the curse," she says. "My mother wasn't without her faults, but she would never create an unbreakable curse. She gave them to me, but no one has been ready until you. They shone for the first time when you volunteered. When a worthy opponent wields these blades, they can break any enchantment. You were gone before I could catch you last time." She winks, but I think there are some things about this woman I could never understand.

I slide the blades into their sheaths.

"Aim true, and they will never fail you." She walks to the door, unlocks it and slides out. The key rests on the table next to the door, shining gold in the candlelight. She tosses me a smile before escaping into the falling snow. "Choose well, young lordling."

I rush through the snow back to my family's manor. Before I go, I have to see my sister—to at least know she's protected and healing. If the task of defeating the beast is as difficult as the witch promises, this could be the last time I speak with her.

There's a loud hum coming from the center of the village. As the sun begins its descent below the horizon, the sky blazes with the light of torches being struck and voices carrying above the buildings lining the streets.

Unease settles in my stomach, but I swallow down the sourness rising in my throat and turn back to my family's home. I sneak in through an opening in the boundary wall, a place only my father and I know about, and slip through the kitchens.

Compared to outside, an eerie silence hangs over the manor, an absence of people besides the ones who live here. I rush to the nearest window and catch flickers of movement in the dark where guards patrol our property.

The sun has almost disappeared below the horizon when I make it upstairs, and silence weighs heavy on the manor. I make for the servant's hall instead of the main staircase and find my sister's room heavily guarded.

"What are you doing?" a voice asks behind me, discovering my hiding spot in the shadows.

I freeze. *Mother.* "I—I was checking on Maris."

She grabs my wrist and pulls into an empty room. "What are you doing here, Will?"

"I came to see Maris."

Mother touches my cheek. "I asked Mistress Gardner to watch after you. Why aren't you resting—"

"I have to save Celia," I interrupt.

"No, you do not." Her voice is sharp, cold. She wrenches her hand away. "You need to go back to the cottage—where you're safe like *she* promised. It's the only way to keep you safe. The castle is still…*alive.*" She chokes on the word, and I wrap her in my arms.

"What happened?" I whisper.

"It's not natural, neither the castle nor what it does to this place when winter comes," she says into my shoulder, but I can't tell if she's speaking to me or through me. "You weren't supposed to live. I mourned you *both.* I can't lose you again." She backs away. "You don't have to go back to the witch, but I didn't know what else to do to keep you away from this—"

I cup her face in my hands. "I have to save Celia," I whisper. "I love her. I'm going to marry her. This is about our *family*, and she is part of that."

She shakes her head. "She will be the death of you."

The words sharpen my resolve and steel my heart. "Not doing anything when there's a chance would be my demise. Please, Mother."

She touches my cheek. "Is there any way to talk you out of it?"

I shake my head. "Let me go."

The door behind her creaks open, and I meet my father's eyes, a bronzed mirror of my own. "Let him go, Lorcella."

Mother spins around, the dissent blooming on her lips. She tenses at the look in his eye, and her head bows.

She turns back to me, cupping my cheek and rubbing her thumb over my skin. Finally, she nods.

"Thank you," I say, kissing her forehead. "I will return. I promise."

She smiles, tears shining in her eyes. "Be safe." She turns away as if unable to watch me go.

The guards don't stop me as I walk into my sister's room, my mother hovering in the hall. Her hair is a fan around her head as her chest rises and falls with each intake of breath.

I lean over her and touch a small cut on her forehead, a scab already starting to form. "At least you're safe," I whisper.

Without waking her, I tuck a strand of hair behind her ear and escape back into the hall, intent on saving another piece of my heart.

The villagers are hysterical, and fire and swords cover the town square as one of the merchants demands vengeance for the decades of suffering. The still-rising winter sent them to the precipice.

I cover my face with the hood of my cloak and slip through the crowd. Frenzied by their anger, no one notices as I disappear into the forest. My lungs ache with each intake of icy air as the winter storms ahead. The castle is fighting back, ready to claim the next girl to keep the curse active. It needs a life to fuel the enchantment, and it needs a hero to sacrifice himself to save the girl.

I step into the courtyard and the ground shifts beneath my feet.

Welcome back, lordling, the voice whispers in my ear. *Have you come to save another?* An echo of a smile at the end of her words is sharper than the sword at my waist.

A grimace works its way onto my lips as snow and ice fill the air. "When I do free her, what becomes of you?"

The temperature around me drops.

Do not speak of what you do not understand, William Rhodes. We come from the same vine, nephew. It's difficult to get rid of the root without destroying the shoot.

Silence settles over the courtyard, and the little warmth available to me rises back in my cheeks. I unsheath my sword and take a step toward the front door, glancing back and searching for signs of the villagers.

Before my hand can wrap around the iron handle, the double doors to the castle creak open.

"Celia?" I whisper into the crumbling space.

My footsteps echo on the cracked floor, clouds forming in front of my face with each breath. Flickers of candlelight illuminate the room and create shadowy figures that move with me.

As soon as I'm through the doors, they slam shut behind me, the lock sliding into place.

The voice's eagerness spreads through me and raises the hair on the back of my neck.

"You want a game? Test me, Rhoswen. Give me your best because I can take anything you throw at me." My words bounce against the stone walls. "To me, this is life or death, and I think you feel the same. I win, you release Celia."

Celia will be your prize. Destroy the heart of the flower in the tower, and she'll be yours. Two souls will leave this place, forever. I promise.

"If you win—"

You presume to understand what I want, lordling. Am I not allowed to name my own prize?

Goosebumps pepper my flesh. The words trace my skin, a snake slithering beneath my clothes. "What is it you want?"

To be truly rid of this prison, to not die inside it. Free me.

I push back the lump in my throat. "How do I free you?"

In order to be free from this curse, a willing vessel has to take my place.

"That's why you're still here, even with Celia. She's not a willing vessel."

She remains silent, but I feel her hovering in the corners of my mind.

Finally she asks, *Do we have a deal, lordling?*

If she wins, Celia and I both die. It would be a worse death to know I tried and wasn't able to save her. "Yes," rises to my lips.

Then let the games begin. I pray you can make it to her tower.

A fierce wind blows through the entryway, robbing the room of light. The castle settles around me, and a slithering sound echoes in the room.

"I told you not to come back," a gravelly voice says. "You were supposed to take her and run."

"Celia? Celia, let me help you—"

I'm knocked to the ground. The air rushes from my lungs, and my blade flies from my hand, skittering farther into the darkness.

"You can't fight this," she says. "You can't fight *her*."

The slithering hiss rises in my ears and wraps around my throat. I reach for the thing holding me to the ground, but my fingers pass through smoke. My body spasms, begging for air, and I force my muscles to relax and my brain to *think*.

I fumble for the dagger at my waist and slash at the invisible creature holding me down. A screech fills the air, and the candles relight with orange and blue flames. I roll onto my side, gulping in lungfuls of air.

I take in the room around me. Thorn-covered vines slither over the floors and up the walls, coming toward me. I slice at them with my dagger, and the blade turns the golden hue of the sun. Pain lances behind my eyes, and I have to squint against the sudden brightness. A shriek erupts from the plant, and the exposed root and vine shrivel and explode in a puff of smoke.

I lunge for my sword, one of the vines grabbing my back foot. I slash at it with my dagger, the piercing scream ringing in my ears. My fingers fumble for my sword, almost in reach, before another vine grabs the blade and throws it across the room.

A scream rips from my throat, and I slash through the next vine trying to grab me. I sprint for the sword and clasp the hilt before the vine latches on. Light pierces the room as my hand meets the blade, and the insidious plant shrivels before it bursts into dust. The debris settles in the air, touching my skin and entering my lungs, but I push past the discomfort and storm upstairs.

A faint glow streams from the next level, and my eyes train on it. Wind whistles through the cracks in the castle, and I almost don't see the beasts until they're on me.

Three wolves launch at me from the shadows, and I swing my sword wide. One of them catches the brunt of my blade and lands in a whimpering heap at the bottom of the stairs. The other two dash forward, lips pulled back in snarls.

One ducks away from my swinging blade as the other pounces. It latches onto my arm, ripping through fabric and skin and drawing blood. I slice at it, cutting its shoulder. It howls in pain and disappears into the shadows, and the other lifts its maw and cries out in agony.

When it comes for me, I'm ready.

We circle each other, one of my eyes trained on the faint glow coming from the next level and the other on the gray wolf. Saliva drips from its teeth and pools on the floor.

"Come on!" I scream.

It pounces.

I dart out of its path and bring up my sword. The blade sinks into the wolf's belly, and it falls to the ground with the cry of death. I rise to my feet and stare at the remains of my battle. The chest rises and falls unsteadily on one of the wolves, but I leave it, hoping that once I break this curse, whatever holds it here will break, too.

I limp up the stairs, holding my arm to my chest and the sword in my other hand. Debris, broken glass, and remains of a life once lived litter the path to the double doors at the end of the hall.

My footsteps slow the closer I get to the light, and I glance around the corners into the shadows for anything to jump out. The wood is cool against my fingers as I press my way into the room, and I'm frozen by the sight in front of me.

My eyes barely register the pulsating rose at the top of the tower, the shining rose rising from the center of the room and hovering waist high. My attention is elsewhere—on the two girls standing behind it.

"Maris, what are you doing?" I ask, the words barely a whisper.

How did she sneak out of the manor?

"What you don't have the power to do," my sister says, the blade in her hand under Celia's throat. A trickle of blood bleeds into the neck of Celia's white dress, tangling with her russet curls.

"Hello, William," Celia whispers, fully herself instead of half hidden by the monster. Her smile stops my heart, and I ache to rush to her and kiss the salted tears from her cheeks, enveloping her in my arms.

"How did you get past the guards?" I ask Maris.

Maris snorts. "I told Mother I needed rest. Alone. Then I used the same secret places you used to sneak through when we were children. You thought you and Father were the only ones who knew about those?"

My eyes flash to Celia. I want to give her all the words I never thought I'd be able to say, but I bottle them inside and turn toward my sister. "Let her go, Maris. We can end this. We can free her—"

"You don't understand! She's in my head! I had to come–this is the only way!" Maris says. Anger colors her cheeks, and tears and snot cover her face. "You weren't held prisoner here. This is the only way! We have to kill the thing that keeps the castle alive."

I lay my sword down. "That's not Celia. Can't you feel it? There's someone else here. That's who we have to destroy, and the only way to do that is to free Celia. If she doesn't have a vessel, then she can't thrive. We can destroy it from the root!"

"There's no destroying it. I've tried! That's why I followed you. Don't you see? She is the root. Celia is connected to it. There was only ever one way to end this." She grabs Celia's wrist and shoves it forward. Roots anchored to the castle dig into Celia's skin, pulsating with their own heartbeat.

I clench my jaw and move toward her. "There is a way, Maris. Put the knife down. Please."

"I can't. I'm sorry."

I reach for the dagger in my belt at the same time Maris begins to slide the knife over Celia's throat. My blade makes impact before my sister can finish her motion, and a scream pierces the air as the blade buries into the flesh of her hand. The knife slides across the floor, half hidden in the shadows.

She drops Celia, and I move my fiancée behind me. "Will—" Celia begins.

"Why would you do that? There was a chance to break this curse!" Maris glares at me, hot tears pouring down her cheeks. "Now we're doomed to forever repeat it because you can't give her up. She needs a willing sacrifice!"

"Will, listen to me," Celia tries to say, but I break away from her and step toward my sister.

"I didn't want to hurt you, Maris, but you don't understand."

My sister yanks the blade out of her hand, her knees hitting the ground with a hard crack as she falls to the floor in agony. I rush toward her, but I'm yanked backward. Thorns dig into my arms, and I'm spun to face the girl I love.

"You should have let me go," Celia whispers, holding onto the vines coming from her wrists. "Maris understands. She's had her *in her head*. You can't save us all. It would have been kinder for you to kill me."

"I can't do that, Celia." I grab onto the vines to pull her closer.

"Stop! Take Maris and *leave,*" Celia says. "Never come back here! I will take her place. I will take Rhoswen's place. The rose's petals have already started to fall." I glance at the flower in the center of the room. "The winter won't last long."

"The winter always returns." I tug hard on the vines, gritting my teeth against the sharp pain in my arms. "You will die here, and then what? What happens when you die?"

She smiles. Her tears flash in the light from the rose still hovering between us. "I won't die. I'll be here until the end of time, keeping the village safe. No girls will be taken, never again."

"But you will die." I tug her another step closer, then one more. "You will die every day you spend here alone. Time will cease to matter, and you will be no more because this place will kill your soul." We're so close now that I can feel the beat of her heart, the beat of the vines against my chest. "And I will not leave you here to die."

I release my hold on the vines and grab the sword at my waist. My hand wraps around the hilt as I'm tugged back and thrown into the nearest wall. I slice the blade out in front of me, and the vines let go.

A piercing scream echoes in the room as they shrivel and die in puffs of dust. Celia falls to the ground with a cry. Two of the women I care most about in the world lie on either side of the rose as I dive my blade into it and release the blinding light of the sun.

Every shadow ceases to exist as the ground shudders beneath my feet. I release the blade, and the weight of endless winters drops from my shoulders.

I leave the sword and dash toward my sister. "Maris, you've got to get up!"

"Will?" she whispers, eyes clearer than before. "What—how—"

"Stand up, Maris! This place is about to fall."

I leave her to rise to her feet and head toward Celia. Blood courses from her wrists and pools on the floor. I rip off my doublet and yank it apart, tying the strips around her wrists to stop the flow.

"Leave me, Will—"

I capture her face in my hands. "There is nothing—*nothing*—in this world or the next that would make me leave you." I pull her close and place my lips on hers, trying to convey every missed moment, forgotten touch, and unspoken word in a single kiss.

Her lips move against mine, quick and fierce, and I pull away and cradle her in my arms.

I search for my sister and find her hovering in the doorway, breathing heavily through her nose. The ground shakes once, twice, three times, and I run for the front door of the castle with Celia in my arms.

"Can you walk?" I ask Maris.

She nods stiffly. "Just my hand," she murmurs.

"Follow me and don't look back."

We race through the castle, and the heavy weight in my chest starts to lift the closer we get to the front entrance. The outside shines brightly with the torchlight of the villagers as they arrive from the forest, but the doors slam shut when we're inches away.

Not so fast, lordling, the voice says, the pain evident in her words. *You . . . must . . . end this.*

"What more do you want?" I demand, spinning in circles with Celia in my arms. "I destroyed the rose! This castle is coming down—"

You must choose . . . you agreed only two souls would leave this place. You're . . . demanding three.

"You lured my sister here" I scream. "She has already been rescued—"

Choose . . .

The castle begins to collapse around us, and I run over to Maris. "Can you carry her, at least over the threshold?"

"William, you can't—" Maris says.

Celia's eyes do not open as I press my lips against her temple.

I look back to my sister. "Can you do it?"

Maris bites back her tears and manages one stiff nod. "I can."

I give Celia to Maris. She strains against her weight, and I reach for the handle.

"I'm sorry," Maris whispers. "I'm so—"

I lean over and cup her cheek. "I love you, Mari. Now, go."

The doors magically wing open, and I watch my sister and the girl I love fall into the waiting crowd. The doors to the castle slam shut behind them, and I spin around to face the voice. A woman staggers into the entryway, the remains of the building falling all around her.

"Have you come to take my place?" she asks, the sound no longer in my mind.

"If that's what I must do, then I will gladly take your place if it saves them."

She slouches on the ground in a mess of black fabric and pain. Her hood falls away, revealing a weary, pale countenance and aged eyes. "Then come end it, William Rhodes. End my suffering."

I lower myself in front of her, and she takes her hands in mine. They're surprisingly warm. She smiles up at me. "Thank you," she whispers before kissing my cheek.

Sound ceases, and I'm left surrounded by darkness, peace, and the flicker of a smile not my own.

I wake with a start, not sure where I am.

"Hello, William Rhodes." I jerk upright and glance to my left to see Mistress Gardner sitting beside me on the grass.

"What happened? Where am I?"

"You broke the curse," she says, not looking at me but gazing at the stars. "We're in the in-between place." The stars take on a life of their own, dancing in the rushing dawn.

I glance around. "Is this my prison? Somewhere in between real life and the curse?"

A laugh rolls from her lips. "No, William. I have come to offer you a choice."

"What kind of choice? I'm done making deals—"

She raises her hand. "This isn't a deal. This is a gift. I have lived more years than some can fathom and seen more things than others can dream up. Your life has barely begun. I wish to take your place. Your life would still be a cursed one since you took Rhoswen's place, but not with my sacrifice. You chose to save the girl you loved, but I am choosing to end this."

"I don't understand," I say, resting my chin on my forearms. "How does your sacrifice end this? I'm a willing vessel for the curse—"

"Your soul would be trapped here, in this place," she says. "What I'm offering you is an end to it. A true break, something only I can give you. I couldn't before, not without your sacrifice. My life is over, William. It has been for a long time. This is my gift to you, my life for yours. All I'm asking is for you to let me end it in the way I want."

"But–are you sure?" I ask.

"This is what I want," she says, still not looking at me. "It's my time to leave. Do you accept the trade?"

Finally, her gaze meets mine, and I see hope mingled with a weary unrest.

"Yes," I say, the word a breath between my lips.

Mistress Gardiner turns her head to the sky and disappears into the night. The world snaps into focus. The delicate breeze dances over my skin as I step back into the winter. Its harshness isn't bitter over my flesh but welcome—hopeful.

I rush outside and down the broken steps of the castle to Celia and Maris and fall down beside them, pulling them into a tight embrace. The growing crowd of villagers stares in shock at the transformation unfolding.

Celia's eyes widen in shock. Maris wraps her arms around me, burying her face in my neck.

"Don't you *ever* do that again," Maris says, hugging me so hard I can't breathe.

"You've exceeded your limit on bad decisions for the rest of your life," Celia says, pulling me down next to her and wrapping her arms tightly around me.

I plant a kiss on her forehead and breathe in the peaceful smell of lavender and frost. "Sacrificing myself for you would have been the best decision I ever made."

"The curse is broken," Mother says, pushing through the crowd. Her eyes never leave us, unlike the villagers who stare in shock at the scene shifting before them. She falls to the ground, wrapping me in her arms.

"Let's go home." She helps us to our feet and leads us back toward the village. "This castle needs to rest as much as we do; it's time for a . . . beautiful winter."

The rest of the villagers follow us back through the rising dawn, blades sheathed and a lightness in the air as snow falls onto the path. Winter continues without its thorns, and the sun blossoms like a rose over the mountains as we make our way home.

Lady of the Roses

Cassandra Hamm

HE STOLE MY heart with a rose. But roses have their thorns.

Lysander's boots thud against the stairs like musket fire. My book hits the table with a muffled thump as I haul myself from the cushions. My ring heats with each step Lysander takes.

"Elaine?"

When I'm in his embrace, my name is a song on his swollen lips. This is entirely different—gravelly and dark, almost… beast-like.

I dart between the bookshelves as though dusty old novels can protect me. Sunlight filters through the windows and highlights dancing dust motes. I shouldn't have tried to leave. I should've waited for tonight, like Miriam and I planned.

Thump. Thump. Thump.

The doors groan as Lysander pushes his way into the library. I flatten myself against a shelf. *Maybe he's not angry anymore. Maybe he just wants to see me.* But the labored huff of his breathing tells me otherwise.

I look down at my hand. Blood-red rubies, carved into petal-like facets, catch a stray ray of sunlight. Lysander's own ruby ring calls to me across the room, a faint pull I once found romantic.

"Elaine, I know you're in here. Stop being such a child." He stalks across the library floor, red coattails flaring behind him. Light glints off his golden boot buckles. I wince at the memory of those buckles slamming into my still-bruised shins.

Lysander lets out a huff. Then, *"Elaine."*

My ring awakens. It sparks white hot and hungry, dragging me toward Lysander, lightly at first, then stronger. I stagger out from the stacks into the open room.

Lysander's gray eyes rake over me, taking in my tangled hair and wrinkled dress. But I am still beautiful. I will always be beautiful, so long as I wear his ring.

Caught up in his command, my hand stretches forward until my fingers touch his. A matching rose ring winks on his hand. Reunited once more. Then my limbs are my own again. I jerk my hand back.

"You know I hate doing that," Lysander says in a soft, flat tone.

Then don't do it. I look at the wooden floor, at the gold-framed window, anything to keep from seeing the disappointed expression on his face. Silver roses bloom on the frosted glass, blocking my view of the outside world. For one terrifying, bleak moment, I contemplate throwing myself from the sill.

"I wouldn't have to use the bond if you'd just come when I asked." He takes my face in his large hands, anchoring me in place. I freeze beneath the touch I once found so alluring.

"Don't shut me out, Elaine. I need you. I can't live without you. Please."

It's the "please" that undoes me. My eyes rove over his long, refined nose and perfectly kissable mouth. It would be too easy to let myself get lost in his touch and forget why I ran in the first place.

That mouth hovers over mine. "Aren't you going to apologize?"

Apologize? When *he* screamed at me earlier for venturing outside the gates? I recoil, gooseflesh rippling on my arms.

"Don't be like that, Elaine."

I want to scream at him. I want to curl into a ball. Instead, I say, "I'm sorry."

Lysander's dimple flashes, making him appear more human than beast. "I forgive you. I'll always forgive you."

For *what?* For daring to leave my gilded cage for a few moments? *"You're* the one who should be apologizing."

He stiffens, eyes hardening, mouth set in a thin line.

Elaine, you fool! I should've placated him or at least let him calm down. He can't be reasoned with when he's in a mood. My breath comes in shallow spurts as I wait for a blow—

Lysander wanders toward the table where I left my book. He lifts it gently, almost reverently. Its cover is as familiar to me as Lysander's face. A feminine silhouette stands amongst a sea of roses—baby pink, creamy white, blood red. Light catches its silver script: *Lady of the Roses.*

The book might belong to him, technically, but it's one of the only things that has felt truly, wholly *mine*. Seeing it in his large hands now...

"*Lady of the Roses.*" He opens the binding, revealing creamy, serrated pages. "One of your favorites, isn't it?"

"Yes." I want to tear the book from his hands. "You, of all people, should understand why I'm drawn to roses."

His lips curl in a smile, but his eyes don't follow. "I didn't know you appreciated our family crest so."

My eyes flick to the wooden shelves and chair backs, inlaid with rose carvings. "Certainly," I say. "But, of course, *Lady* is more than just a book that uses the language of flowers in both subtle and non-subtle ways. Aurelia herself is what makes the book beautiful. The world has given her nothing but pain, yet she still tries to save it."

If only I could be like her. I know she's just a fictional character, but her love for people, her empathy for those who suffer...

But it seems all I can do is care about myself.

"It sounds quite touching." Lysander's fingers tighten on the page right before he tears it from the binding. The page floats mid-air, joining the dust, before settling against the carpet.

I keep my mouth clamped shut, my body stiff, hiding a silent scream. That book has kept me sane. It has helped me through the long nights as I nurse both physical bruises and invisible wounds. And now it has been irreparably damaged.

How dare he. How. Dare. He.

I inhale deeply, trying to exude serenity and composure, but moisture still pricks at my eyes. I blink hard and turn away, hating that he saw even a glimpse of my pain.

The slight tearing sound brings me back to Lysander. He pulls lazily at another page, his gaze on me the entire time, as though to say, *Your move.*

"I'm sorry," I whisper.

"What was that?" Lysander pauses. The page—the start of a new chapter, with looping numbers and a hand-painted rose—is still attached to the binding. At least, for now.

"I'm. Sorry." I grit my teeth and force the words out, but saying them still feels like a betrayal of everything I am.

"Are you now?" He gives me a lazy smile.

He's waiting, but for *what?* I swallow hard and survey the partially-torn page. Aurelia and her eventual husband, Alistair, have escaped from the dark lord and found themselves by a rosebush. Alistair breaks off a stem, ignoring the blood that drips from his hands, and gives her a single red rose. There is so much in that one gesture—*you are beautiful. You are courageous. I love you.*

My romantic heart reread the pages over and over, wishing that someone would care for me like that.

Maybe I found my prince... but I wish I hadn't.

He tugs on the page, and my heart rips along with it. I can't stop a whimper. "Please, Lysander. Please."

His eyes burn into mine. I can almost hear him say, *I can and will take everything and everyone you love from you.*

I think of Miriam, the bondservant who has risked everything to help me. I can't let him find out about her, or... I don't want to think about what he'd do.

Lysander closes *Lady of the Roses* and sets it down.

I let out a shuddering breath and grab his hand—the hand that just defiled a piece of my heart. "I'm sorry I disobeyed you. I'll never do it again, I swear." The words taste foul, but I need to make him believe I'm fully, truly broken. And the worst thing is... it might be true.

His lips curl into a smile. "I know." Then he claims my mouth.

Something sparks within me at his touch, something traitorous. His hands cradle my cheeks as he kisses me slowly, tenderly, like I'm as fragile as a petal. He pulls back, murmuring, "I love you so much, Elaine."

It was so easy to love him. It still is.

He'd seemed like such a gentleman. I was hot and bored at my mother's latest social event, waiting for my older sister to finish flirting, when he approached. When he held out a blood-red rose, my heart stopped. No one had ever approached me, let alone a man who looked like *this.*

"A flower for a lady," he'd said.

When I moved into his castle, he gave me the rose ring that now graces my finger. My sister would've died for such a ring. "We are bonded for life now," he told me.

How do you break an unbreakable bond?

"You are so lovely," Lysander whispers against my lips.

I hate how those words fill the hollow places in me, the ones my mother and sister carved up long ago. And he knows it.

You're only beautiful because of him.

When he's gone, I kneel and take the fallen page in trembling hands. It's fragile, brittle, jagged, like my heart.

Aurelia would be disappointed in you.

I press it to my chest and finally let myself cry.

Lysander is almost boyish while he sleeps. His red-brown hair is rumpled, his face slack and sweet. I prop myself onto my elbow and watch him for a moment longer, hating myself for wanting to smooth his stubbled jaw.

At this rate, I'll be late to meet Miriam. But shouldn't I enjoy my last moment with Lysander?

He put you in a cage. So, why do I feel such a pang at leaving him?

Extracting myself from his arm, I slide from the bed. I don the leggings and blouse Miriam stole when she was on laundry duty, then kick my discarded nightgown under the bed. I don't ever want to see that piece of flimsy fabric again.

But what if it doesn't work?

I refuse to acknowledge the idea. I *have* to escape. I can't take another night here.

Satchel slung over my shoulder, I creep through the dark hallway. Lysander's ancestors glare down at me from golden picture frames. *What are you without him?* they seem to say. *He made you beautiful. He made you something of value.*

Moonlight filters through the library's frosted windows, highlighting the roses and casting the shelves in an eerie silver glow.

Will I truly be free tonight? Lysander slowly restricted my access to the outside world, too gradually for me to notice until I was locked inside the gates. Then there's the ring—it doesn't like being separated from its mate. Once, Lysander left me at the castle while he traveled to the very outskirts of town. My scalding ring slammed me against the walls, trying to reunite me with Lysander.

He never tries to push the bond limits anymore.

But what if my idea doesn't work? What if my hope is shattered? I'm not sure I could take it.

"Miss Elaine?"

I nearly jump out of my skin before recognizing Miriam's rough drawl. "Yes, it's me."

The bondservant detaches herself from the shelves and wrings her hands. Her stained, rough-spun dress and pinned up curls tell me she must've come straight from her duties.

Suddenly, I can't look at her. Can't think of what I'll be doing to her.

I turn aside, find *Lady of the Roses* on the shelf, and shove it inside my satchel, which bulges with clothing and supplies. The torn page is safe between its binding. I'll find a way to mend it once I escape. *If* I escape.

Miriam doesn't say a word, but I feel her eyes on me. How can she possibly be so *calm* right now? Or maybe she isn't calm at all. Maybe her placid exterior hides a storm.

Lysander didn't want me talking to the bondservants, let alone making friends with them. Maybe because he knew they would understand my captivity better than anyone else could.

I can't take it any longer. I turn to her and blurt, "Are you sure you want to do this?"

Miriam looks at her boots. "Better me than you, miss."

My eyes sting. I throw my arms around her and hug tightly.

While hiding from Lysander a few nights ago, I discovered a book on soul binding magic. I already knew that the bond was linked to objects—specifically to matching sets, which was why jewelry was often used. What I *didn't* know was that bonds could be transferred.

"You could come with me," I say. "I can go a certain distance from him. I don't *have* to give you the ring."

But I know it won't work. He'd just call me back with his soul magic.

Miriam gives me a sad smile as though thinking the same thing. Then she leads me to the back of the library. Of course the spell requires a mirror. It just *has* to torment me in every way possible.

As I peer into the glass, I can almost believe this is my true face—my flawless, porcelain skin; my large, long-lashed eyes; my thin, elegant nose; my straight, blindingly white teeth; my plump, trembling lips.

Miriam will receive the entirety of my curse—not just Lysander, but my beauty, too. Is that why she's willing to take on this burden? Because she wants to be noticed?

We yank strands of hair from our scalps. Miriam draws a kitchen knife from her dress and slices her palm. Crimson droplets gather in the lines on her well-worked skin. I take my own knife and do the same. It stings, but nothing so bad as what I've faced from Lysander.

The rubies in my ring catch the moonlight, bright and impossibly lovely. To think that such a small thing keeps me captive. I could almost believe it's all in my head, that I've concocted this entire torment.

"It's not an order, you know," I say. "I'm not your master, Miriam. You don't have to obey me."

Miriam's throat works up and down as though no one has ever said that to her. Maybe they haven't. Maybe she's only ever known commands. Maybe being bonded to Lysander wouldn't be so different from her life right now.

"I know, miss." Her voice is just a breath.

Our hands join, mixed with the hair and the blood. Now, it's time for me to speak the ancient language to transfer the bond.

I know the words, of course. I memorized it, obsessed over it, fantasized what it would be like to break the bond. Yet, now that it's here...

My chest tightens. I gaze at my perfect face, my slender neck, and imagine all of it gone—leaving me the wallflower, the embarrassment, the failure.

"Miss?" Miriam prompts.

I tear my hand from hers. Her blood stains my palm, and I suddenly want to scrub it away. "I can't."

Her eyebrows knit together. "What do you mean?"

"I can't... I won't be..." I take in a shuddering breath. "I want to be *pretty*, Miriam. I know it's selfish and ridiculous, but..." I think of my life before Lysander. Were the social snubs really better than Lysander's passive aggression? At least he *loves* me.

"Oh, don't worry!" Miriam says. "You're a pretty one, and that's no mistake, miss!"

"But this isn't my *real* face." Heat fills my unpainted cheeks. "It's close to my real face, but it's... altered. It was part of the bond magic."

Her mouth parts in an 'o.'

Eyes burning, I turn away. My sister called me "the ugly one" and refused to acknowledge me in society. Only my late grandfather seemed to think differently, but he was old and touched in the head.

I don't know why Lysander even noticed me. Maybe because my face had been slathered in paint. Maybe because my dress showed off my curves to their best effect. Or maybe he saw someone so desperate for love that she'd leave everything behind—someone who could be easily manipulated.

Will anyone ever find me attractive again?

"You're pretty," Miriam says, "but that's not why you're my . . . well, my *friend,* miss." Her cheeks darken as though she's afraid to call her mistress such a familiar word. "It's what's inside."

I sigh. Sweet, simple Miriam. She doesn't understand that beauty ensures survival.

"It's true, Elaine. I mean, miss."

"Call me Elaine. I'm not your mistress anymore. Or, I won't be soon."

"Hurry up and get that ring off, then," she says.

I falter. Can I really do this to her? Can I transfer my pain to her?

I could try taking it off myself. Last time, it nearly killed me, but it'd be better than putting Miriam through this.

I eye the rose-decorated window, wondering, not for the first time, what it would be like to throw myself from the sill. If the world would be better without me in it.

"Don't you second guess yourself now, Elaine." Miriam watches me with such serenity, such gentleness. "You deserve to be free from Master Godfrey."

"But so do you!"

"I've never been free," she says.

"After all I've done for you." Lysander's words cut through the dust-strewn air, slamming right into my gut. Maybe it's the magic of our rings, but I crumple in front of the mirror as though I've been stabbed.

How did I not notice when he arrived? How could I have been so stupid as to think I could get away with this?

"Elaine!" Miriam reaches for me. "Are you all right, miss?"

"I'm . . . fine." I straighten, trying to ignore the cold creeping over my skin. Miriam can't be here right now. Should I order her to leave? Would Lysander allow it?

"Who is this?" Lysander asks, watching Miriam like she is an insect to be squashed.

"Just one of the bondservants." I force the words out. "She was assisting me with . . . well, I've been looking for a certain book, you know, and she—"

"I doubt the girl can even read." His gray eyes are as impenetrable as stone. "If you're going to lie, do it *well.*"

I think of torn pages and shattered dreams, of Aurelia's bravery and my own cowardice.

Lysander's hand catches mine, twisting my palm to face his. His face pales at the dried blood on my hand. When he turns to Miriam and finds a similar stain, an agonized cry rips from his mouth. "You were trying to break our bond!"

I don't know what to say. Everything is unraveling. I look to Miriam, silently begging, *You need to leave!* But she stands, frozen, a perfect target.

"Hit her."

The command seizes my limbs. I whip my hand back and slap Miriam across the face. The rubies draw blood on her cheek.

My soul cracks. I ache to throw myself at him, to beat him until my fists bleed, to scream and scream until my throat is raw.

I'm sorry, Miriam. I'm so—

"Hit her."

Miriam flinches away from me, but not before my hand cracks across her face again. Tears pour down my cheeks.

How could I ever have *considered* inflicting this on someone else? Am I really that selfish?

A thought hits me. *What if...what if the control goes both ways?*

I focus on the bond between our souls and imagine tugging that cord like a marionette's strings.

"Stop!" I say.

Lysander freezes.

For a moment, all I can do is gape. Lysander, my beast, my prince, is *powerless.* His features are fixed in that terrible smile, his limbs stiff, his chest barely rising and falling.

"What did you do, Elaine?" Miriam's eyes are wide, terrified. Blood streaks her round cheeks.

I could hurt him now. The thought sends a thrill through me. I could make him sorry he ever gave me that rose. I might even be able to kill him with a word—

Ice creeps over my skin at the horrifying thought. Maybe this is how he started. Maybe he lashed out at someone to get back at them. And now...he's *this.*

I don't want to be like him.

I release the magic. Lysander hurtles toward me. I don't have time to react before he crushes me to his chest. I try to suck in air.

"How *dare* you." Each word drips with unbridled fury. "I should kill you for that."

Do it, I want to say. Except...I don't *want* to die. Not really. I don't want to be in pain, but I don't want to be gone from the world either.

He has stolen everything from me. But he will not steal my desire to live.

"You created the bond," I say tightly. "You should've realized it went both ways."

He opens his mouth, but then something crashes into his back. He stumbles forward, nearly knocking me off my feet, but I use his surprise to free myself from his grip. Miriam stands behind him, a tome in hand.

"Get out of here!" I hiss, swaying on my feet.

She shakes her head, face pale. "Not without you!"

I have to stop this. But how? Even if we could still finish the transfer, I don't *want* to give this burden to Miriam.

I yank on the ring. Heat floods my body, searing my skin, penetrating my muscles and bones. I gasp, lungs shuddering, heart refusing to beat.

I might die without the ring. But if I don't try to remove it, he'll kill Miriam.

You could grovel. You could beg—

But I don't want to beg. I don't want to walk on eggshells my whole life, placating and pleasing, always wondering when the next blow will come, either physical or mental.

Without him, you are nothing!

I clench my jaw and shut out the voice.

"You can't break the soul bond. Not without another host." Lysander gives me a calm, cruel smile, the one he wears before the impending torment. But instead of inflicting it on me, he turns toward Miriam.

Miriam darts into the shelves, her dress flaring behind her. Lysander's boots pound against the wooden beams in pursuit. His legs are so much longer than hers.

If I remove the ring, will it weaken him too? Maybe my sacrifice could save Miriam.

But you can't remove it. Not unless...

I know what's tying me to the ring. Not love for Lysander, not anymore. That died long ago. Love for my *beauty.*

A lump forms in my throat. I knew it would come to this, and yet to have to consciously do so...

"Ugly little thing, isn't she?" My sister's words come back to me, as biting as the first time I heard them. *"Mother will have a terrible time marrying her off."*

I shove aside the thought and tug on the ring again. My vision spots as fire rips up my arm, searing straight to my heart.

Lysander lets out a cry.

I pull harder. Tears pour down my cheeks. Soon, this skin will be bumpy and acne-ridden, assuming I survive.

"You can't remove it!" Lysander's shout is closer to me than before. He must've abandoned his chase, at least temporarily. "You know what will happen."

I know.

The ring scrapes against my skin, drawing blood to match the blood on my palms.

He bursts out from the shelves. "You are only beautiful because of *me.* You have value because of *me.*"

I think of Miriam, who cares more for my heart than my outward appearance. I think of my late grandfather, who called me pretty when I had crooked teeth and a bumpy nose, and he *meant* it.

"I had value before you ever came into my life," I say. "You just couldn't see it."

And neither could I.

I pull. The ring flies off my finger and disappears into the library's shadows.

Pain rips through my chest, deeper than anything I've ever felt. Worse than any of my mother or sister's rejections, fiercer than any command Lysander gave me. Our souls separate with a vicious tearing.

I collapse, surrounded by the scent of phantom rose petals.

"Miss? Are you awake?"

I groan. My lungs shudder, and my skin aches, something bone deep, like I've been crushed beneath Lysander's castle.

Lysander! My eyes flash open. Miriam sits over me, her gaze gentle. I'm lying down on something long and soft—a bed. The walls are creamy brown, and the window is plain, with a wooden frame and normal glass, no roses in sight.

I must be in the village. Does that mean I escaped Lysander? I can't remember what happened after my collapse.

"Oh, thank the Lord." Miriam clasps her hands together and nods up at the sky. "You gave us a mighty scare, miss."

"Where is he?" I croak.

She doesn't answer for a moment. My throat tightens.

"Master Godfrey..." She fidgets. "I'm afraid he didn't survive."

Lysander... is *dead?* Was he that dependent on me that my separation cost him everything?

I did this to him. I'm the reason he's gone from this world. Shudders wrack my body.

"If you don't mind my saying, miss, he did this to himself," Miriam says quietly. "You didn't make him give you that ring."

My jaw works up and down. I'm numb, unable to summon any tears. I hear him say, *"I can't live without you, Elaine."*

If I'd stayed, I'd still be broken, but he'd be alive.

"Here. This might cheer you up. 'Sides, you'll need something to do, being stuck in this bed and all." She hands me a book—*Lady of the Roses.*

I clutch it to my chest, my breaths swift and shallow. It survived. Yes, it's a bit torn, but it's still lovely.

"Thank you, Miriam. For everything. I... needed you back there." And in every moment between. If not for her, I might've succumbed to the urge to end my own life.

Her dimples flash with her smile. "Of course, miss."

"Does this mean you're free now?"

She drops her gaze. "I'll be passed on to a new owner, I suppose."

What? Even after all this?

No. I can't accept that. Her new owner might end up being better than Lysander, but she'll still be *owned.*

"I'm your mistress," I say. "Aren't I?"

She frowns at me.

"That means I can free you."

Her eyes widen. "You mean it, miss?"

"Yes." No one deserves to endure what I endured. Least of all this sweet, selfless girl. "All of you. All the bondservants."

She presses a hand to her mouth. I can almost see the chains snapping.

"I'll see if you can live at my mother's place..." If I'm still allowed there or even *want* to go there. Still, I'm sure I still have a trust fund of some kind, and if not, I don't mind working. "You won't be without help."

"Thank you," Miriam squeaks. "Thank you so much, miss."

I don't know what to do with my hands, so I run my fingers through my tangled hair. It feels thick and coarse, somehow, not silky and fine like I'm used to—

I nearly choke on my own breath. "Bring me a mirror."

Miriam's brow furrows, her mouth turning downward. "Miss, I don't think now is the best time—"

"Now!" I snap.

With a sigh, she gives me a plain hand mirror. I almost drop it.

A bump protrudes from my nose. My eyes are too close-set, my chin indented, my cheeks too round. My teeth—oh, Lord, my teeth are yellowed, my right canine twisted.

But as I consider my eyes, a little green, a little gold, and the freckles dotting my bumpy nose, and the dimples tugging at my round cheeks, I realize—maybe there *are* parts of me that I like. Because they're *me*. They're *real*.

I missed this face.

"Are you okay, miss?" Miriam asks.

"I am," I say, and I mean it. Yes, I left part of my soul with Lysander, and I may never feel beautiful or whole again. But Miriam and I are both *free*. "And please... call me Elaine."

PURER THAN POISON

PART TWO

THE SLEEPING DRAGON

Beka Gremikova

THE SLEEPING DRAGON Teashop was known in Quira for its spiced apple blend. Nobles often used Ximena's teas to help them sleep—and sometimes, they requested her to ensure their political opponents slept . . . longer.

One such note slipped through the letter slot just before her shop opened its doors for the day.

X,

Today, the princess will arrive for tea. She's embroiled herself in the political turmoil between ylvens and Quirans, and I think she deserves a nice, long rest. Please use your spiced apple blend with its special ingredient, and take care of her for me.

Another missive from Queen Kadira, who had commissioned Ximena just last week to take care of an incompetent huntsman.

And now, the *princess.*

The letter flared under a self-destruct spell, crumbling into ash. Ximena wiped her soot-streaked fingers on her robes, then shook out her hands until her wrists ached. Kadira always hated it when she did that, but Ximena found the motion soothing. Her nerves slightly settled, she let out a gusting breath.

The huntsman—old, weary, longing to simply chat and sip tea—had been an easy target. A stranger. He'd fallen asleep so quickly, she'd almost forgotten he'd never wake up.

But the princess was another matter.

Shivers swept through her as she stepped into the back kitchens. Memories gnawed at her, sharp and painful....

"I can't keep her," Ximena whispered, blinking into the gloom. A ylven midwife pressed a damp cloth to her cheek while others cleaned the baby. Younger ylvens held torches and sang soothing lullabies to the newborn. Their voices, soft and keening, rippled through the yawning caverns.

The eldest midwife glanced at Ximena keenly. "You don't want to?"

Ximena's cheeks heated. She looked away. "Her father wishes to raise her with his new wife." She blinked rapidly against the sting of tears.

"Oh, child..."

Ximena shrugged, her chin trembling. "I should have expected it, I suppose. His family pressured him to marry within his rank. I'm just a lowly tea seller, and he's... the future king."

"You could always stay here."

"You're very kind, but the mountains aren't my home." She longed for the comfort of her brews and the familiarity of her shop.

The midwife clasped her hand. "Well, know that there's always a place here for you and your daughter. Should you ever need it."

The chime of the doorbell broke Ximena from her reverie. She blinked. Oh, yes. Her teashop. And the *princess*. Her stomach churned. Leaving the water to boil, she returned to the front of the shop.

A girl stood in the middle of the room, gazing at the dragon-shaped decorations hanging from the ceiling.

Princess Kuly was beautiful, with dark lips, soft black hair, and a round, plump face that Ximena's fingers suddenly itched to cradle. The sort of girl most Quiran mothers would boast about.

The sort of girl Kadira *hated*.

Though the queen didn't know Ximena's connection to Kuly, Ximena doubted that knowledge would matter.

Ximena reminded herself sharply that it *didn't* matter. Kuly wasn't her daughter. Not anymore. She was a target.

And if Ximena wanted to keep her home and her cozy, familiar life, she couldn't let her longing for what had never been get in the way. She served the queen, who hadn't abandoned her—who, instead, gave her purpose.

Ximena straightened. "Welcome," she murmured and tilted her head in greeting.

"Miss Ximena." Princess Kuly smoothed her skirt, bowing. "My stepmother praises your tea-steeping talents very highly." Her voice held the sweet formality and distance of a stranger.

Ximena's shoulders relaxed slightly. *A stranger. Yes, just a stranger. Like the huntsman.* She didn't owe strangers anything.

"I'm honored." Ximena nearly walked into one of the dangling dragons, its lips curved in a snarl, its eyes flashing.

"I've been very stressed lately, and she insisted I try your spiced apple blend," Kuly continued. She scowled slightly. "She's so *pushy*." Her hands rose, and she shook them out violently. Then she flushed, dropping her hands. "I'm sorry, the queen hates when I...."

Ximena pressed her palms against her robe, her heart thumping. She barely resisted the urge to shake out her hands, to relieve the tension in her fingers. That one gesture was so small, so simple... And yet...

There's always a place for you—and your daughter—here.

Your daughter.

Your daughter.

No manner of special requests, no manner of money, no manner of queenly wrath could change that fact. Could turn this child into a complete stranger. Ximena stared at Kuly, a smiling mirror of her own soul.

"She hates it, does she?" Ximena croaked.

Kuly swallowed, fidgeting with the folds of her robes. "It—it drives her mad." Her dark brown eyes glinted. "Though she drives *me* mad with her politics. She thinks I should leave it all to her—"

Ximena's mind whirled. She grasped for something to say. "Now, now, you're supposed to be relaxing, aren't you?"

Kuly shook her head. "Do you always mother your customers?"

A lump lodged in Ximena's throat. Then she said hoarsely, "Only on special occasions." Before Kuly said anything more, Ximena ushered her into a booth and hurried to the kitchens.

Not a stranger. Not a stranger. My . . . Trembling, Ximena picked a tea blend and brought the tray out, pouring a cup to set before Kuly.

Kuly inhaled, her nose wrinkling. "Such a sweet smell... Apple?"

"Mountain apple, a ylven blend. Easier on the stomach than the spiced." Ximena folded her fingers together tightly. *It's not too late. You can serve the usual. . . .*

No. She clenched her fingers together.

"It smells lovely." Kuly inhaled deeply, her eyelashes fluttering, and took a long sip of her tea.

A few moments later, the princess slumped across the table.

That night, a package from The Sleeping Dragon arrived at the palace alongside a note.

Your Highness,

I took great care with the princess. To celebrate, enjoy this special blend—a personal favorite. I'm closing my shop and moving to the mountains with family for a while. I don't expect you'll need me anytime soon.

Take care of yourself.

X

The Hunter

Anne J. Hill

THE LEGEND TELLS of a hooded man, cloaked in darkness, roaming the land between forests and towns. He swings a battle-axe in his right hand and a dagger in his left. The blood of shifters and wild creatures drips off his blades.

His first kill was witnessed in an elvish village known for its strong ale. A wild wolf with raven black fur chased a boy through the streets, snarling and clawing for blood.

The hooded man stepped out from the shadows of a tavern, jumped between the boy and beast, and stabbed the wolf in the side. She yelped and toppled over, but it wasn't enough.

The town watched in horror as she picked herself back up and lunged for the man, teeth gnashing. With one powerful blow, his axe cleaved her neck from her shoulders and down tumbled the head of a woman. Her body shifted from fur to flesh, and there in the stunned village, her blood ran red.

The man scooped up her body and detached head, and glided down the middle of the street. The townspeople watched silently, some in awe, others in terror.

No one saw the tears that trickled down and landed on the woman's whitening face, and no one felt his heart ache for the life he ended. And no one watched a tired man digging a lonely grave for a beautiful woman.

But someone had to keep people like the young boy alive.

And so, from that day forward, he vowed to roam the land, slaying the damned on his own accord.

Now, sometimes, for a few coins, you can pay him to rid of dangerous monsters. It is a low price to pay. Some call him cheap, others call him noble, and some call him a devil. But they all know him by one name:

The Hunter.

Related to Thorn Tower *by Anne J. Hill*

SNOW DARK

Cassandra Hamm

She is alive, but she isn't living.

She moves, she speaks, she breathes—
but the hole inside her chest widens
with each inhale and exhale.
Her heart fractures
with each fragile beat, nearly lifeless
because if she let herself feel,
the pain would pull her under.

Her stepmother's words embed like barbs
in her sensitive skin, stinging, slicing,
feeding on her insecurities.
The place where her father used to be
is a yawning ache inside her chest.
You aren't enough.
You'll never be enough.

She is so tired
of pushing back the exhaustion
sweeping over her like a tide,
longing to pull her under.
It would be easier to let go and
sink into forever sleep.

Just give up.
It'll be easier that way.

He rides in on glorious promises
he never intends to keep.
His lips are so warm, so soft—
Surely they will wake
her cold, dying heart.

He takes and takes and takes
and she gives and gives and gives
until there is nothing left of her—

Too needy, he says
before vanishing into the night.
Tears stain her sheets like blood.
Screams and sobs scrape her lungs raw.
Her chest rattles with reed-thin breaths.

Not enough, not enough, not enough.

Not even the food she consumes
eases the ache inside.
She eats and eats and eats,
her lips stained blood-red,
her throat full of acid
as she expels the calories,
trying to erase the damage
she inflicted on her imperfect body.

She is so, so tired.
No one will notice if you are gone.

Arms wrap around her, squeezing,
willing her to see clearly.
Some have stayed despite her darkness.
Their words bounce off her walls—

I love you.
So common, so powerful, so ridiculous—
I would miss you if you were gone.
A trite, untrue sentiment—
she is not the sort who
makes a mark on the world.
Stay with me.

Ever so slowly, the words
slip past her defenses and
warm her deadened heart.

I love you. I love you. I love you.

What if her hollow, fragile self is enough?
Light penetrates her walls
and soaks into her soul.
She tries to remember
how life tasted sweet,
how each breath was a
terrifying new adventure.
The fog in her brain clears
for one beautiful moment.

I want to live.

There is still darkness
in her stepmother's taunts,

in boys like the one who
stole her first kiss and her dying heart.
There is still darkness
inside her, searching for cracks
in her fragile interior so she'll
spiral into the depths of her mind
where no one will pull her out.
Food won't fill the hole her father left,
but still she aches to gorge and expel.

But she holds tight to the
family she found
and stays upright.
She will fight.
She will *live.*

I will live.

QUEENSIDE

T.H. Forster

THE FIRST SNOWFALL arrives early that year, in mid-October. As the flakes drift down before daybreak, the villagers in the city streets pour out of their homes, their faces turned up with astonishment. Many stretch out their hands to catch the fragile crystals that melt into their palms, as though they believe the weather to be some illusion that will vanish in a moment.

As the hours pass and the snow dusts the roofs, gardens, and roads—undeniably real and pure white—the hushed voices and stunned silences turn into frantic whispers, whoops of laughter, and soon, cheers as throngs of citizens begin to make their way toward the tower. Their new queen has promised them. They know what today means.

In the castle, Queen Elizabeth sips at her wine and watches the crowds winding through the streets toward the dark, distant structure. The tower. Her childhood home.

She runs a thin, pale finger along the stained-glass window before opening it and reaching out to the snow. A handful of flakes disintegrate along her forearm, the crystals matching the white of her skin.

No illusion.

The door to her study swings open, and she hurriedly shuts the window. It's Phillip. He bows, kneels, kisses her hand, then her lips. He smells like moss. She frowns.

"Good morning, my Queen." He smiles, taking a seat across from her.

She smiles back. She can't help it. "Good morning, love."

Phillip pulls a roll of parchment from his cloak and sets it in front of her. "Lord Walpole finished writing this just now. All it requires is Your Majesty's signature."

Her stomach twists with unease. She knows what it says, but she reads it all the same.

Isabella, Former Queen and Traitor to the Nation,

You are hereto notified of your execution, scheduled for sunset on this, the first snowfall in the first year of our Majesty's Queen Elizabeth's rule, long may she Reign, as sentence for your previously convicted crimes against the kingdom, Her Majesty, and our late king Henry, your husband, God rest His soul. You have until sunset to make peace with our Lord.

Elizabeth, Regnant

She stares at the parchment for a long moment, barely noticing as Phillip nudges an ink bottle toward her and presses a quill into her hands.

"Elizabeth?" he says at last.

She looks up. Her husband's dark eyes are flooded with concern. "Is everything all right?"

"Perfectly. Of course. Yes. It's just . . ." She looks again at the paper before slowly setting the quill on the table. "I thought I would have more time."

"What difference would another month or two make?" Phillip kneels by her, his hands toying with her ruffled collar. "Let's be grateful she didn't find a way to stop the snow from coming at all! You gave her a very obvious loophole with that sentence—death on the first snowfall? Elizabeth, with no snow in *seven years*—"

"I know, I know." Elizabeth brushes him aside, her eyes drifting back to the snow, the flakes thickening as they cascade down in perfect silence. "I... I had just hoped... to..."

"What, my Queen?"

She stops. "Nothing. Whatever it was, it doesn't matter." She immerses the quill in ink, signing her name in smooth, stately strokes. This is the last communication Isabella will have from her. She has to be sure her stepmother won't find a flaw in a single letter.

Elizabeth knew that finding flaws had been a gift of Isabella's. On the day Isabella married Elizabeth's father, the King, the new queen was devastated to find white roses had been gathered for her hair.

"White shows dirt," she declared to a maidservant and the five-year-old Elizabeth. "It draws grime and decay to itself. Red fixes everything."

She produced a vial of clear liquid from the sleeve of her gown and scattered a few drops along the blossoms. Within moments, the white had bled to scarlet red.

"How—" Elizabeth gaped. "How did you do that?"

"Family secret, my dear." Then she tucked a red blossom into Elizabeth's hair and winked.

Isabella was lovely. Everyone said so. Hair like cornsilk which somehow shone brighter on cloudy days, sparkling green eyes that seemed to see everything at once, a full mouth which smiled easily but laughed only for the blessed few. Elizabeth had been in awe of her beauty.

She was sharp too. They said she could debate matters of state with the most intelligent minds in the land. Everyone praised the king for such a brilliant choice of wife, the last member from such a wealthy family line, too. With a fortune like that, it was a match made in heaven.

Those years were golden for Elizabeth. Her father dancing with all the ladies of the court while Isabella entertained guests with her sweet song and wit. Isabella never failed to notice if she was tired, or hungry, or needed a new gown because she was "growing so very fast."

When Elizabeth was eleven, her father took ill with a sore throat. Three days later, he died. She and Isabella watched the funeral from the castle window, both garbed in black. That night, Isabella was proclaimed Queen, and she called Elizabeth to her room.

"You understand, my dear, it's only temporary?" she asked. "My advisors feared if you were named your father's heir, some courtiers would take advantage of your age and rule in your place. I plan to abdicate once you are old enough."

"I suppose," Elizabeth said. "I think you will be a very good queen, Mama."

"Thank you, my darling. I hope so." She turned back to her mirror, adjusting the thick gold band atop her head. "There's a little tear in your dress. Better change before dinner, and I'll see that one of the ladies mends it."

Two weeks after her twelfth birthday, Elizabeth awoke to the sobs and screams of her ladies-in-waiting. Four guards stood over her bed, and two roughly grabbed her by the arms and dragged her down the long castle corridors to the Queen's staterooms.

She stumbled as they dumped her at her stepmother's feet. Isabella was dressed, but her hair was unbound, her face bare, her eyes wild. The handful of courtiers behind her looked like malevolent gray shadows forming a shield around their mistress.

Elizabeth climbed to her feet, pulling her shawl tightly around her. "Your Majesty?"

"Princess Elizabeth," she said. Her voice was ice. "You are hereby placed under arrest on suspicion of conspiring against the Crown."

Her breath stalled in her throat. "What?"

"Your guards will escort you to your quarters in the tower, where you will await trial and sentencing."

"Your Majesty!" The room was spinning. "Mother, no!"

"If you are found to be innocent, no harm will come to you." Isabella gestured, and the guards seized her arms again, dragging her out of the room.

"Wait!" She kicked at them, straining to look back at the woman who wouldn't meet her eyes. "Mama! Please, I don't understand! Mama!"

The doors slammed shut, and she would never see her mother again.

Twelve became thirteen, then fourteen, fifteen. And still, Elizabeth waited in her rooms, watching the guards pace on their watchtowers below, the clouds shifting in infinite, ever-changing shapes.

She was given no servants, no change of clothes, only a single dress every year to keep up with her as she grew. To occupy her mind, the guards allowed her to clean her chambers and the rooms of other prisoners. She sang, danced, and read the few books she was permitted. When a wealthy courtier was occasionally imprisoned for a brief time, she was hidden from their sight—an entity meant to be forgotten.

But she remembered. She remembered the castle gardens and playing with her ladies by the river. She remembered riding with her childhood friend, Phillip, or reading with her tutor in the library. Most of all, she remembered her parents and grieved for them.

She listened to the guards' conversation, getting to know them and their lives. They were uncouth, uneducated, by her standards. But they were entertaining. She liked some of them. Others not as well.

They eventually listened to her, too, noting when she pointed out a certain moss was difficult to remove, or a step on the staircase was extra creaky. They stopped yelling at her to shut up when she sang and started asking if she had any requests for meals.

Fear lessened its grip on her heart day by day. Until the morning before her seventeenth birthday, when a note arrived from the castle informing her that Isabella had ordered her execution.

It was a private affair. The guards thought this was Isabella's last great mercy towards her stepdaughter, granting her an execution hidden from the prying eyes of the people. Elizabeth looked for her stepmother at the platform, but she was alone with her guards. "Please," she said as they wrapped the blindfold around her eyes. "Please, I have done nothing wrong. I never—"

"I'm sorry, Your Ladyship," one of the guards said. He sounded genuine, too. "We have our orders."

Her head was lowered onto the chopping block. Large steps echoed toward her, and then came the sharpening of an axe.

"Have you made peace with the Lord, Your Highness?" a gruff voice asked.

She lifted her head. "Captain? Is that you?" The Captain of the Guard was Chief Executioner at the tower and perhaps one of her only true friends.

A thick silence, then, "This brings me no pleasure, Your Highness."

"Captain, please," she whispered.

There was another long silence, then the swish of a blade in the air. She winced, but no pain came. Suddenly, the blindfold was whipped off her face.

The Captain's gray eyes stared into hers. "Take my horse. Ride for the woods. Now."

"What?"

"Be safe, little princess." He tossed her off the platform onto the steed waiting below. "Go!"

And with that, the horse took off. She was gone before she had a chance to thank him.

The Tower, for all its foreboding nature, could be worse on the inside. That's what Isabella tells herself, at least, as she watches the snow pile up on her windowsill, the glass mercifully sealed enough to keep water from leaking through. The fire crackles behind her, firelight growing ever stronger against the fading afternoon light.

The last of which will signal her death.

She turns and picks up the parchment left sitting on her cot, reading and rereading the handful of sentences her stepdaughter has deigned to send her way.

"'Make peace,'" she mutters before crumpling up the parchment and tossing it into the flames. A year ago, a document like that would have been invaluable for her work—examples of someone's handwriting could be necessary for taking on their likeness or causing them injury. But that doesn't matter anymore. Her gift has cost her everything.

It was her gift that won her the King's attention in the first place, though he didn't know it. She was being presented at court, the last of a wealthy, noble lineage from the North, and she was terrified. That was to be her life now—dances and jewels and politics and power, the very thing for which she'd been trained the last seventeen years. Her parents were gone, and there was no one to guide her, protect her as she sought the power she was destined to wield.

So on that night she had erred on the side of caution, and taken a draught to enhance her features. It was one that her parents had taught her to brew years ago. She needed self-assurance, not insecurities. She needed to look like a queen.

Her timidity squashed, she did not hesitate to make eyes at the King, did not titter like the other air-headed girls when he asked her to dance. They conversed and dined. She found him intelligent, passionate, ruthless. A good partner for a life of power, and even better, he was already well into his middle age. She would easily out-live him.

They were married within three months. Elizabeth was her maid of honor. She was a sweet child, and from what Isabella had heard of the last queen, much like her mother. Elizabeth clearly adored Isabella, so there was no problem there. The princess's nose was a little snub-shaped, and her posture a bit poor, but with her fair skin and raven hair she would grow into a beautiful young woman and no doubt make a fine foreign match for their country.

There would be no need for Elizabeth to rule, of course. Isabella would give birth to sons. She knew that, Henry knew that, everyone knew that.

She became pregnant weeks after the wedding.

They announced the pregnancy after two months, and all the court rejoiced, her husband with them. It was the happiest day of her life.

But one night, she awoke to pain in her abdomen like nothing she'd ever known. By daybreak, the doctors told her and the King the child was gone.

The disappointment on the king's face was a weight on her chest for months, especially when no pregnancy followed afterward.

The first time she found her husband with another woman, it felt as though her heart had been crushed by a wine press. She refused to shed a tear, but the woman was thrown from their quarters.

"You knew how it would be," he crooned in her ear. "Give me a son, and all will be yours. Give me a son, and you'll have your reward."

The months passed. A second pregnancy, then a third. No child came. Whispers flitted through court, and soon those whispers cared not who heard them.

She tried everything. She consulted all of her family's knowledge of herbs and poultices, potions and draughts. Her desperation fueled her power, but even she had her limits. For all her magic, she could not make her body carry a child.

Elizabeth remained her only source of joy, the one person who did not seem to know or care she had no sons. The two of them were often together, and as her hope for a child began to fade, she began to teach Elizabeth about ambassadors, court functions, finances, and languages. The day may come when she would have need of it.

Years went by, and as she continued to try, the strain began to take its toll on her body. As her health and beauty faded, the whispers grew to a roar of mockery and hostility, so she took to crafting illusions of health and youth to be the woman she'd once been, smoothing out wrinkles, concealing gray hairs. But her illusions of youth changed nothing. Six years after her marriage, the king ceased pretending their union existed, and divorce was openly discussed at feasts and state meetings.

She had failed.

There were some at court, however, whose loyalty she held. Courtiers who recognized the savvy with which she had navigated the pitfalls and traps His Majesty had set for her. Enemies of the King who saw something to gain in supporting his intelligent, estranged wife.

The final straw came during the late summer, as the court was returning from a hunting trip on a nobleman's country seat. King Henry had been in an especially foul mood that day, the hunt having gone poorly. Isabella rode further back, allowing the King to flirt with his newest favorite, a fifteen-year-old contessa whose uncle had recently been promoted to Chancellor.

The Chancellor rode beside Isabella now. He was a warm sort of man, who led the majority of social events at court, but he had been a vocal opponent of hers for many years. He leaned over to her, a broad smile on his face.

"I was sorry to hear, Highness, of your recent loss. I imagine His Majesty was laid low by the news."

She had lost her fifth and final baby seven months ago. The King had sought comfort in the arms of one of his mistresses and left her alone in her quarters for good.

"He bore the news tolerably, Chancellor. His Majesty bears bad news with strong spirits, as I'm sure you know."

"Indeed." The Chancellor ducked to avoid a low-hanging branch; his dark eyes fixed on his niece and the King up ahead. "He rallies well, I think. Always looking forward to the next solution. And what does Your Highness think of his latest stratagem?"

A knot formed in her stomach. "The Chancellor mocks me."

"I think not." He glanced over at her, eyebrows raised. "I will speak bluntly if that will assuage your doubts. There are fears in court that you will not go quietly."

She was silent a long moment as they rode on. Her husband's laughter drifted back on the air, deep and proud, the contessa apparently having lifted his spirits. "Why does the Chancellor feel the need to tell me this?"

"To ensure that you will." His voice took on a sharp edge she had never heard from him before. "His Majesty needs heirs, Highness. Do you think the Princess Elizabeth will be able to rule this kingdom when he is gone?"

"She may be a woman—"

"It is worse than that. She is a *kind* woman. All who meet her cannot help but praise the sweetness and gentleness of that child. A soft hand will not guide this kingdom. Elizabeth will be ruled by whomever she weds. And that is a dangerous game for politicians to play. His Majesty needs a son, and you have failed."

She raised an eyebrow. "Do not pass judgment on that which I could not control, Chancellor."

The Chancellor looked around and lowered his voice. "I know you practice the craft of which we do not speak."

She fought to conceal her surprise as their horses halted beneath a tree.

"If you wished to give His Majesty a son, he would have one by now." He plucked a leaf from the tree and twirled it between his fingers, the yellowed hue catching the sun's rays. "I know not for what purpose you leave him childless, but I warn you that I will not hesitate to remove any threats to the Crown." He looked up then. "His Majesty thinks you may be handled with the question of divorce. I think not. You are, forgive me, Highness, quite proud. And more powerful than he realizes. But you have a weakness of which our King is equally ignorant." He dropped the leaf, watched it spin toward the ground. "You do have a child."

She stared.

"It is said the Princess Elizabeth calls you 'Mother.' She would be devastated to see you meet an end of violence, I think. So I ask you to consider her in this as well. Do not force her to question her loyalties." The Chancellor tapped his horse, and the steed began to walk off. "Consider my advice, Highness," he called back. "The match is set; it is your choice in what manner you lose."

She sat rooted to the spot for several minutes, and only the crack of a branch spooking her steed brought her back.

When they returned to the castle a week later, she knew what she must do. She kept a vial of dried herbs stored in the back of her cabinets, behind a hidden door, mixed with a few carefully chosen items from around the palace. Dinner saw her seated next to Henry, like always. She slipped a mere spoonful in his wine. No one glimpsed anything suspicious.

The additions to her poultice were designed to slow the poison. What should have been a death brought on in mere hours took three long, painful days. A natural illness. It gave her no pleasure to watch. A quick death would have been kinder. But if The Chancellor knew of her gift, she had to make it look as though she had nothing to do with it.

What was more, those three days gave her time to gather her support. The Chancellor had been right about one thing– Elizabeth was too young, too gentle. She would be ruled by politicians, seized in a mad grab for power, and would probably be overthrown in revolt. Isabella had to protect her daughter.

She had to become the Queen.

The first revolt came a year into Isabella's rule, on Elizabeth's twelfth birthday. An uprising in the city led by the Chancellor.

She rallied her troops and rode out into battle, swallowing her fear and wielding as much magic as she dared. When the tide turned against them, she abandoned restraint and set the field around her ablaze, carving a path of ruin in her wake.

They fled before her. The now-former Chancellor and his family narrowly escaped capture in the confusion of battle. The officers she did capture alive revealed his plan to depose Isabella and have Elizabeth marry his eldest son, so he would rule Elizabeth.

Isabella had the officers beheaded. She was cold rage. The Chancellor had escaped. He would return. He had made his agenda of crowning Elizabeth in her place perfectly clear. Her advisors urged her to execute Elizabeth as a traitor and eliminate the threat, but that was out of the question.

But his spies could be anywhere. They could kidnap Elizabeth, smuggle her away, use her for their ends. She had to keep her safe, had to protect her in a way that pacified those loyal to Isabella.

It was for her own good. She would be released when the threat of revolt was gone, when the Chancellor had been dealt with.

The day she sent Elizabeth to the tower, the last of the snow melted in the city and would not fall again for seven years.

The people had stopped cheering when Isabella's carriage rolled through the streets. It didn't matter that the kingdom no longer had debt, that crops were good, that she toured the land each year to know her people. She was a witch, and they all knew it. They feared her.

Her spies got wind of a second revolt brewing in the north, planned for Elizabeth's seventeenth birthday. A larger force this round. Not for the first time, she suggested visiting Elizabeth in the tower, but her advisors would not hear of it. They were urging her to order her daughter's death.

"It will be kinder in the long run, Majesty." They said, twittering and passing warrant after warrant through her hands.

"She is my heir. I have no children. Without her, where will we be?"

"There are distant cousins, Majesty. Cousins who will support you, who will not seek to depose you." Her bishop rolled out the newest warrant, brandishing a quill.

She was tired. Tired of this long, silent war. She wanted to be left to rule in peace.

Princess Elizabeth,

You are hereto notified of your execution, scheduled for sunrise on this, the seventh year of our Majesty's Queen Isabella's rule, long may she reign, as sentence for your crimes of conspiring against the Crown. You have until sunrise to make peace with our Lord.

Isabella, Regnant

She signed it.

She awoke the next morning from a dream of blood filling her nostrils. "Wait!" she cried, leaping from her bed. Brushing off her ladies, she rushed down the hall. "Guards! Get me to the Tower. I have made a mistake!"

By the time she arrived, the tower was in chaos, and Elizabeth had already escaped.

"You have damned me!" Isabella threw a knife into the table with enough force to rock the furniture. "You have damned us both!"

The Captain of the Guard flinched and backed toward the door, trembling. "Us?" he asked.

"Not you, you fool," she spat. "Her. In their hands, she will be their pawn, to move about and do what they will. And I—I will lose everything."

The Captain furrowed his brows. "But—"

"Find her! Now, or it will be *your* head on that chopping block!" Isabella threw another knife, this time at his cap, pinning it to the wall above his head. His eyes widened, and he scurried out of the room.

She slouched in her throne, watching the last of the autumn leaves wave in the wind. The lack of snowfall in recent years had not gone unnoticed by the people. Although those loyal to her deemed it a sign of God's blessing, others took it as an omen of death, that her rule was dishonest.

Perhaps they were right. She had been willing to kill her own daughter to keep her power, the power she had once told herself was to keep Elizabeth safe. Perhaps death was all she brought.

The new uprising was put down, and the Chancellor's head was brought to her on a pike. She did not take the comfort in it she once might have.

She slept ill that night and for many nights after. Her draughts for maintaining beauty and health were nearly doubled in strength from when she first began using them.

Then came the day the Captain of the Guard reported the Chancellor's son was rallying troops at an encampment in the north. Rumor had it that the princess was hidden there.

She left the meeting with her councilors without another word and descended to her workroom below the castle.

Elizabeth had been taken. They would use her, destroy her.

She had to get her back.

The idea came easily enough. The castle orchards were bursting with apples, the red fruit a spot of color in a world of stone and iron. She chose one and crafted a sleeping draught so strong it would give the drinker a deathly stillness and pale face. She slipped away to the rebellion's encampment and removed her illusions of youth. The years of stress and pain had not been kind. Her golden hair had long since faded to a brittle gray, her emerald green eyes were now pale and hollowed, her body frail and twisted. For this, she would, for once, appear to her daughter as she truly was. Why? She could not say. Penance, perhaps. For what she'd done and had yet to do.

She recognized Elizabeth instantly, despite not having laid eyes on her daughter in five years. She was lovely, grown into a truly regal girl. The Chancellor's son had provided her with fine clothes, and she seemed content as she wound her way through the tents and people, smiling and laughing.

Isabella shifted her basket in her lap and held up the spelled fruit.

"Apples!" she called, her voice cracked and breathy. "Fresh apples, the last of the harvest! Enjoy them before the frost!"

Clear blue eyes found her milky green ones. No hint of recognition passed across Elizabeth's face.

"Hello, madam," the princess called. "From what orchard do you grow your produce?"

"My child's home," Isabella responded with a wide smile. "She lives here now."

Elizabeth fished around in her coin purse. "I will take a few back to Lord Phillip's estate. He is fond of the fruit."

"Oh, but Your Highness must try one now!" Isabella insisted, standing with her spindly body. "Let me gift it to you; it would be an honor."

"Oh, but I couldn't."

"Please."

Was it pity in her daughter's eyes then? Isabella watched as Elizabeth picked up the fruit, its glossy skin red like rubies in the late afternoon sun. She took one small, perfect bite, and smiled.

"The taste is truly delicious—" She frowned, then stumbled.

Isabella gripped her daughter's body as she collapsed and slowly lowered her to the ground. She fished out another vial and quickly downed it, grimacing as she vanished into the air, watching, unseen.

If she took Elizabeth with her back to the castle, her advisors would demand the girl's blood, and this third revolt would descend from the north. Neither she nor Elizabeth would survive.

Both her supporters and enemies had to believe her daughter was dead, had to believe the reason for rebellion was gone.

Let them bury the girl. She would find her and then rescue her and hide her away. Somewhere only she knew.

She would keep Elizabeth safe.

She watched the first screams go up in the crowds, the first tears. A few rebel leaders descended upon the body, and panic followed. They believed her dead. Her work was done.

She returned to the castle to await the news of her rival's death. To play the part of a triumphant queen.

Word never came.

A week later, an army decimated hers just outside the city. When she made ready to meet them, icy fury coursing through her, her advisors said Elizabeth was leading the forces.

The rage died in her instantly, replaced by panic. How? How had she awoken? Isabella had not undone the spell's effects, she was sure of it. It made no sense.

And now Elizabeth fought against her.

She scanned her cabinet of draughts. She had potions that cast fire at her enemies, spells that turned soldiers to stone. She could topple the entire castle and crush the advancing armies beneath the rubble if she chose.

But Elizabeth would perish. Either in the battlefield, or on the executioner's block.

The distant screams of the dying rang in her ears, and she made her way toward the drawbridge.

Soldiers parted before her. She conjured illusions of terror to rain down upon the rebellion, but paused at the sight of ravens black hair waving in the distance. Elizabeth had woven a white ribbon in her tresses. Like she had on Isabella's wedding day.

Isabella's hand, readied with potions, trembled, and a glass jar shattered on the cobblestone beneath her.

She had no choice. She would not raise a weapon against her daughter ever again, no matter what it cost her.

She surrendered and was thrown in the tower. Requests to meet with the new Queen were denied, and her sentence was delivered by one of the prison guards.

She threw him out of her cell with a final cry of anger and watched the February sky resolutely refuse to snow.

Isabella had known her death was to come before the first flake fell. Six months in captivity. Six months rotting in her tower and not one word, one visitor from the castle since that moronic guard had delivered her sentence.

Until today.

Prince Phillip stood before her, his face impassive as the flames from her hearth shed dim light over the room. His eyes were dark, hair cropped short, clothes black but embroidered in gold thread.

Unmemorable, she thought.

"To what do I owe the pleasure, Your Highness?" Isabella asked.

Phillip took a seat across from her, his eyes taking in every inch of the space. "I thought it was high time we met face-to-face, madam."

She kept her gaze fixed on his hand resting uneasily on his sword hilt, the firelight glinting off his wedding band. "I meant why today?"

"Any number of reasons could be provided, none of which I believe would be to your satisfaction." Phillip leaned forward in his chair. "I have come simply to reassure myself that you have no means by which to stall your execution."

Blunt. Unafraid but cautious. Less than civil, given the lack of proper title in her address.

"Does my daughter know you're here?"

"*Step-daughter*, and I am not at liberty to divulge what Her Majesty does and does not know."

In other words, no, she didn't know.

Isabella stood and crossed the room. "I can assure you, sir, I have nothing I would require to practice my gift. And even if I did, I am not certain that I would use it. It has failed me thus far. I have no reason to think it would succeed now."

"You'll forgive me if I find that difficult to believe."

She looked at him, raising an eyebrow. "Would you believe me if I told you I love my daughter?"

He scoffed. "You loved what she gave you. When she was of no more use, you tried to kill her."

"Strange." She smiled slowly. "I often wonder if the same could be said of you."

He drew his sword in an instant, eyes blazing. "What did you say to me, witch?"

She gently rested a finger on the sword's tip, nudging it aside. "Your father once told me Elizabeth would be unfit to rule because of her kindness. That she would be ruled by whomever she wed. It was a truth he used to manipulate me into drastic action. It strikes me that we are at the end of a very long game, a game that your father played with all of us, and that it is you, Your Highness, who have come out the winner. The knight who gained a crown."

"Your false speeches on a forked tongue will do you no good here," he said, trembling with emotion.

"Unlike your father, I have long had a knack for speaking plainly, much like yourself." She sighed. "Everyone around me simply assumes I speak deceitfully."

He slowly sheathed his sword, eyes still alit with rage. "You mock me."

"I sense you will not be swayed in your opinion." She shook her head. "You have the love of my daughter for reasons I do not understand, but I must trust her judgment, given our current states. I promise you I am in no position to interfere with your lives, however much I may wish to."

He looked at her a long moment, eyes narrowed with distrust. "I won't forget this conversation, madam." He turned to go.

"And Phillip?" she said. He paused, his hand on the door. "You may have won my daughter, but my daughter has not won her kingdom—not yet. See to it you do not lose one for the sake of the other."

There was real fear in his eyes as he shut the door behind him.

She stood in the silence that followed, shoulders back, her head held high.

He'd won.

Elizabeth was a Queen. And a pawn. But perhaps—perhaps she would have greater success than Isabella had. Perhaps she would be happy.

That was all that mattered now.

When she awoke to find the snow drifting down in clumps, she laughed. One of her rare, beautiful laughs, for the last time.

When the guards came at sunset, she stood, having recited the last of her prayers, and walked to her death with a heart that was already dead.

Phillip stormed out of the tower, the wind whipping his cloak around him as he peered into the darkening sky. Fear and anger clawed at his chest. Isabella had to be dealt with. She would destroy everything they'd—everything his father had—

Elizabeth. She would destroy Elizabeth.

He mounted his horse and rode to the castle as fast as he could. The guards lowered the drawbridge at a snail's pace, and he careened past them, the torches mere blurs of light as he headed for the stables. From there, he ran to the castle, hat lost in the wind, cloak a ragged banner behind him as he sought out the dungeons.

Isabella had practiced her art in secret, but everyone in court had known it existed. No dark place contained more royal secrets than the dungeons.

He wandered through the maze of darkness, carrying a single torch with him for light, looking for that sign he was certain he'd find.

Then, there it was. A streak of enamel carved onto the mossy stones above his head.

A red rose.

He pressed it, and it slid away, revealing a stairway descending into the earth. He followed it, and the staircase emptied into a room filled with jars, books, plants, and bottles of every kind.

He looked around the space for a moment, catching his breath, then set to work.

Slicing, bottling, boiling, mumbling. He paused in his work now and then to double-check an ingredient or strengthen the spell.

It would take hours for the potion to brew. The stench of moss filled his nostrils. He fought down the panic in his throat and forced himself to clear his mind. He knew his work. Anger and fear would cast an illusion, yes, and a convincing one at that, but he needed something real for this to work.

He needed stronger motivations.

He needed Elizabeth.

He thought about the first time he'd seen the princess, now his queen. He and his father had been visiting the castle for the King's birthday. Phillip, at nine, had finally been deemed old enough to make the trip.

Elizabeth had been seven and the most beautiful thing he's ever seen. Dark hair, raven's black, with skin whiter than porcelain as she danced with her ladies at the feast. She was a gem even then, and Phillip had watched from a distance, wondering why so many people around him talked of the princess with sadness in their eyes when she was joy incarnate.

They'd visited court once or twice every year after that, and he always looked forward to visiting the raven-haired princess who smiled at him.

His father had started training him in witchcraft that year, teaching him how to gather herbs, cast illusions, hide in the shadows.

"It does not make you more powerful than anyone else," he had said. "You only wield power in a different way. Abuse it too openly, and it will be your doom."

It was his father's illusions that had enabled them to escape Isabella's wrath when their first revolt failed and they'd fled into exile.

When Isabella had thrown Elizabeth in prison, Phillip had wanted to cast a cavalcade of illusions to ferry her out of prison to safety. But his father had stopped him.

"Isabella won't harm her," he promised. "This prison is her way of protecting the girl from us. Magic will do you no good."

Then, in the span of a day, he'd lost his father to blood and battle, but Elizabeth had come back to him. It was his task now to protect her, to overthrow the witch.

By any means necessary.

Finding Elizabeth in the field that evening would haunt his dreams for the remainder of his days. Her already white skin near blue in the fading light. Her lips pale, face slack.

He cried out, knelt by her side, frantically searching for the cause of her death.

The apple, one bite missing. He sniffed it.

Sleeping draught, like death. Isabella. She'd been there.

He paused. Sleeping Death… It had a cure. She…she was still alive.

"Do not bury her," he instructed the men. "Do not let Isabella get her hands on…on her body. I will return."

It took seven days to gather everything he needed, but gather them he did. He didn't think, his mind awash with terror as he cut and boiled and brewed.

He returned at sunrise, a small vial in his bag, and found they had placed Elizabeth in a glass coffin near the campsite.

In a movement unseen by the crowd, he unstoppered the bottle and placed three drops on her tongue.

It took all of a minute for the color to return to her cheeks, her eyes to flutter open. A minute more for her to explain what had happened, for it to become clear Isabella would stop at nothing to keep her crown and eliminate Elizabeth's claim. He said nothing to Elizabeth about the Sleeping Death potion or cure. That was information he wasn't supposed to know.

He led the third and final revolt that week to victory, his magic carrying them on an undercurrent of rage and power. It took all he had to conceal the effects of his power from the others, but conceal it he did.

Now again, Phillip strode to the castle walls, a vial tucked in his bag. The full moon filtered through the cloud cover, lighting his way. Elizabeth would expect him home soon. He needed to move quickly.

He clasped the vial in one hand, raising it up to the sky, muttering the necessary words, before throwing it to the ground with as much force as he could muster.

The explosion threw him against the castle walls, a silver cloud blooming over the grounds. He coughed, inhaling what felt like shards of ice working their way towards his heart. He watched the cloud disperse heavenward, collecting vapor. A chill wracked the air, and he nodded, satisfied, before turning back toward home.

The first flake of his snow fell less than an hour before dawn. He stole silently from their bed to ensure that the drops were real, that he wasn't dreaming. They melted in his palm. His power had been strong enough. It had worked.

Elizabeth would be safe

They'd won.

Isabella, the Wicked Queen, is beheaded at sunset, and Elizabeth eats her supper alone. The snowfall has let up by the evening, the land coated in a band of white icing. Despite the weather, Elizabeth is able to wander the castle grounds with her ladies after the meal, her feet propped up with platforms to avoid tracking her gown in the icy slush.

The frost has come on so suddenly that the last of the rose blossoms are still in the garden, their small, frail petals curling up toward the setting sky, the snow dusted like powder over their faded colors.

Elizabeth lets out a cloudy breath as she watches the last of the sun's light vanish from the horizon. She did not attend the execution. Phillip thought it wouldn't be seemly, and she wasn't certain she wanted to anyways.

This woman has taken so much from her. She had probably killed Elizabeth's father. She had left her to rot in the tower, stolen her throne, tried to kill her—twice. They said Elizabeth had been like the dead for a week after the wizened old peddler woman with milky green eyes had gifted her an apple. She still can not reconcile that frail, cracked voice and hollow eyes with her mother. She still can not understand why.

A gust of wind blows back the hood of her cloak, and she revels in the air. Even after all this time being free, she still bristles at being confined in the castle for too long, resents the stifling air of the indoors. It is all too easy for her to relive the moss and filth of the Tower.

Beside her, one of her maids pulls out some shears and reaches for a few of the faded roses. “For Your Majesty’s chamber?”

“No,” Elizabeth says. “Not the white. Bring in the red ones.”

Red fixes everything.

The Garden

Emily Barnett

IT HAD BEEN one bite. My teeth sunk in sweet flesh that turned bitter in my core.

The old woman cackled, slithering from the garden with her basket of apples and lies, leaving me to rot amongst the trees. To die in the garden my friends and I had toiled in—laughter and sweat growing flowers and plants and memories. Life.

Now, the fruits stained my dress where I lay. Gnarled branches became my tomb, cutting red stripes in my snowy skin. Twigs tangled my midnight hair.

Death blanketed me.

Years I slept with bones and decay. Cold and immovable.

Helpless.

Then—a kiss.

A warm breath became my own, and I sucked in life.

I rose.

A man—a Prince—lay still against a tree. His hands splayed to his sides, palms open to the skies. Gone without a fight. Stealing poison from my veins, the infection from my blood.

I hadn't known him, but his gentle, glazed eyes spoke of knowing me. His sacrifice sang of loving me. But the garden was dark, and I shivered, cold and scared.

Rising, I took his cloak and kissed his icy cheek, then fled from the garden—the tomb built for me. Shame and gratefulness entwined in my chest, grafting into something new.

The taste of death's flesh was still caught in my teeth.

I found my little friends, and we grieved and rejoiced. But my tears ran only for the Prince who I'd left behind. Who saved me. Who loved me.

But my friends shook their little beards and their gazes misted with joy.

They knew the Prince. They knew where he lived and where he came from. And as their words spilled over me like sunbeams on a blooming rose, I smiled.

He's no longer in the garden, they assured me. A world like ours has no hold on a Prince like him.

My limbs stopped trembling. My heart was furrowed, its soil readying for the spring.

And I planted my garden again.

Fragile
They call me fragile
Lips red like an apple
Hair so black it dazzles
Skin white as mountain snow
So
I must be fragile
to obtain and maintain
such a facade and
to remain in the ruling class
is it not a requirement to be
obtusely vain? And
so
I must be fragile
As even in death I was regarded in
a such delicate way
encased like fine china and
set out to be seen

but not touched
So
they call me fragile
I was supposed to be queen
but they forced me to clean and
become unseen
a servant in my own home
before I was thirteen
but
they call me fragile
My own protector became
a defector when he
thrust a knife at me and
I was forced to flee to
realms unknown
But
they call me fragile
And that apple
poisoned by the one
from whom all this began
yet I could not be undone
As the poison infused my veins
even Death refrained from breaking me
For
I am anything but fragile

Soul Poison

Beka Gremikova

THEY NO LONGER had to warn her not to talk to strangers. As soon as the seven men had left, she locked the door, drew the bolt, and slammed the shutters closed on all the windows, save one. That last peek to the outside world was propped open, allowing just enough light to fall across the cold dirt floor.

She huddled beneath the window, her head brushing the ledge, too afraid of the darkness to veer beyond the pool of sunshine.

When they returned home from the mines, she still sat there. Her head lolled to one side, her mop of dark hair shadowing her face.

They glanced at one another, their lips tight.

"Don't tell me she's…" one whispered. Though the queen had been dead now for years, their hearts still stuttered to find their little girl slumped across the floor.

The youngest man knelt by the girl and gently touched her shoulder. Her eyes flew open, and she gasped a little. Then color returned to her cheeks, and she smiled. It didn't reach her large dark eyes. "I–I'm sorry."

"No apologies!" one whispered fiercely.

"Did you have a bad dream?" another asked.

She shook her head.

Lies. They could see it in the trembling of her lips, the shortness of her breath.

She had escaped one nightmare to fall into another. In unison, their fingers clenched into fists. Out of grief and desperate hope, they had pushed their beloved girl into the claws of a monster worse than the one that had killed her. They had ripped her from death at the hands of one villain to throw her onto the mercy of a man whose tyranny gripped a kingdom.

"I shall love her all my days," the king had vowed.

Until she objected to the way he treated his subjects. Until she learned that she preferred kindness to a handsome face. Then she had turned into his enemy.

The girl rose to her feet and threw open the rest of the shutters. The tiny cottage glowed in the soft evening light, but she could only shiver. The seven men took up their guard at the door. If the man who called himself a king ever came again, they would know what to do. Until then, they waited in fear, the darkness within gnawing away at the sunshine without.

It was a poison worse than any the girl had tasted—a poison that killed not only the body, but the soul.

Mirror of Ice

Julia Skinner

THE FACE IN the crystalline mirror isn't the one I remember. Cold eyes, a crown of perfectly pressed hair, expression like fine stone glazed in ice.

No one told me becoming the fae Queen would result in... *this*.

I strain to catch even the slightest glimpse of fire in the depths of her eyes—the spark I always used to have. But there is nothing familiar about the face looking back at me.

"Please." I press my hand against the chilled glass, and my reflection does the same. "I don't want this. I want to be *me* again. My kingdom needs the real me."

Not this perfect, queenly statue.

They do not need you, the Queen whispers in my head. *No one has ever needed you.*

I squeeze my eyes closed.

You were not enough to save your people.

The girl I used to be stirs in the back of my memory, faint wisps of an image that has almost entirely faded away.

"You killed her," I whisper. The Queen in the mirror doesn't even flinch. She doesn't care about the past she left behind.

Or the girl she had to kill to be who she is now.

To be who *I* am, now.

Ice weaves through my veins as my magic slowly takes control. Once upon a time, we were a broken people. Forgotten by all of our supposed allies. Enslaved by the Darkness my magic now holds at bay. *Never again,* the Queen promises in my mind.

For a moment, the face in the mirror flickers, blurring. "I'm . . ." my voice catches, "I'm sorry."

There is no place for a weak, foolish child here.

The last memory of *me* slips from my grasp. I straighten, turning from the mirror. The cavernous room is empty—just a looming box lined with colorless, chilled walls. I loosen my fisted hands and feel my shivering magic flood through the castle like a silent winter storm. I can sense it reaching invisible frozen fingers over every servant and soldier in the castle, creeping out across the land. *Across my land.*

Striding to the door, I throw my head back and straighten my shoulders like the monarch the kingdom knows me to be.

The world will be ours starting today. And no one will ever hurt us again.

As I reach the throne room, my black-suited soldiers stand a little straighter, and the servants quickly bow in perfect unison—except for one. One who looks far too much like a memory I've forgotten. The maid swirls across the white floor as she sweeps, oblivious to my presence. Her hair tangles around her tanned face with every move, flaring and curling and dancing in the air. She's like *fire*—a single spark in my kingdom of ice.

Still watching her, I beckon to the Captain of the Guard. He approaches and kneels stiffly, gripping the hilt of his polished sword. I can feel my magic filling his veins, chilling away the warmth that used to flow through him.

I knew his name, once upon a time.

"That girl," I say, "lock her away."

He freezes, though his face remains as blank as the walls of this castle. Finally—*finally*—he speaks, his voice barely audible. "In the dungeons?"

There is a flicker of rebellion in his question.

Leaning down, I grip his shoulder in my cold hand, smothering his emotions with my powers. "*Yes.*"

Without another word, he moves to obey. The perfect soldier of ice.

I will remove everyone who could ever stand in my way. Until all that is left are those who have forgotten every trace of the people they used to be.

I snap my fingers, and a servant scrambles over. "Yes, your Majesty?"

"Send out a message to the kingdom for every mirror to be destroyed."

My people will not see what they are becoming until it is too late.

Stone glazed in ice.

Just like their Queen.

They called
him the
Snow
Whisperer

SNOW WHISPERER

Anne J. Hill

They called him the Snow Whisperer
Slinking into town once each winter
Bringing frost on his fingertips
Smiling through icy blue eyes

Skin white as the snow he spun
With hair whiter still
Passed through the red apple trees
And filled his fruit basket full

He'd freeze the round red fruit
A delicious winter treat
For all the boys and girls to bite
Juice turning their chins to ice

Children would sing of his deeds
Snow flowing from his fingers
Flakes dropping on their noses
And ice sculptures to carry home

They called him the Snow Whisperer
The man who controlled the skies
For only one day he'd come
Leaving the rest of winter black

Related to Thorn Tower *by Anne J. Hill*

A Lesson in Apples

Beka Gremikova

JACK TORE INTO the roasted chicken thigh, the heat of his anger suffusing with the warm tingling of his mother's herb blend. The flavors of rosemary and thyme soothed him, their homey familiarity pushing against the sting of resentment.

He crunched down on a bone and spat it onto the ground.

"What's that you got there?" asked the old woman sitting beside him on the bench.

Jack dropped the chicken thigh back into his food sack, sighing. Of all the seats the king had built along the Heroes' Highway, he'd chosen the one with the nosy neighbor. The little old ladies always looked harmless—that was to gain your trust before they guilt-tripped you into giving up your lunch.

Though, he conceded, he'd needed to sit *somewhere*. After walking through towns and forests all day, he was famished. The other benches he spotted along the tree-lined lane were all full. With rest spots and water fountains dotting the highway, would-be heroes thronged like pilgrims.

Jack licked his lips, about to tell her to mind her own business. But he could almost feel his mother breathing down his neck—his mother, who had handed the bag of food to him with a kiss on the cheek, murmuring, "Be generous to strangers."

Still, he couldn't stop his slight impudence. "Food."

The old woman pressed gnarled hands to her pale, sunken cheeks, her red lips pursed in an exaggerated 'o.' "Bless me soul! A young man on a Hero's Journey carrying food! Well, I never!"

Jack tilted his head. "Sarcasm actually becomes you."

The old woman's thin lips stretched in a smile. "It's not just a gift—it's a skill." Her gaze drifted to his sack. "Just like a well-cooked meal. Did your mother make it?" Her voice sounded creased and worn now, and her eyes shone.

Not the guilt trip, Jack thought. *Please, no.* "Yes…"

No wheedling response came. A gnarled, quivering hand reached up to adjust the hood around her face.

Jack leaned forward, curious. She was weeping. "Are you all right?"

She sucked in a breath. "Forgive me." She gave a creaky laugh. "It's been years, but sometimes the pain is still fresh." She spread out her hands. "It's like homemade bread—you forever remember the taste, and it never really leaves you."

"You lost your mother?" he whispered.

She nodded. "I was only a baby, but losing her…." Her eyes, dark and wise, clouded. "If my mother had been around, my father never would have remarried…." A crooked finger traced the deep wrinkles in her snow-pale skin.

"I'm sorry." Jack glanced down at the bag, full to bursting with more roasted chicken, cheese quarters, bread slices, fresh fruit. His mother had splurged what little she had to buy the cheese and fruit for his quest.

His cheeks burned as he recalled his mother filling that sack before he left home. He'd declared that he would return in a few months if he didn't find a princess to rescue. "Don't give up so easily," his mother had told him. "Give yourself more time." He'd completely snapped then.

How could she believe in him so much when he couldn't believe in himself?

Rather than squabble with him, she'd simply filled his traveling sack to the brim.

"Would you like to join me for my meal?" he finally asked the old woman. Although he couldn't erase his horrid words to Mother, he *could* honor her generous soul.

The old woman clasped her hands together. "I would enjoy that very much."

He reached into the bag, pulling out a shiny, red apple.

She flinched away from him.

He raised a brow, and she gave a huffing laugh.

"Sorry. Reflexes." Tugging down her hood, she released a tumble of salt and pepper hair.

"They're good for you." He bit into it, relishing the taste of a new spring morning—crisp, fresh, with the slightest sour tang to make his mouth water. "An apple a day—"

"Won't keep evil queens away," she muttered, eyeing the fruit. "Must be nice to have a loving mother."

Jack opened his bag to hide his embarrassment, lifting out a homemade loaf. He held out a thick slab to the woman, who took it with a big smile.

He bit off a mouthful of his own slice. Just the right kind of chewy, the crust tasted as rich as his favorite ale, frothy and deep.

The old woman stared at the bread. "It doesn't even need butter!"

Jack shook his head. "We're too poor to own a cow, so Mother perfected a loaf that's delicious by itself."

They made short work of the bread, cheese, and fruit that Jack retrieved from the bag, and stripped every bite of roast chicken from the bone. A few loaves and bundles of cheese remained, sustenance for the rest of his Hero's Journey.

The old woman leaned back at last. "Thank you, child, for sharing that delicious meal with me."

"Thank my mother," Jack said, wishing *he* could.

"You'll continue on your Journey now, I imagine?"

He nodded, staring down the highway that wound through the thin trees. "I hope to rescue a princess." Then he'd build his mother a palace.

The woman rummaged in her pocket, producing a shiny, red apple with one bite out of it. "I'm not magical, myself. But this apple killed me once. Maybe it'll take down a monster for you."

"It *killed* you?"

"Well, momentarily. I was revived by a prince on his own Hero's Journey."

Jack hoped the princess he eventually saved was half as nice as this woman. He took the apple, wrapped it in a napkin, and stuck it into the front pocket of his bag. "You didn't have to give me anything."

"I have a soft spot for those on Heroes' Journeys." Her lips quirked. "Good luck with your quest."

His heart warmed. The last bitter taste of his anger dissipated. He leaned down and kissed her cheek. "Thank you."

She waved him away, but her eyes twinkled. “My compliments to your mother.” She stood, hobbling in the other direction. “She’s done a hero’s work—cooked a fine meal *and* raised a fine son.”

A fine son? He’d try to live up to that.

FAIREST VILLAIN

Kaitlyn Emery

I HEARD THE RUMORS whispered on the lips of courtiers. They believed I was obsessed with my reflection, or perhaps a witch and the mirror before me contained magical properties, causing my vanity to need constant satisfaction.

What a ridiculous notion. Simpletons.

But, truth be told, reality was stranger than the rumors. Perhaps, had I not known the truth, I too would have believed the lies.

My eyes dropped to the bloodstone around my neck, cut in the shape of a heart, placed there by my late husband. It nearly glowed in the morning light as a stream of warm rays burst over the rise of the mountains. I knew it was time.

Every predator, no matter how strong, can meet its end. And now, with the sun spilling into my chambers, I knew my husband's daughter would be at her weakest. I had hoped it wouldn't come to this, that I would not have to be there to witness her fate, but after the Huntsman failed me, I knew I must end my stepdaughter's story before it was too late for us all.

I took one last look in the mirror, checking for a reflection to reassure myself it had not been erased by her curse, like so many others. My beautiful face stared back. My husband had always admired the high arch of my brows and chiseled features, like they had been cut from alabaster stone, he would say. Statuesque and perfect. Thankfully, he was not there to see the dark circles forming under my eyes from the stress his daughter wreaked in my life. It was the only consolation to his absence.

If I didn't put an end to this madness now, the entire castle would fall prey to the princess. And I couldn't let that happen. My husband's legacy was too important.

A vase of roses sat beside my dressing table. Such a treacherous little flower. Beloved by all, yet encased in perilous thorns. Just like my stepdaughter. She was an object of desire, coveted by many, but beneath the flawless exterior was something far more sinister. She held a bite to her beauty, like the thorns adorning the rose. I leaned over to inhale the potent perfume and plucked a bloom.

Such a delicate weapon...

I pierced one of the thorns into my skin, and a drop of blood formed along the tip of my finger before splattering onto the marble floor. Pressing the offending plant deeper into my finger, I let the blood drip freely, patiently waiting for the bait to take effect.

As if on cue, there was a knock at my door.

"Who is it?"

"It is I, stepmother." Her voice was soft, weakened by the daylight.

I knew she couldn't resist the temptation of fresh blood.

"Come in, Snow."

The doors before me opened, and the fairest creature in the land appeared, her eyes wide and nostrils flared ever so slightly. Her silk dress whispered across the marble floors as she entered my room, the seven guards that followed her everywhere closing the doors behind her to stand guard outside my chambers.

Midnight locks wisped down her back like smoke, adorned by a silver band embellished with a single emerald. Her skin was as white as freshly fallen snow, giving her an almost lifeless look, but her lips were as red as the blood on my finger.

She was enchanting. Beautiful. Her odd extremes made her seem exotic. A smile from those full, stained lips could compel anyone. And had. Many, many times. But not me. The crimson stone around my neck kept me immune to her charms.

"You are hurt, Stepmother."

I glanced down at the delicate floral weapon in my hand. "So it seems, child."

Her eyes darted erratically from the blood dripping off my finger to my eyes. "Sh-Should I call for help?" She struggled to maintain eye contact.

She acted so innocent, and when she was a child, I had perceived her to be a gentle soul. I even cared for her back then, motherless and frail as she was. By day she seemed so sickly, avoiding the sunlight and keeping indoors. But by night she grew stronger, her beauty flourishing beneath candlelight.

"Stepmother?"

"No need to call for help, Snow. It's just a small trickle of blood. Nothing to worry about."

The girl's pupils were huge as she tried to pry her gaze from the red liquid weeping from my body.

"Come here, child. I picked these apples from our orchards. I thought we might enjoy them together."

Confusion flickered over Snow's porcelain features. "I don't like apples, Stepmother. You know that."

I carefully selected the chosen apple, letting the blood from my finger permeate its flesh. She didn't like the fruit, but she would like what I added to it.

Snow watched my every move.

"I think you will like this one, my dear." I held the apple out to her, the metallic scent of my blood clashing against the tangy-sweet aroma of the fruit.

I could see distrust flicker across the girl's face before she dropped her gaze, voice flat. "You already know what I am… Why are you toying with me?"

I tried to school my features and keep my anger from boiling over. My plan would go better if she cooperated.

"Of course I know, child. But we don't talk about it, do we?"

I never understood why everyone seemed to turn a blind eye to her secret. More people knew than let on, they just ignored it. There were legends and myths told about her kind, but no one was brave enough to expose this wretched girl for what she truly was.

A cold-blooded monster.

A calculating demon.

I was going to change that. "Did you really think I wouldn't know after I found your father gasping for his last breath, drained of his blood?"

Tears pricked her eyes, but I would not be fooled.

"I didn't mean to!" Her voice cracked.

Lies! Still, I forced my voice to soften. "I know, darling. You would never hurt your father on purpose." I held the apple out further. "Come, sit with me at my mirror. I will brush your hair, and we can talk. But first, a precaution. Eat, that you might not be hungry, child."

Her lower lip trembled. Many suitors had praised her for their perfection, but every time I looked at their soft, red fullness, all I could see was the blood of her father.

"I don't like mirrors."

I had learned that long ago. As a child, she abhorred them, which was very strange for a girl blessed with such beauty. "I know, but now that we both know what you are, there is no sense in avoiding them any longer. Come. Sit."

Reluctantly, she moved toward the chair and sat, the reflective surface opposite her refusing to display her likeness in its reflection. It was as if she were a ghost.

I picked up the brush from the dressing table and, like I had so many times since she was a child, began to brush her long, dark curls.

Snow followed my reflection in the mirror, a look of longing in her eyes, before her gaze dropped to the stone around my neck."It was my mother's," she whispered.

"What was?" I asked, confused.

"The necklace." She nodded toward the bloodstone, and my fingers sought the comfort of the hard surface, as they always did when I thought of her father.

I feigned a smile and returned to brushing her hair. "No. It was your father's. He gave it to me as a gift." She would not mar my memories.

Snow nodded sadly. "I know. That's why he died."

Fury pricked my back like a thousand needles, and this time I didn't bother to keep my anger in check. "You killed him for giving me something you thought was your mother's?"

The girl winced as if I had struck her with my words and rose from the chair, pushing away my ministrations. "No! You don't understand.... I couldn't help it!"

Of course she couldn't. It was always someone else's fault. Never Snow's fault. The apple with my blood seeping into its flesh sat on the dressing table where I had left it. It was time her lies and deceit stopped. She would eat that apple! I clenched it in my fist, my grip so tight my nails impaled its red skin. "What do you mean you couldn't help it?"

Snow fell to her knees, weeping. Such a spectacle. "The witch who cursed me gave my mother the bloodstone—a talisman to protect one life. Mother chose to give it to Father. She always took care of us. That's why... that's why she was my first... I was so young; I hadn't learned to control the thirst!"

"*You* killed your mother?" If it was true— What kind of child would kill her own mother?

"I didn't know what I was doing! I just wanted the hunger to go away! When I realized I had killed her…I tried so hard to control it after that. I tried to stick to rats and small animals, but the hunger just grew. No matter how much I tried to stop it. Until one night when Father was trying to help me manage the hunger, I lost control again. I don't even remember doing it; I just remember waking up to Father, cold in my arms, his blood in my mouth…. Why won't the blood curse be satisfied? Why?" She wailed, grabbing at my skirts.

I lifted her chin slowly, staring into those frosted eyes. "All of the pain can go away, Snow. Take a bite." I held up the apple, bruised but still tantalizing with my blood.

She looked from the fruit to me as if offended by my suggestion. "How will an apple help me?"

"Eat it, Snow," I insisted.

Something flickered in her eyes. Fear, then acceptance. "You poisoned it?"

I held her gaze, my heart unmoved by the sadness in her eyes. "You killed your father and mother; you must atone for your sins."

"But what about the kingdom—"

"I will do what must be done to protect your father's legacy and his people. Even if that means killing you."

Snow raised an eyebrow as if to challenge me. "I may not lose control when I am near you because of that stone, but that doesn't mean I couldn't *choose* to sink my teeth into you." As if to make her point, she parted her lips to reveal pointed fangs.

I held my position. "If you are truly sorry for what you did, you will take the bite."

Her eyes filled with tears as my words sunk in. With resignation, she took the apple from me and brought it to her lips.

Our eyes locked for a moment.

"Thank you," she whispered.

What? "Thank you?" I questioned.

A small smile tugged at the corners of her mouth. "Now, the people will remember you as the villain of my story. Not me."

"What do you—"

She sank her pointed teeth into the fruit. "Guards!" she shrieked right before she began convulsing, spitting blood out of her mouth. "Help me!"

Horror clawed at my throat. She played me. The realization of my mistake hit me as furry raged through my veins. She would not make me the villain! She would not make herself the martyr and turn the kingdom against me in her death.

"No!" I tried to pry the chunk of apple from her throat, but she had already swallowed. "No! You are the monster!" The apple rolled from her hand and across the floor as I shook her limp body. "You're the monster, not me!"

My chamber doors burst open. "Your Majesty?"

I dragged my gaze from Snow's body. The Princess' seven guards stood there, swords drawn, eyes taking in the situation. My poisoned apple lay at their feet, red as the blood that now stained my soul.

FIERCER THAN FANGS

PART THREE

You kill the
ones you love
to create a
better world.

SEQUEL TO *LIGHT DAWNS IN DARKNESS*

I FOLLOW MY FATHER in the veil of the setting sun. He knocks on a mansion door, and a woman with a red ribbon in her hair opens, then vanishes inside the house. I crouch behind a tree and watch as the traitorous duke steps out and my father hands over his satchel.

My father fights on the wrong side of the war with the Revolters, enemies of the Emperor—my enemies. But I've seen him whisper in the night, playing friendly with the Loyals. He is a spy; I know this now—wooing the Emperor while kissing his enemy.

So I've become the monster this war needs.

I don't know what lies inside his satchel, but it cannot be good. He was eager to bring it, so I must ensure it never reaches the Revolters.

I slink through the grass, and just as my father hands the bag over, I dig my claws into his back. We scramble in a mess of fur and flesh until the woman cracks the door open, and I lunge for her.

But the duke grabs me and yells, "You can't have her! Stay off her path," and calls me names I won't repeat.

Teeth gnash, claws fly, hands yank.

I dig my teeth into my father's leg, and an accidental gunshot fires.

Blood blooms across the duke's stomach.

I killed the duke.

The woman grabs the satchel and takes off into the night, and I lay by my father, watching the life drain from him. Too many slashes, too many bites. And with his remaining strength, he tells me he still loves me.

Even after I've killed him, too.

Now he lays beside the duke. I'm sorry for what I've done and let out one wail for the dead.

But that's how war goes. You kill the ones you love to create a better world.

Without seconds to spare, I pick myself up and chase the woman through the forest. Each attempt I make to step on her path thrusts me back, and I can never reach her.

Something in the duke's words must be keeping me from her; I know not what.

But still, I hunt her down, through branches and graveyards...

Because curses can't stop me.

I pause when she reaches the Emperor's castle, watching her beg to be let in.

This I did not expect. The satchel was meant for the Revolters, but here she is, at the castle gate. I question myself for a moment.

But I cannot be wrong. Because if I am, that'd mean I killed my father for no reason. And that I can't bear.

So I harden my heart.

And bare my teeth.

And plan to devour the red ribbon woman.

When something in me freezes.

She looks over her shoulder in my direction. I feel a prick in my head. And like she can read my mind, her face falls into sorrow. She calls out from the gate, "I'm on your side, wolfman."

She could be lying, but dread fills me because maybe she isn't.

And I've become the wrong sort of monster in this war.

I lock eyes with her, and she holds out her hand in my direction, even though I'm hidden behind the thicket in the night.

She says, voice sweet as honey, "I've got powers too. Blood-born. You're not alone. We're on the same side. Your father was indeed a spy, but not in the way you think. He was a Loyal, just like you, spying against the Revolters. But don't blame yourself. You didn't know or understand. You did what you thought you had to do. You're not a wolf inside."

I dip my head, flashes of memories coming to my mind. Memories I could have misunderstood. Misplaced hatred and wrongful accusations.

All these years, he'd been fighting for me?

Fighting to create a world where blood-borns with powers like mine can live without fear of being rejected, or worse, killed?

All these years as I've hated him and reasoned he wasn't actually my father. I was adopted, so of course, he had no real love for me, I'd told myself many times. He had no genuine desire to fight for a world I could live freely in.

But all these years…

I've been wrong.

I cry wolfish tears for the lives I ended and the lies I've believed. And there I lay, a monster forevermore, because this is guilt I'll never rid.

But as the sun slowly rises, light shines on the woman's face, and she utters words I'll never forget, "I forgive you, wolfman."

The wolf within stirs and cries for forgiveness I do not deserve.

I might never forgive myself, but she has, so there is hope…

Forevermore.

LIKE A FOX

Beka Gremikova

SPLASHING AND LAUGHTER drifted to Veya from the hot springs. She peeked over the clump of sunbaked rocks to where her sister, Vasilisa, treaded water with her two attendants. Though she did not boast the keen hearing of the Pelted shapeshifters, Veya still caught a snippet of their conversation, and her stomach churned.

"I heard Petrov's wife just gave birth." Vasilisa combed her fingers through her gleaming dark brown hair. "And Telkov has *finally* gotten betrothed." She gave a delicate snort.

Marriages. Births.

Both things denied to Veya because of her Peltless rank in the Fox Clan. Her fingers twisted into her own coppery locks, her nails digging into her skull.

One of the attendants glanced up toward Veya. Her lips twisted.

"How do the pelts look, Veya?" she called. "Her Ladyship would like to know."

Veya's cheeks burned. She dragged her gaze to the three fiery-red fox furs laid out on the rocks. Fitting her high status, Vasilisa's was the largest. "There are a few dirty spots," Veya forced out as she brushed the bristly hair. "Your Ladyship," she added hastily when another of the attendants glowered at her.

It didn't matter that she and Vasilisa were blood-related—since she'd been born without the magical pelt that allowed her to shapeshift, Veya would never be considered a true member of their Clan.

Vasilisa sighed. "We did trek through lots of mud, but I'm sure you'll get it clean. It's seen worse."

"At least the Peltless make fantastic groomers." The first attendant leaned back against the rock wall behind her and closed her eyes as the hot water bubbled.

"Don't they? Oh! Hurry, though, Veya—the Wolf Clan ladies' turn to wash is in an hour, and you know how they get if we take too long. Though... we could just blame you if we need to." Vasilisa yipped in laughter, and her attendants joined in.

The sound stabbed Veya's ears; she snatched up the pelts and staggered away. The foxes' laughter rang through her mind, reminding her how little she belonged with her own family. Without a pelt of her own, she couldn't even *laugh* like a fox, loud and joyful.

She stared down at the bright copper bundle in her hands. She needed a pelt, and here she was with an entire stack of them...

Take one and run!

Surely, being family, she could meld with her sister's pelt magic. She could run away, start fresh in another part of the Fox Clan... She swallowed. How many times had she thought of this very thing—and never dared?

Her steps slowed, and she stopped in the middle of the path to the cleaning hut. The scent of pine from the nearby forest flared in her nostrils. The trees' shadows beckoned her, offering her a place to escape, to hide...

Something scuffed the ground in front of her. She glanced up and froze.

A large black wolf, eyes solemn and dark, watched her from a few feet away. A bright crimson sash was braided around his neck, decorated with small, gleaming beads.

Lord Mishak. One of the Wolf Clan's prime picks for a future alpha.

Her heart thundered in her ears. If he wanted to, he could take her down with one leap, one bite from his massive jaws... After all, despite the neutral ground of the hot springs, wolves and foxes weren't friends. Outside of places like the hot springs, the Clans avoided each other as much as possible.

She shrank back to let him pass, and he slipped by with a regal nod. He trotted away down the road, his tail swishing.

Tears pricked her eyes as she swiped her arm across her face. She was so *tired* of scraping for favor from every Pelted she came across. She didn't even *know* Mishak, yet the rules of Fox Clan society dictated that she should always make way before him.

Her arms tightened around her sister's pelt, and the others dropped from her arms to the path. *Let them get dirty. I won't be cleaning them anymore!* She snuck a look over her shoulder. In the distance, Vasilisa's high, mocking laughter echoed, but nobody else walked the stretch of dirt between Veya and the hot springs.

Her stomach tightened, and she darted into the surrounding forest with Vasilisa's pelt. The trees closed in around her. Cool shadows rippled across her skin and *almost* banished her panicked, tangled thoughts.

If she got caught... If the foxes overlooked their hatred of the wolves and asked them to hunt her down....

No. She had to do this. She ducked under a branch and veered toward her grandmother's old den, huddled in a cluster of oaks deep in the forest. As a child, she'd played there safely under her grandmother's watchful eye, away from the Pelted children who considered Veya a disease. Away from the family who gnawed on what little she had and spat it back in her face.

After half an hour of running, Veya stumbled into the familiar clearing. Oaks crowded around her, surrounded by shrubs and toddling trees. Her grandmother's abandoned den gaped from the shadows of two leafy saplings. Acorns and pine needles crunched underfoot. Veya keeled over, gasping for breath, the pelt still scrunched in her arms. It tingled against her skin as though daring her to claim it for herself.

Her entire body trembled at the notion of owning *anything*.

She licked her lips and swiped her sweaty, drooping curls out of her eyes. Shaking out her limbs, she planted her feet squarely amongst the acorns and pine needles and tugged the pelt around her shoulders.

She pressed her eyes closed. Maybe, just maybe, she could shift...

Pain tore through her, the magic pointed and sharp like fox teeth all along her limbs. Every strand of the fur hummed with her sister's voice, as if embedded with Vasilisa's imprint: *I belong to no one but Lady Vasilisa herself. You're* nothing *but a thief!*

Her knees buckled; her chest constricted. Her fingers numb, she crumpled to the pine needles, and her vision swam into darkness.

Veya woke to late afternoon sunshine shifting through the treetops. Pine needles crunched under her body as she struggled to her hands and knees, limbs stiff and sore. The pelt lay sprawled across the ground, its reddish hues streaked with dirt.

Nothing but a thief. Nothing but a thief. The pelt's accusation rang through her mind, its echo as searing as a fox's piercing laughter.

She wrapped her arms around herself. What could she do now? Her plan hadn't worked, and… A shadow stirred amongst the trees.

Terror pinned her to the spot.

The shadow solidified into a large black wolf, crimson beads hanging from his neck.

"L-lord Mishak!" She gasped and tried to stagger to her feet, but her legs felt as light and fragile as the pine needles.

Lord Mishak sniffed at the air, his nostrils flaring. "You must be Veya." He tilted his head, his eyes bright and searing. As if in response to her panicked expression, he murmured, "Your family asked for my help to track you down. You can trust me." His voice wasn't as deep as she'd expected. It lilted a little, as if he spent much of his time laughing at a joke no one else cared to hear.

But he was still an enemy. Any ally of her family, however begrudging, could *only* be her enemy.

She had to get away.

She threw herself forward, but her body buckled, and she crashed back to the ground. Pain shot through her limbs. A massive paw pinned her leg, firm yet gentle. A glance over her shoulder had her staring straight into Mishak's keen gaze.

Panic clawed at her. "Please!" she blurted. Tears threatened, but she blinked them back. "Please don't take me back to them!"

"I don't plan to hurt you or bring you back to your family without hearing your story first." His voice was level, soothing. "You mustn't harm yourself trying to get away."

"What would you care about that?" Heat burned through her stomach, and her fear faded under a wave of anger. She glared at the nearby pelt, which, despite the grime that coated it, still shone a deep orange-red in the dappled sunlight. "I'm just a Peltless."

His eyes narrowed. "All the more reason you must show care to yourself." He lifted his paw from her skin.

"Why bother? Nobody else cares." She slowly sat up, shivering.

He blinked at her. "Are you saying your Clan doesn't care if you're hurt?" He shifted, and a hulking wolf no longer crouched beside her—instead, a tall, brown-skinned young man with long black hair and kind, somber eyes knelt on the forest floor. His pelt lay wrapped around his shoulders. "Wolves revere their Peltless members—do not foxes do the same?"

Shame clogged her throat. She buried her face in her hands. Only a traitor would want to reveal her family's secrets to a stranger. But Mishak leaned forward, his brow creased, lips pursed, gaze searing and attentive. Like he might actually care. Like, with him, her words might truly matter. She swallowed. "No," she whispered between her fingers. Guilt churned in her stomach. *Thief. Traitor.*

A hiss escaped his lips. "Please, help me understand. What do you mean?" He sounded astonished and bewildered.

At least the Peltless make fantastic groomers. But never friends, never students, never wives, never mothers. She dragged her fingers through her snarled curls in an attempt to hide their trembling. "What I mean is… Without a pelt, I'm not allowed to marry, or have kits, or receive any education."

Mishak reeled back as though she'd lunged at his throat. His fingers clenched around the delicate scarlet beads of his necklace. "I…I'm so sorry." He hesitated, and his eyelashes lowered. "Have you any idea as to why?"

She shrugged. "I think you're asking the wrong person. I don't know why the Fox Clan elders decided Peltless weren't worth their effort." She studied the dirt-streaked fox fur, its individual hairs glistening. She imagined it wrapped around Vasilisa's body, nestled against her skin, both claiming her and obeying her commands—a power Vasilisa couldn't hope to understand or appreciate. A power that made her strong and healthy and desired. A power that would carry her and the Clan into the future and leave Veya in the dust. "I…I suppose foxes still fear the Wolf Clan and want only the strongest to pass along their genes."

"So you stole the pelt to…to *join* this society?" His tone wasn't accusatory; he merely tilted his head like a befuddled fox kit.

"What other society *could* I join?" she snapped as fury boiled up in her. "I suppose *your* wonderful, perfect Clan is open to applicants?"

He flinched, then bowed his head. "It's not as ideal as I may have made it sound." He traced his fingers through the muddle of sticks, leaves and acorns around them, stacking the pine needles into little heaps. "High-ranking positions are very respected—and closely guarded. If you are born into an alpha position, you're expected to accept it... whether you want to or not."

"Why wouldn't you want to be alpha?" Was this wolf saying he'd prefer *not* to be in a position of power?

"There are... certain qualities that alphas must possess, in the Clan's opinion," Mishak muttered. "Qualities that *I* don't have, or ever want to have."

She shouldn't care, but she was curious anyway. "Such as?" She bit her lip. Did that sound too rude, too disrespectful? Would he turn around and snap at her, as she'd heard about other wolves doing?

But Mishak seemed unperturbed. "Alphas must always ensure others know who they are—to throw their weight around, as it were. To be the loudest and meanest in the room. To make sure other Clans know we are not to be messed with."

"They sound annoying," she muttered before she could stop herself. She froze, eyes darting to his face.

Mishak grinned with a flash of sharp white teeth as his eyes crinkled. "My thoughts exactly. Annoying, and rude."

"And your Clan... wants *you* to do all that someday?"

"Because I was born to alphas, and was the largest of my litter."

She stared at his long, jagged canines, still intimidating even in his human shape. "I suppose you must be a great hunter, too. No wonder my kin turned to you."

"Very begrudgingly."

The fear that had faded returned with the chill of a northern wind. "I suppose you—you *have* to bring me back?"

His lips twitched, and he stretched, cracking his knuckles. "No fox has any authority over me. Your kin asked for my help in hunting you down... but my mind is my own whether I decide to be their huntsman or *your* helper."

She sucked in a ragged breath, afraid to believe her ears. "You... you would help a *Peltless*?" she squeaked.

He waved his hand at her. "Whatever beliefs your kin holds toward you, I don't share. But stealing is still a crime, in either Wolf or Fox's opinion."

Run! Her instincts screamed, despite the weakness in her limbs. *Before they find you and kill you!*

But Veya couldn't run—all she could do was trust in this man's sense of mercy. She swallowed. "What if I returned the Pelt?" she whispered. "Could you—would you take it back for me?"

He regarded her steadily. "And what would you do?"

Why did he still care so much? What was she to him, to anyone? She blinked back tears and wrapped her arms around herself. "I don't know. I just need to get away from here."

Behind them, bushes rustled. In a blink, Mishak shifted back to wolf form, a towering surge of muscle and fangs. She shrank back, heart in her mouth, but the wolf stepped closer—and *over* her, until she lay nestled between his front paws.

He lowered his head with a rising growl. His long black fur brushed against her cheek.

A large grey wolf and two foxes emerged from the undergrowth. Veya, her face pressed against Mishak's leg, sucked in a deep breath before panic could turn her insides to mush.

"Well done, Lord Mishak," one of the foxes said. Veya recognized the grey-and-black fur and bright eyes of Telkov. He trotted forward, gaze narrowed on Veya, the other fox at his heels. "We will take charge of her from here. We owe your Clan a great debt—"

"You owe us nothing." Mishak crouched, his chin skimming Veya's hair. The tiny *clink* of his beads echoed in her ears. "Because she's not returning with you."

Veya bit back a gasp. The foxes stared at each other, jaws agape, while the grey wolf's ears flattened. "What are you *doing*?" he growled.

Mishak bristled and lifted his chin high in the air until he appeared taller than the other wolf. "Throwing my weight around." His voice came out a deep, threatening rumble. Chills skittered along Veya's neck, and she pressed her hands into the dirt, her fingers closing around a sharp stick.

The grey wolf snarled, his teeth glistening in the deep shadows of the clearing. "You're not alpha yet, *milord*."

"But I will be." Gone was the quiet, oddly unassuming wolf Veya had talked with not long before.

"You would risk further enmity with an entire Clan over a single Peltless fox?" The other wolf shook his head, his silver fur rippling. "It's *madness*. We have *our* family to protect!"

"And as a future alpha, *I* have a say in *who* that family is."

The grey wolf snarled. "As your family, allow me to tell you you're a *fool*!" He sprang forward with a snap of his jaws. The foxes glanced at each other uncertainly, then followed after, nipping at Mishak's heels.

Mishak swiveled his head and bared his teeth. Saliva splattered against Veya's hair. A blur of teeth and fur hurtled toward them, aimed for Mishak's throat. She hadn't stopped to consider that Mishak might have enemies that would take advantage of finding him alone in the woods. Faster than she could think, she threw herself forward, fingers tight around the sharp, jagged stick she held. She jabbed it at the grey wolf and felt the burst of skin giving way.

A ragged yelp, and a paw smacked her in the face. Pain sprang through her head; her ears rang. Something yanked at her tunic and dragged her backward. Dazedly, she blinked up into Mishak's blazing eyes. "*What* are you doing?" he snapped.

She licked at the blood that dribbled between her lips. "Throwing my weight around." She smiled up at him crookedly, then winced as her head panged.

"Next time, stay back. It's better for our defense."

"Next time?" She sat up. The other wolf, the fur around his throat bloodstained, had regrouped. With a gulp, she realized just how *huge* he was—easily Mishak's equal, if not even larger. She glanced up at Mishak, but he wouldn't meet her gaze. His eyes were narrowed in on his opponent.

He lowered his head and spread his legs wider. "Stand down, cousin. You may be the alpha of *your* pack, but you're not the alpha of mine."

"*Every* pack in the Wolf Clan will be affected by your actions," the grey wolf snarled. "Don't fool yourself into thinking otherwise."

"Are you saying we shouldn't help those in need?"

"We help *our* people," the grey wolf said. "Wolves for the wolves."

"Sage advice." Telkov nodded.

Mishak's ears flattened. Then he stiffened. "Wolves for the wolves," he murmured. He glanced down at Veya. "Would you... would you like to become an honorary wolf, then?"

"*What*?" she yelped.

A strangled howl ripped from the other wolf. He darted forward. "No!"

Mishak threw all his weight into the grey wolf in a clash of fur. Mishak's opponent staggered back and tumbled to the ground with Mishak pinned against him. Mishak closed his jaws over the grey wolf's snout. The grey wolf whimpered, rolled over, and flashed his stomach in what Veya assumed to be a sign of submission.

Her shoulders sagged with relief.

Nearby came the slightest crackling of underbrush, so faint Veya nearly missed it. Mishak started, and the grey wolf stiffened, his eyes flying to the trees.

Someone else was coming.

Mishak cursed and quickly turned human, keeping his hand pressed on the grey wolf's snout. Though the other wolf could have obviously fought back, he did not move. He breathed heavily, his gaze glazed.

Mishak glanced at Veya. "Quickly!" His dark eyes snagged hers. "Yes or no? Will you join the Wolf Clan?"

A wolf—fierce, respected, powerful. Unyielding.

And, sometimes, terrifying.

Yet Mishak had been kind, too. Perhaps…perhaps there might be others….

"Yes," she whispered. "But—"

Mishak wrapped his pelt around her shoulders and snugged it tight under her chin. His lips moved silently, even as his hands trembled. His eyes shone with tears, but he offered her a tiny smile.

The pelt did not resist her. Rather, it *melted* into her skin. Magic, smooth and soft, rippled through her body, tugging at her joints, tickling her stomach. Scents and sounds like she'd never experienced overwhelmed her senses. She staggered—and found herself stumbling on all fours.

More wolves burst into the clearing, and a dazzle of howls pierced her ears. Mishak stood, fists clenched at his sides. The wolves skittered to a stop, wide eyes fixed on Veya. One of them, a large white wolf, stepped forward, nostrils flaring. "Mishak, who is this? Why does she smell like your pelt?"

Mishak rubbed the back of his neck. A deep flush crept over his skin. "Greetings, Mother. This… this is my friend Veya. She seeks refuge from the Fox Clan, and I granted it the only way I know." After a moment's hesitation, he raised his chin. His fingers fidgeted with his beaded necklace. His hair shone with streaks of red in the fading afternoon sunlight. "I am now Peltless."

His declaration was met with stunned silence.

He turned to the foxes. "As a wolf, she falls under *our* laws." He picked up the discarded fox fur, now a crumpled mess, from the forest floor and tossed it at Telkov's feet. "Take your pelt back to your princess. You have no further business here."

Telkov opened his mouth but shrank back when the female wolf sent him a glare. He and his fellow fox scattered back into the woods.

The white wolf gave a long-suffering sigh. "A Peltless Alpha. I've never seen such a thing."

So the wolves took care of their Peltless, but didn't offer them ruling positions, Veya realized, biting her lip. Her mind still rang with Mishak's words. He'd traded places with her of his own volition, but had she just left him to the same fate she'd suffered for so long?

The wolves crept forward to snuffle Mishak's arms, his face, his hair. He smiled, then laughed, rubbing his hands through one's fur, nipping at another's ears. He grinned up at his mother. "Perhaps it's time things were different. Not just for us, Mother, but all the Clans. A Peltless shouldn't have to flee her family to find a normal life."

"You little troublemaker." His mother shook out her fur, though her tongue lolled in a smile. She bowed her head to Veya. "Welcome to the Wolf Clan. Even I cannot argue with the magic of the pelt. It has accepted you, and, therefore, so must I, by the Wolf Laws. We will do our best by you." With another glance toward her son, she turned and melted back into the forest, the rest of the pack close behind.

Except for Mishak, who lingered on the edge of the clearing, his eyes on Veya.

"Why did you do it?" she asked him, now in human form, his pelt—no, *her* pelt—curled up in her arms. She ran a finger through the thick, bristly fur. She was still a fox—still felt that deep, knowing bond to her old Clan—but now she felt another kind of belonging . . . something that had been freely offered, something that she hadn't had to scrape and scrimp for. She bowed her head to hide the tears that stung her eyes.

"I can't protect you on my own." He smiled ruefully. "I can help you better with my pack on my side—and there's only one way they'd accept you. You had to smell like a wolf." He shrugged his shoulders. "When I'm truly alpha, we can start changing things from the inside. Then, if you don't want to be amongst my Clan any longer, you won't need to be. Perhaps we can change the Clans' mindsets for good, and you can rejoin the Foxes if you wish."

Her heart stirred at the determination and hope in his voice. A giddy grin twitched at the corners of her lips. "*Only* if I wish."

A deep flush crept into his cheeks. He ran his fingers along his beads, shoulders hunched slightly. He coughed. "Of course. I'd—we'd . . . be happy to have you as part of our pack as long as you want to be part of it." Skimming his fingers across his beads, he dug his sharp canines into his bottom lip, now looking like a bashful kit.

She bit back a giggle. Did it even matter anymore that she couldn't laugh like a fox or would never look like a fox?

She wrapped the pelt tightly around herself and gave a gleeful howl.

Darkness falls

with a

howl.

He stalks through the woods,
His footsteps bold and swift.
He lures in the helpless
At every midnight shift.

His ears catch the cries,
His fur blends in the dark.
His teeth snap and break bones,
His claws, cold and stark.

Hunting from the shadows
His yellow eyes glow.
Seeking out lost children,
His greedy thirst grows.

He is the wolf.

I tread through the woods
My footsteps soft and meek.
I'm a child, and I'm helpless
My courage is weak.

At every twist and turn
Hiding 'neath my scarlet hood.
My heart shakes inside me
At the sounds in the wood.

I hide from the shadows
My eyes cast to and fro.
The danger draws nearer
While my terror still grows.

I am the girl.

He walks through the woods
His footsteps sure and steady.
He seeks out the helpless,
Ever at the ready.

Lumberjack of all trades
His axe in his hand,
He works day and night
A brave, good-hearted man.

He checks every shadow
With wise, careful eyes.
He stops, and he answers
The fearful night cries.

He is the woodsman.

But then the dread night comes.
My hands weak and shaking,
We three meet in the woods,
My heart frail and quaking.

But I stand against the wolf,
As the woodsman swings his blade.
And though I fall beneath his bite,
The enemy is slayed.

Life passes under the moon,
Time is lost in teeth and growls.
My senses fill with blood and pain.
Darkness falls with a howl.

That was the night.

But now I hunt in the woods,
My footsteps sure and bold.
I am no longer helpless,
My courage still holds.

My hood does not hide me.
The weak, I now shield.
Side-by-side with the woodsman
We neither falter nor yield.

My ears catch the whispers.
My yellow eyes glow.
My bite swift and vicious,
Against every dark foe.

Now I...am the wolf.

The greatest
weapon against
any beast
is its own.

HOPE IS A DANGEROUS THING

Maseeha Seedat

SEQUEL TO *THE GUARDIAN OF THE MAELSTROM*

HOPE IS A dangerous thing. It can drive a man mad.

My father's words echoed in my mind as I stood at the gates to the port of Cádiz.

Well, good thing I'm a woman.

Gulls screeched across the sky as the sun rose on the horizon, rousing the sailors and dockworkers to prepare themselves for the day ahead. Most of the boats would return to the harbor tonight full of fish, others in a few weeks with precious treasures from Turkey and America.

I, on the other hand, didn't know if we would ever make it back home again.

"Ready to go, Captain Isla?" A hand squeezed my shoulder reassuringly.

I looked up, face-to-face with Ray and his silver-streaked dreadlocks—my first mate, my father's best friend. My fingers drummed against the copper-red hilt of my sword—my mother's technically, but it was all I had left of her now.

"Hoist the anchor," I said, forcing a smile. Ray had no idea what was to come on the journey ahead. None of the crew did. And I couldn't let them find out. As far as they were concerned, we were going to Tenerife to preserve the trade relations my father had made twenty years ago, a year after my mother died bringing me into this world.

Ray ushered me up the gangplank to *Valka*, hollering orders to the crew as I snuck to my quarters. I placed my satchel on my bed. It was empty for now, but I would fill it by the time we reached Tenerife, by the time I abandoned my crew, my ship—my home.

No.

I wasn't abandoning them. I would survive Tenerife. I would survive the caves of Don Gaspar.

But the caves had haunted the seas for centuries, their legends claiming an evil spirit roamed in its shadows, that a darkness lived there capable of consuming you whole. If that was true, my chances of returning home alive were almost non-existent.

I strolled to my father's desk in the far corner of my room. I hadn't touched it since he died on our last adventure. All his papers were still scattered, his maps filled with his illustrations, and his drawers held every record of his journeys.

No one would search here for my secret.

I opened the top drawer, pulling out a letter with a blood-red wax seal, with a stamp from Tenerife. We had journeyed there a few moons ago to rekindle my father's trade connections. That was when I found the letter on my desk.

At first, I assumed it was a record of the new deals we made. Those thoughts vanished when I saw the name on the back.

Valka.

My mother's name.

I rubbed the weathered parchment between my fingers, resisting the urge to reread it even though I knew it by heart. In her cursive hand, my mother detailed how much she missed my father, how much she longed to see me, and how some curse trapped her in the caves of Don Gaspar, waiting for her savior.

Hope is a dangerous thing, my father would say. *It kindles a fire that cannot be doused without killing a little of your soul.*

But the fire had already sparked within me. The only way to extinguish it was to find her. I had to go to Don Gaspar. I had to survive the caves. If there was even the slightest possibility of rebuilding my family, I had to risk it all.

A lone tear trailed down my cheek.

"Isla, you in here?" Ray called, knocking on my door.

I flicked away the tear, racing to the door. It swung wide open, almost knocking me off my feet.

I had to hide my nerves a lot better.

"I'm here, Ray." I smiled again. "I was on my way to take the wheel."

"All yours, Captain." He bowed theatrically, his dreadlocks dancing in the wind.

I edged past him, trying to walk calmly as his stare burned into my back. The helmsman handed me the wheel with a bow, the familiar grain of the wood comforting against my trembling hands. It felt like home, freedom, and the chance for me to finally steer my own course without my father worrying about his 'little girl.'

The summer breeze filled *Valka*'s sail, rippling through my red frock coat as I set our course southwest. We would reach Tenerife in one week. I had plenty of time to plan my escape off *Valka*.

Our third night to Tenerife carried a full moon. It wafted in and out of the clouds as the crew drew straws for their watch shifts. I hooked my arm into the rope net I sat in, listening to the gentle melody of the waves lapping against *Valka*'s side. Ray scrambled up the net to join me.

"It's time for us to draw our straws, Captain." He rattled the sticks in his fist, a sly glimmer in his eyes.

Of course. It was my father's tradition to tell legends on the night of the full moon. Either the captain or the first mate had the honor, so it was me against Ray.

I closed my eyes, waving my hands over his fist as I picked out a straw. He did the same, pulling his out with an extravagant flourish.

Mine was shorter.

Ray whooped with delight, hollering to the crew below us, "Oy! Gather round. Time for our captain to share her wisdom. Whether it is wise or dumb, that will be up to interpretation."

The men gathered on crates and barrels around the mainmast as the cook emerged from the galley, a massive pot in his burly arms. Whatever it was, it smelled delicious. Bowls were passed around as I swung down from the nets, my mother's sword swinging in its scabbard at my waist. I took my bowl and stood on a barrel in the center, flicking through the stories in my mind.

Only one stood out.

"All right, all right, save your interpretations for later." The crew fell silent, waiting for me to speak. "Now, this story was first told to me by my father, Captain Adrian. May he rest in peace—"

"May he rest in peace," echoed the crew.

"—and tonight, we'll see if I can live up to his legacy."

I cleared my throat, easing my voice into the rhythm and cadence my father had taught me.

"Beyond seven mountain ranges, beyond seven seas," I began, my tone echoing the days of old, "a little girl lived on the coast of Ireland. Now, this little girl loved the ocean, and she spent every spare moment she could muster in a cove hidden in the craggy cliffs of her island.

"'Be careful,' her mother would warn her. 'There are beasts in these waters, and little girls like you are their favorite snack.'"

The crew chuckled at this. Fine, the story was childish, but my father had designed it for the six-year-old I once was. It was meant to be that way.

"One day, the girl sat in the crashing waves, eyes closed, lost in her daydreams of sailing around the world. She was so consumed in her thoughts that she didn't notice the roaring thunder even though there were no clouds. She didn't see the shadow lurking in the waters, getting closer to shore."

Gasps fluttered across the ring, echoing in the silence of the open ocean. A grin crept across my face. The crew always played along with my extravagant bedtime stories.

"The shadow rose out of the water, taking the form of a kelpie, a sea monster that could easily be mistaken for a horse. Its body was dark and slick like oil, its mane made of tangled seaweed.

"But the girl was still lost in her dreams. The beast bent low, loosening its enormous jaw. Its teeth clamped over her foot, and her eyes shot open as it threw her onto its back. The girl screamed for help, struggling against the sticky black fur of the kelpie. No one came.

"The beast dove deeper into the ocean, deeper and deeper, until all she could see was the swirling, twirling mane of her kidnapper. But then, she noticed something. Hidden in the seaweed strands, the kelpie had a bridle and razor-edged metal reins draped over its neck."

"The Bane!" the men yelled, just like I did as a child. Every monster had a Bane, something that could be used against it, part of the curse that made them what they were.

"That's right." I grinned. "It was the only way to steer the beast. Even if she cut her hands off in the process, the little girl had to take this chance. She had to get home."

I paused, drawing out the tension. The crew was still, silent.

A deep breath filled my lungs. "The little girl grabbed the reins, bubbles rushing out of her mouth as she screamed from the pain. The metal sliced into her palms as she forced the kelpie back to shore. The beast had to obey, for the bridle slit into his jaw, spewing a dark liquid through his teeth.

"Once back on shore, the little girl dismounted, still holding the reins. Her blood dripped into the ocean as the kelpie whinnied, black ooze streaking down its marsh-green neck. It yanked its head back, wrenching the reins free of the girl's hands, and sped through the crashing waves as fast as it could. The little girl never saw it again, and she lived happily until the end of her days."

That was how I ended my stories.

My father had used his own style. *What was the moral of the story?* he would ask. I always knew the answer. Every story he told me had the same answer.

The greatest weapon against any beast is its own.

I strolled across *Valka*'s deck as the sun rose on the sixth day, my arms shuddering even though I tried to stay calm. If the crew felt I was up to something, all of this would be for nothing. The keys to the hull rattled on my belt loop, clattering even more when I shoved them into the lock.

The door creaked open, and I peered through the darkness.

I reached out for a bag half-filled with salted beef. No one would find it missing, not when we had about a dozen bags still full in the pantry. I crept back to my quarters, locking the door behind me, and strode across the wooden floor until my footsteps made a hollow *thump.* I pulled the floorboard away, revealing a small compartment filled with my stolen goods. A few water skins, an array of food, some alcohol and bandages—everything I could possibly need for Tenerife. I hoped it was enough.

My mind began to wander, trying to picture my mother when I'd save her, when I'd break her curse and bring her back home. My memory conjured up a woman, but I couldn't distinguish her features. I couldn't remember her face.

"Captain?" Ray's voice yanked me out of my daydreams. "Isla? Are you alright?"

I glanced at the red clock hanging on the wall. *Blast it.* I was usually at breakfast by now.

"Coming!" I said, my voice shrill as I kicked the floorboard back into place.

I opened the door, barrelling into Ray's chest as he stood there, patiently waiting.

His brows furrowed, concerned. "Isla, what's going on? You cried when we left Cádiz, and now you're all flustered. Is everything all right?"

"Yes!" My cheeks burned red. They had to be as bright as my hair, *at least.* "I haven't been sleeping well. But I'll take it easy today, I promise."

Ray placed his hands on my shoulders, pushing me back into the room. His worried expression turned cold, hard. My heart pounded faster. "Sit," he said. I obeyed as he locked the door behind him.

"Are you okay, Ray?" I tilted my head, trying to turn the tables. "Something's going on."

"Don't even try it," he said, his voice taking on his 'serious-father' tone. "Listen, the last promise I made your father was that I would keep you safe. How can I honor that vow if you're keeping secrets from me?"

"What secrets?" I squeaked.

"Why are we going to Tenerife?"

I crossed my arms defensively. "Because that island has treasures beyond our wildest dreams. My father knew that. We need to maintain the relationships he made and keep the trade running—"

"Isla…" He tapped his foot impatiently. "What's the real reason?"

"That is the real reason."

Ray sighed, shaking his head. He walked to my father's desk, pulling open the top drawer.

"Oy, that's captain's property!" I jumped off the bed. "You have no right—"

He pulled out my mother's letter. I froze.

"You're going to Tenerife because of this," he said. "You think she's still alive, don't you?" I was silent. "Don't you?"

I hung my head, defeated. "Yes."

Ray's glare softened. "Of course you do. Your father did the same thing. You're identical."

"My father? You mean he got a letter like this?"

Ray rummaged around in his pockets until he wrenched out a crinkled piece of parchment. The handwriting, the seal, the stamp—they all matched my letter.

"Why didn't he tell me about it?" I asked.

"Because this letter destroyed him, Isla. You don't want to find what's waiting for you there, trust me."

Tears trickled down my face. Ray pulled out his patchwork hankie, placing it firmly in my hand.

"I know what's there." I sniffled. "My *mother* is there, waiting for me to save her."

"No, she's not." Ray sat me in my father's chair, kneeling before me so his eyes were level with mine. "Isla, she's dead. I saw her chest still after you were born. I saw them bury her at sea. She can't be—"

"Don't! Don't say it." The flame in my chest burned brighter, refusing to die with Ray's concern.

"Fine, but you can't go," Ray insisted. "You're going to fall into the same trap as your father."

"What trap?"

Ray's gaze dropped, focusing on the mud splatters on his boots.

"What trap?" I insisted.

"This letter is not from Valka," Ray explained. "It came from a siren who lurks in the caves of Don Gaspar. Your father saw her when he reached the island, and she morphed her appearance, taking the form of the person dearest in his memory: your mother." He held my father's letter between his fingers. "She slipped this into his bag while he was asleep. By the time I woke up the next morning...he was already on his way to the caves. I couldn't stop him, but *please* let me stop you. Let me save you."

His eyes met mine, and I felt the pain in them, the regret in his glistening tears. I didn't believe him. How could I? Yes, I believed in monsters. Every good sailor did. But Ray never told me about the letter, and now he was creating an elaborate story to keep me from finding my family?

I grabbed my letter back from Ray, stuffing it into my pocket. "Not a word of this to the crew."

He stiffened, glaring at me. "No.... Isla, you can't be serious. You're putting their lives in danger. Your father did the same thing on our last adventure and look what happened to him."

"You think I don't know that?" I threw the handkerchief in his face. "You think I want to hurt you? I don't have a choice, Ray. If she's alive, I have to find her!"

Ray bent to pick up his hankie, turning his back on me. He unlocked the door and stood, waiting.

"I just realized something," he whispered.

"What?"

He glanced over his shoulder. "We're not the same height."

I rolled my eyes. "So?"

"So...that means we don't have to see eye to eye on everything."

He shut the door firmly.

I stayed in my quarters the whole day, twirling the emerald ring on my finger. Sunlight glinted off the gold band as dusk approached. A knock at the door came from one of the deckhands as he brought me a bowl of stew. I wolfed it down greedily.

It would be my last meal before Tenerife.

That night, I didn't sleep. I lay in bed, watching the moonlight flicker across the clock on the wall until, at last, it struck five.

It was time.

I crept out of my quarters, checking if the coast was clear. There was no time to bump into Ray and endure another lecture. He would be mopping the decks for a month if he stood up to his captain again.

I knew *Valka* like the back of my hand. All her secrets, her hidden passages, all of them were engraved in the creases of my skin. It was easy to reach the galley without being discovered. A warm glow radiated from the coal fire in the back, casting shadows across the tabletops and crates that filled the cramped room. The cook bustled through the mess, chopping slimy carrots in one corner, stewing salted meat in a pot on the stove—a whirling tornado as he prepared breakfast.

He almost tripped over his feet when he saw me in the doorway.

"Captain, I didn't notice you there." He bowed, taking off his hat.

"Don't worry, Cookie. Do you have a minute?"

He guffawed, the motion wobbling his enormous belly. "Of course I do. You were always in the galley as a child, sneaking off with biscuits and the rare strawberry. I couldn't get rid of you then, and I doubt I could get you out of my kitchen now."

Perfect. It was time to use my charms to my advantage.

I sighed, faking relief. "Oh, thank goodness. I really need your help."

"What's the matter, Captain? I'm all yours."

"A few of the lads got bored in the middle of the night, so one decided to show off his knots and unraveled the rope holding the cargo below deck. Now all the barrels are rolling about and crashing into the crates, ruining all of our goods from Cádiz. We could use someone with muscles like yours to fix the whole mess."

"Me?" he gasped. "Surely there are younger, stronger men above deck who can help."

"They're not as strong as you, Cookie. Everyone knows you're the toughest man on board."

Cookie puffed out his chest, rolling his shoulders in bravado. This was too easy.

"You can count on me, Captain. Keep an eye on the pot, would you?"

"Will do, Cookie. Thank you."

He hurtled down the hallway. By the time he would return, confused by the lack of broken cargo, I would be at the helm like nothing was wrong. He would be busy with breakfast. I had plenty of time to cook up another lie to explain his little trip to the hold.

I peered into the pot. The murky liquid bubbled excitedly as I lifted the emerald off my ring, revealing a hidden capsule filled with valerian oil. I had bought it back in Cádiz from a healer, claiming I had insomnia. Just a drop of the liquid could put a grown man to sleep in an hour. A whole vial split between thirty men? They wouldn't notice I had left them for Tenerife until they woke up tonight.

The sun started to rise as I took the helm. It wasn't long before the breakfast bell was rung, and Cookie brought out the stew. Confusion crossed his face as he brought my bowl to me.

"Captain, about the hold...."

"Yes, Cookie?"

"It was sorted by the time I got there."

"Oh. The boys must have cleaned it themselves." I chuckled innocently as I placed a spoonful of stew between my lips, speaking with my mouth full. "This is delicious, by the way. You have to teach me the recipe one day."

Cookie's chest puffed out again. Nothing like complimenting a chef's cooking to make him all warm and fuzzy inside. He rushed back to his pot as I spewed my mouthful of broth back into the bowl. I wouldn't fall victim to my own tricks.

I scanned the deck, making sure every man had at least a bite of the broth. My eyes met Ray's. He scowled at me as he slurped up a spoonful.

As the sun rose, scattering shimmering diamonds in the ocean, the island of Tenerife loomed ahead. Sunlight trickled through the clouds smothering the mountain peaks, illuminating little details across the island: the shadows falling down the cliffs, the birds circling the volcano, the waves crashing on the shore.

"Land ho!" yelled a deckhand from the crow's nest. His voice trailed off in a yawn.

We had to dock the ship before everyone fell asleep.

"Ready the anchor!" I ordered. "Ease the sails."

"Yes, Captain!" the crew hollered as they leaped into action. Well, they tried to, but the sleeping draught had already taken effect. The helmsman took the wheel from me as I raced to join the men and speed up their sluggish pace. A few hobbled to release the anchor while the deckhands hauled in the sails with gaping yawns.

That's when they started to drop. At first, no one noticed, but more started to pass out across the deck.

We had to dock *now*.

"Release the anchor!" I ordered, and a chain of voices carried my message to the men below. A deep whirring filled the air as they released the anchor, and the chain unwound until it hit the ocean floor. The helmsman carried us a bit further, nestling the anchor into place when he slumped against the wheel.

I stared at the crew around me, all of them asleep. My plan had worked. All I had to do now was find my mother.

"Isla!"

I gulped. I knew that voice. I whirled around as Ray clambered out of the hold, his firm grip heavier on my shoulders from his drowsiness.

"Isla, what did you do?" he whispered, forcing his eyes open as he battled against my poison.

"I'm sorry, Ray, I really am." I shoved his hand off my shoulder, and he stumbled to his knees.

"Isla, don't go.... Please, don't."

He sank to the floor as his eyes fluttered shut. I turned him onto his side, brushing the dreadlocks away from his eyes.

"I have to," I whispered, and the flame in me burned brighter.

Ray was safe here. They were all safe. If Don Gaspar took a turn for the worse, at least I would be the only one going down. He could still lead the crew and get them all home safely.

On the plus side, he would make sure I went down as a legend.

I grabbed my satchel from under the floorboards, draping it across my chest as I dropped into the rowboat.

I severed the ropes tethering me to *Valka*.

It was time to see my mother.

The boat scraped against craggy pebbles as I pulled it onto shore. The stones poked through my boots, chipping away at the flickering hope inside me. But even this pain wasn't enough to destroy it.

The wilderness of Tenerife was nothing like the ports back home in Cádiz. We didn't have many trees, not to mention the bushes and cacti scattered across the rocky plains of this island. I wandered along the dirt roads to the heart of the isle, to the little valley where the caves rested in their slumber. The locals paid no attention to me. I probably wasn't the first explorer searching for Don Gaspar's caverns.

Around noon, the plains dropped into a canyon, shelves of rock forming a path to the babbling waters of the lazy river below. At the base of the canyon, hidden in the shadows, was a gaping dark inlet. The entrance to the caves.

My fingers drummed against my hilt as I descended into the murky waters. Mother probably wouldn't recognize me. I was a newborn the last time we were together. But that didn't mean she couldn't get to know me. I could fill her in on everything. My first sword fight. The day I mastered all my knots. It would be like she was never gone.

I jumped the last few feet, my boots splashing in the algae-ridden river, the spray soaking my clothes. I shook myself dry and ducked into the cool shadows of the cliffs, unsheathing my mother's sword. Maybe now I could finally return it to her.

The cavern mouth was pitch black, darker than the bottom of the sea, like a deep, eternal slumber. A shudder crept through my bones.

Before I could change my mind, I entered the caves, blinking rapidly as my eyes adjusted to the black world before me.

My hope burned brighter, smoldering in my chest, lighting the path ahead. Through the gloom, the dusted sienna rock formed terraces cascading from ceiling to floor, each filled with bubbling pools of water. Stalactites hanging from the arches overhead dripped down to the flooded floor, every splash reverberating in the vast, empty space.

The rhythm of my heartbeat pounded in my ears. Hopefully, I could break her curse so she could finally return to civilization.

"Mother?" I called out.

Buffoon. She's never been called Mother in her life.

I cleared my throat. "Valka?"

It was the first time I had said the word without thinking of my majestic ship.

Something splashed in the water a few feet ahead. I dropped my satchel, gripping my sword tighter. "Valka?" I inched forward.

A light flickered at the back of the cave, casting long, terrifying shadows across the arches. Adrenaline coursed through my veins, setting my blood aflame as I inched closer.

The cave opened into a small chamber, a thick column with weathered rings holding the roof up. Gemstones were scattered in the rockface, glittering in the glow of a nearby campfire. Beside the fire stood a woman, her flaming red hair streaked with gray, permanent wrinkles around her eyes. Could it be? A flimsy seaweed-green dress was wrapped over her body, barely covering the sickly glow of her blotchy skin.

She was there. She was right there.

"Are you—" My breath rattled through my lips. "Are you Valka?"

She nodded, walking over to me. *She's real.* My breath caught in my throat as she ran her fingers through my carbine braid. Her hands trailed down to my shoulders, resting there while she stared deep into my eyes. I gulped hard. She was real….

"It's me," I said, praying she remembered. "Isla."

"Isla…." she whispered as if testing the taste of the word in her mouth. She smiled, her teeth still pearly white after all this time. From this angle, they were pointed like daggers. I blinked, and they were normal, humane. Maybe it had been a trick of the light.

"How long has it been?" she asked.

"Too long." Tears streaked through my dust-ridden face.

She is real, said the voice in my head, trying to convince my heart.

She pulled me in, wrapping her arms around my shoulders. My sword slipped from my fingers in shock as I embraced her. I inhaled sharply, her musty scent something I never wanted to forget. My head started to spin.

She was *real.*

Then why did this feel so wrong?

Something spat against my hope, threatening to kill the flames just before they rose to their glory.

Doubt.

No. This was my mother. She was right there in front of me, holding me in her arms, her wild hair trailing over my shoulders.

I had to test her. I had to prove that she was real, or else she would never feel like home to me.

"Do you remember me?" I asked, loosening my embrace, but she held on tighter.

See? I tried to convince myself. *She never wants to let me go.*

"Of course I do," she said.

"Do you remember our home?"

She sat near the fire, pulling me to the ground with her. "How could I forget?"

"Can you tell me about it? Father never went back there after you... left."

She took my hands in hers, her yellowing nails digging into my skin. I winced, wriggling my fingers free of her grip. As soon as we got out of the caves, I was taking her to the best salon in all of Spain. "Well, it's probably changed since then. We used to live in a beautiful city called Barcelona."

I felt a sledgehammer slam into my gut.

"What was it like?" I asked, even though my home was in Cádiz.

She was my mother. She was my *mother.*

"There were forests everywhere, as far as the eye could see, almost like the wildlife here in Tenerife. Your father and I built a treehouse in one of the elder trees. We used to go there every summer to get away from the bustling ships."

Forests? The closest forests to Cádiz were a day's hike away at least.

Tears pricked my eyes. She had to be my mother. She just had to. She was all the family I had left in this world. She couldn't be a lie.

"Oh, you're crying," she said, cupping my face in her hands. "Here, let me get some water for you."

I nodded, the fire in my chest sizzling out as she strolled to a spring at the back of the cave. *This can't be happening.*

Valka— No, this was not my mother. Ray had been right.

How had I been so foolish? Of course, my mother was dead. Of course, it just had to be a siren trying to scrape together its next meal instead of *my mother* waiting for me to rescue her. Of course, none of this was real.

Anger replaced my hope, bubbling deep in my stomach. It twisted itself around inside me, warping over my judgment, taking over my every thought and movement.

With her back turned to me, I reached into my boot, pulling out my hidden dagger. The siren turned back to face me and I tucked it into my sleeve.

"Is everything all right?" she asked, handing me a roughly-carved wooden dish.

"Everything's fine." I placed the bowl beside me. I couldn't tell if she poisoned it. "I just can't believe I found you."

I pulled the siren close to my chest, holding her there with all my strength.

"Isla, darling, you're squeezing a little too tight."

I bit back my tears. *This is not my mother.*

"Isla? Isla, stop it!"

The siren hissed furiously, struggling against my grip. Her hands clawed at my spine, ripping through my red coat and burrowing into my skin. I ignored the pain and gripped my dagger, willing my hand to slice the little hollow at the back of her neck.

This is not my mother. She isn't real.

I shut my eyes and bared my teeth. Kill her! Kill her, and it would all be over, and I could go back to Ray, the crew—back to my *Valka*.

But I couldn't. How could I kill someone who looked so much like me, so much like *her*?

My fingers went numb, and the next thing I knew, I was crying into the siren's shoulder. She stopped clawing and instead ran her fingers through my hair to comfort me. With the other hand, she threw my dagger across the room.

"I'm sorry!" I said, and I meant it. "I'm so sorry."

The siren sighed and pulled me in closer. "Well, I'm still hungry."

Thick black ooze slid through her crimson locks, covering her entire body as she closed her jaw over my shoulder. I winced and pushed myself off her chest, scrambling for my sword as blood dripped down my arm. The siren slithered across the ground and slammed into my chest.

I landed on my back, bashing my head against a protruding rock.

The world started to spin as black spots clouded my vision. The siren dug her thumb into my shoulder, and a scream escaped my lips. I had never felt pain like this in my entire life. I writhed furiously, reaching for a slab of firewood, for my sword—anything to slam into her skull.

She pinned my arms under her knees as the ooze sizzled away, revealing the beast that trapped me, that had fooled me. *Why had I trusted that letter?* Her large pointed ears towered over her head as darkness consumed her eyes. Her dagger-like grin glittered in the firelight, dribbling spit onto my face.

My vision swam as her grip tightened over my throat.

This was what hope brought.

This was the end.

Why have I been so foolish?

My eyes fluttered shut. I listened to my pounding heart, my rasping breaths for one last time.

A clatter of stones echoed through the caves, followed by the faint splash of feet against water.

The siren hissed as the splashing came to a stop. A dull *thwack* rang against the rock, trembling the overhanging stalactites.

The siren ripped her hands off my throat and landed to my right, growling furiously. A torrent of stones rained from the cavern roof, followed by something warm and heavy landing on my lap.

I sputtered, blinking rapidly to clear my darkening vision. Even though it was blurred, I recognized the object on my lap. My satchel.

"Sorry I'm late," laughed a familiar voice. "Someone wanted me to sleep through the party!"

There in the half-light stood Ray, his coat in tatters, sword in hand as he ducked and swerved around the siren. He chuckled as she dived at him and missed, which only angered the beast further. Her legs merged into a shimmering fishtail—the final step to destroy her human disguise. Ray swung his sword around, bashing the hilt against her head, effortlessly knocking her to the ground.

He turned to me, urgency in his gaze. "Isla, you need to find her Bane, now!"

Of course. Her Bane. *The greatest weapon against any beast is its own.*

As the siren clawed at Ray, I dashed around the cave, teetering from the lack of oxygen. Where could it be?

Ray grunted as the siren dug her talons into his leg. "Isla! Any minute now."

"I'm trying!" I coughed and stumbled sideways, bashing into the cavern wall.

A loose rock dislodged itself as I fell to the ground. I clung to the wall as I pushed myself up, and my hand fell into a small crevice. Inside, my fingers closed over a gleaming dagger; shimmering scales etched into its bone hilt.

It had to be her Bane.

"Got it!" I wheezed, and I chucked the dagger to Ray.

He caught it and pinned the siren's arms under his knees. He raised the dagger over his head, knuckles white against the hilt. I shut my eyes, shivering as the squelch of spurting blood echoed through the cavern.

I peeked one eye open, instantly regretting it as Ray wrenched the Bane free of her throat. He thrust it into her stomach, and the siren's whimpering cries soon faded to silence.

My legs finally gave in, and I collapsed onto my back, my insides shattered into a million pieces. Tears streamed through my sand-ridden face as my mind stretched across the cave, desperately searching for the broken shards of my soul. It reached into the shadows and crevices and rebuilt me until I was whole—almost. I couldn't find all the pieces. Part of me had died with the siren, leaving a hollow emptiness deep in my crux.

Hope is a dangerous thing.

I turned to face the siren. Even in her beast-form, she had red hair, a slender body. She could have been my mother with a fishtail.

It will be the loose thread that pulls your sanity apart.

"She's not Valka," Ray said. "She tried to kill you."

"Yeah, I can tell," I muttered, pulling off my red coat to reveal the blood-stained shirt beneath it. "Can you grab my satchel for me?"

Ray's eyes widened, rummaging in my bag as I eased my shirt off my shoulder. He took out the alcohol and bandages, then hesitated. "This might sting a little."

"I know." I needed a distraction from the pain. "How are you awake?"

Ray poured the alcohol over the bandages as he sat beside me, reeking of sweat. "Because I knew your father. He used a sleeping draught on me when he went after the siren." He chuckled as he rinsed my wound in the alcohol. I screamed, and it echoed across the cave as I squeezed Ray's forearm. "Sorry, kid, I did warn you."

"Just keep talking," I winced.

"Aye, Captain." Ray started to wrap my shoulder in the bandages. "I faked breakfast this morning, just like you, then I faked passing out, which I did pretty well if I do say so myself. But once I got to the island, one of the local's bulls broke loose, and guess who they decided to go after?" He turned to show me the rips along the back of his jacket. "Destiny really didn't want me to save your life."

My gaze fell to the siren's lifeless body. "I'm sorry I didn't listen to you."

"I'm sorry I didn't lock you in your room." Ray traced his fingers along his sword. "Part of me hoped she would be gone. Your father tried to kill her after her illusion faded, but you know how the stories work. A siren can only be killed with her own Bane. But Adrian couldn't find where the beast hid her dagger, so he tried to kill her with his own sword. Of course, she regenerated. I just thought she would have left this dump after all these years."

I sat up, taking out my disheveled braids and layering my hair over my shoulders. "I don't want to be here anymore. Let's go home."

I stood up, but Ray grabbed my hand, pulling me back beside him. I leaned against him, listening to the soothing rhythm of his heart.

"Isla, you didn't do anything wrong. You followed your heart, kid. Just listen to me next time so you don't act like a fool." He elbowed me playfully, but I kept my gaze steady on my trembling hands. He squeezed them tight. "You know, you still have me, right? You still have the crew. Cádiz. You have our *Valka*. You still have a family."

I grinned through my tears. "Are you going soft on me, Ray?"

He pushed me off his chest, striding across the room to retrieve his sword. I stood as he handed me my mother's sword— No, it was mine. I was sure of that.

"Of course not, Captain." He kneeled before me, holding the siren's blood-stained dagger. "A token of your victory."

"My victory?" I laughed. "I think you slew her while I tried to breathe."

"Let's just say it was you." He winked. "The crew would probably respect you a lot more after learning you found, spoke to, and 'slew' a siren in one day."

"And if they discover it's a lie? What will happen to my reputation then?"

"Come on. It will be fun!" He pouted like a child.

I couldn't help laughing. "All right, fine, but only for a few days. Then we'll tell them the truth."

"Fine." He rolled his eyes as I tucked the dagger in my belt, looping my arm into Ray's.

Something ancient and familiar bubbled inside me, something I hadn't felt since I found the siren's letter.

I was home, and I'd never doubt that again.

I would never
be helpless
again.

DEVIL HUNT

Kaitlyn Emery

I SIT, ENTHRONED IN the branches of a mighty oak. Waiting…

Grandmother warned us not to gather herbs in the woods. "Beware the wolf who hunts the forest for unsuspecting souls."

That day, I forgot.

I should have known better, but I was drawn by a man more beautiful than anyone I'd ever seen. That was how they got you. With a face like an angel, but the soul of the devil.

He's close now, his foul stench floating on the breeze. From my perch among the trees, hiding between the forest's branches as they swallow me in their boney jaws, my gaze shifts toward the small clearing below. The fog clears, and the moonlight shines like a beacon upon a fair figure shrouded in a blood-red cloak.

Her cheeks hold the softness of early womanhood, making her the ideal target. She picks flowers from the clearing with a steady hand, placing them in the basket beside her while humming a soft, lilting tune.

I feel like my brain is misfiring as memories flash at the forefront of my mind. My stomach clenches while I work to suppress them.

I could never remember why I felt such a strong desire to follow him, nor what he said when I reached him. I could only recall pieces of what happened after.

He pinned me to the ground, his intent obvious. He planned to devour me in every way possible. My virginity. My body. And my soul.

Then blood. Lots of blood. Searing pain as teeth sunk deep into my face. The screams of my grandmother running at the demon with an ax raised above her head.

I blacked out then, venom coursing through my body. When I woke up, my sister was carrying me through the dark forest, my grandmother's crimson cloak draped over me. Grandmother's ax swung at my sister's waist.

My survival was a miracle. I was meant to die that day. But instead, I received a gift my attacker never meant to give. The Bite. It left my face disfigured but imparted to me the heightened senses of my assailant. I had vision that could pierce the dark even when there was no moon. Hearing that could detect the slightest breath. And smell…

I could never forget that vile half-wolf scent carried by my attacker and his kind. It was imprinted on my senses the same way half his disease imbued my bloodstream.

I focus on the whispering trees and the approaching devil's padded steps. Innocence will not be the victim tonight.

In the distance, I see him approach. His steel-gray and pupil-slit eyes greedily drink in the sight before him. The moon lights the way for the young woman as she picks up her basket and wanders toward my hiding place. The wolf prowls through the shadows with teeth bared.

When he reaches the edge of the darkness, he grows taller; his back straightens, and fur falls away to reveal the face of a man as he steps into the light.

His red-hooded target continues to hum her tune, never faltering. She seems blissfully unaware of the stalking predator. Then the wolfman calls to her, his voice alluring as heavy perfume. She turns towards him. Her lips curl into a dreamy smile, and her voice, steady and sure, beckons him to approach.

I take a deep breath and almost gag on the violent stench of my target. Slowly, I pull a silver-tipped arrow from the quiver on my back. I notch it into place and draw the string, brushing the feather along my scarred cheek.

I fix my gaze on my prey and remember.

Grandmother perished at the hands of the wolf. The wolf perished at the hands of my sister. I survived because of Marian. She helped me to endure the changes but also to harness them. She knew once I mastered my abilities, I would never be helpless again.

"My, what big teeth you have." The girl's voice in the clearing below is controlled.

"All the better to devour you with, my sweet!"

I've heard this line a half dozen times. Werewolves are rarely original.

The attacker lunges, bloodthirst in his eyes, but his mark is ready. She throws back her cloak, and the moon's rays catch on the vicious blade of my Grandmother's axe. I release arrows, my aim true as they pierce the monster's hide, causing his back to arch as he stumbles forward.

My sister does not falter. She is a crimson crusader. An avenging angel. She is sure of her destiny. My sister swings her axe in a silver arc, lopping the beast's head from his shoulders and breaking the spell that transformed him. The wolf's head tumbles to the forest floor with a satisfying *splat.*

Marian throws back her crimson hood and howls at the moon in open defiance, daring any other wolf to challenge her. The shadows seem to shrink around her. She steps over her fallen foe and hums again, the wolf's blood dripping from her axe as she walks toward me.

I drop out of the trees to meet her, my heart racing. I embrace my sister and fill my heightened senses with her scent. I smell no fear when she holds me, and my pulse slows to match the steady beat of her heart.

"It will be dangerous, but I promise no wolf can stand against us if we're together."

Fearless Marian. I wasn't sure I could do this when I first received The Bite, but her faith in me transformed me from the helpless girl covered in blood to the dark-clad figure protecting the innocent from the shadows.

Every werewolf hunt, I am afraid I might lose her, but Marian never wavers. The day of The Bite, Marian told me I would never be hunted again. Instead, we hunt.

Moonlight finds me once again

Beast of Lore

AJ Skelly

Tiptoe softly, big beast creeping
Through these woods, next meal seeking
In the moonlight, shadow looming
Hear his growl . . . it's dooming

Running quickly, don't look back
Lungs are aching, branches crack.
Alert the creature to my presence
Squawking shrieks, ghostly essence.

Running faster, scared and panting
Red cape billows, body canting.
Tripping over roots asunder
Too late now to fix my blunder.

Moonlight streaming down
Catches on my red-hood crown.

Screaming, gnashing fills the night,
No one near to hear my plight.

The beast descends, teeth extended.
Ripping tears that can't be mended.
Pain lashes me from inside.
Gasping, clawing, have I died?

Laying, panting on the ground,
Blood pools all around.
No humanity is left
The wolf is gone, my soul his theft.

Life is slowly leaving,
Fading, broken, grieving.
Fluttering eyelids,
Death makes his bids.

But as moonlight finds me once again
Dead heart inside me . . . beats begin
Round my neck still dangle,
Red shreds of a life now mangled.

Rising from the gore
I have become the beast of lore

There are Wolves in These Woods

Erin Della Mattia

THE WOODSMAN SIGHS as he resets the trap. As with all the others, the spring was set off—the snare empty of prey. Perhaps, he considers, it once held some small creature, but another beast heard its screams and got to it before him. He prays this might be true. The carpet of snow beneath the trees is undisturbed save for his own footprints. No blood splatter, tufts of fur, snapped branches. No sign that anything larger than a snow flea crossed paths with his trap. And so, yes, the woodsman prays.

He breathes into his cupped hands and rubs them together, thinking longingly of his pale calf-hide gloves. Gone now, like so much else. Surrendered—willingly—to his family, so that they could gnaw on the leather and dampen the hideous echoes of their stomachs. It is now a week since they enjoyed that so-called meat. And so, with flakes crystallizing in his nose, the woodsman plods wearily through the snow to try to trap whatever elusive creatures still live within these woods.

All around him is quiet. As usual, now. Some months ago, as the villagers labored in the fields collecting their second harvest, the animals of the forest disappeared. Slowly, oh, it happened slowly, but as if by malevolent design. Birdsong faded. Squirrels, weasels, foxes, all seemed to rustle away into other lands. Hunters and trappers went out and returned with less and less, and, then, nothing. Then, worse: the harvest turned moldy. Preserves spoiled. Smoked meats were gobbled up under cover of midnight. Then the snows came and didn't stop. The villagers were forced to carry their bows and traps deeper into the woods, until some did not return at all. Anxious voices spoke of unseen and unheard creatures moving in the night, making off with the little livestock that remained. And then, horribly, a baby. Another. Another. A child aged three, five, nine. Children snatched off forest paths while searching for acorns; children left to wander alone by families abundant with gaping mouths and protruding ribs.

The woodsman heard stories worse than the disappearances; there is always a fate worse than being eaten by beasts. The beasts, at least, cannot control themselves. They act according to their needs without consciousness. No, he cannot blame a beast for acting in its nature. But, a person... Desperation he understands, but there is more honor in death than in survival at such a price.

But those are rumors, only rumors. He endeavors to put it all from his mind and focus on the task at hand, for it would not do to retch his already empty guts.

Despite his frozen fingers, the empty snares, his disappointment, hunger, exhaustion, he relishes this time in the woods. Beneath the grey canopy drooping with snow, he is free from his family's thin faces and pitiful moans. Their eyes that linger too long upon his back, as if to silently berate him for his failure to provide. But he knows that were he to catch something, he would gorge himself on it, raw and bloodied, and feel neither pride nor shame, for he is beyond such feelings now.

Something in the forest intrudes on his quiet. A hollow yet plaintive whistling. The woodsman follows the sound through the leafless undergrowth to a footpath. There stands a small girl. At his approach, the child steps backward on the path, ducking her head further into the recesses of her crimson hood.

The woodsman holds his hands out in front of him to show that they are empty, as he might do when approaching an unfamiliar dog or his wife when she is enraged.

"Fear me not, young one. I am a simple woodsman. I mean you no harm." He intends to speak gently to the child, so he is surprised when what emerges from him is a raspy, grating voice, like a boulder being dragged across a cavern floor.

The girl neither responds nor flees. She seems as gaunt and ragged as any child in the village. Her dress sits low on her chest; it must be a cast-off from an older woman, her mother, perhaps. Its end trails in dampened tatters in the snow. The woodsman can just see the girl's frost-blackened toes peeking out from beneath the hem. Her family must have eaten her boots before sending her out into the world, alone.

The woodsman has a daughter. Her cheeks hollowed by hunger, eyes bulging from loosened sockets. He can scarcely stand to look at her, only glimpse her from the corner of his eyes, a wispy shape on the stool where she practices her stitching, tsking when she pricks her finger on the needle. She is careless, like she has blood to spare. But always so mild, as if resigned to a death by hunger. How different this girl is before him, with her frostbitten feet and ragged cape. She is one who would defy death, he thinks, would scream and flail against it with what little strength she has. How proud he would be to have her as his daughter.

"You ought to beware," he continues, "walking through these woods, as young as you are. And alone." He pauses. A feeling like a warm poker traces his spine as though some secret eyes are on him. He wavers on the spot, his face flush. Perhaps it is the girl's brother and father, hiding just out of sight, ready to pounce on him should he so much as touch the girl. He has heard of such things, such traps.

He speaks more loudly so they might hear him. "These woods are hardly safe, even for myself, with my knife and hatchet." He rests his hands on his belt, nearer to his weapons.

The girl lifts her head, pushing her hood back just so. Her face is long, both sorrowful and haughty, and her eyes are frenzied like many of the village children. Eyes that shift too quickly, too appraisingly for a child. Her hair is a matted mane around her face. When she speaks, her teeth are yellow and pointed, like a rat.

"Good sir." Her voice is soft, scarcely above a whisper. The woodsman finds himself leaning in closer, the better to hear her.

"I am going to my grandmother's cottage. It lies just past a thicket of white birch." She holds up a rotting wicker basket in which clank several bottles. "My mother is a brewer. She bid me bring this ale to my grandmother, for she is too frail to visit us herself."

"Ale for your grandmother," he repeats, thinking of his own grandmother, whose bones lay deep beneath the roots of an old oak tree. In life, her cheeks were round and rosy as sun-gorged strawberries, her hair thick and golden like corn tassels. She had come from a distant land and could hardly speak the language of his village, but she always had a bright smile ready for any gentle soul who crossed her path. The woodsman smiles to himself, imagining this girl's grandmother as kindred to his own.

"Take care you get there quickly," he tells her. "Do not stray from your course."

"Nor you, good woodsman," she lisps. "There are wolves in these woods."

He has a thought—very brief—of simply knocking the girl on the head and taking the treasures of her basket for himself. The weight of his arms and measure of his hands tell him how easy it would be. After all, he has done it many a time with his prey, animals he found caught in his traps while their persistent hearts still beat. How much different is a little girl from a fox?

The girl shivers, as if her body understands his thoughts and would fall to the ground on its own.

He is about to take a step towards her when his shoulder flinches. He feels those eyes again. A breathless watching, waiting. The crouching that comes before the pounce.

"Yes," says the woodsman, steadying himself. "Yes. All should beware in these woods."

The girl nods. The corners of her cracked lips pull back into something like a smile. Then she continues past him along the path, leaving a waft of damp flesh in her wake.

The woodsman looks at his hands, thickened with years of hard labor and creviced with everlasting dirt. For all their strength, they shake like withered leaves. He tells himself it is hunger, the frigid cold air, and he tries to forget about the girl.

For a time, he allows himself to be distracted by his empty snares until the rumbles of his stomach reproach him for not thinking to beg a bottle of ale from the girl. He might have offered to protect her through her journey in the woods, and she would have been gracious enough to bestow on him some ale without his asking. But, he reasons, if she has not made it to her grandmother's cottage by now, then something else must have caught up with her, something not worth the trouble of protecting her.

It is late into the afternoon, the sun's faint light dipping below the horizon, when the woodsman comes across a small stone cottage beyond a thicket of white birch. Just where the girl said it would be. The door stands ajar, and snow has blown into the threshold.

The woodsman approaches the side of the cottage. Chunks of stone have toppled from the chimney and lie in a bed of weedy snow at the woodsman's feet. There is a tiny window in the wall; he moves to peer inside.

The cottage appears empty of life. There are two chairs, one knocked to the ground, and a table. A hutch at one wall bears some rough pottery and a puddle of dried wax. But, there. In a gloomy corner of the cottage, he spies a bed with a mound beneath the quilt.

He tears his gaze away and squats to the ground, his face in his weary hands. *Grandmother.* It is as if she is before him in this strange place, in this other woman's bed. He sees her again, her feverish red skin sunk to bone, decaying while yet alive. *Grandmother, what big teeth you had, for your skin had pulled back from your mouth, and you could do naught else but smile.*

The woodsman whimpers. His fingers collect frozen tears from his cheeks and dash them away into the forest grown long with shadows.

The sun is almost set, and so, with a grim expression, the woodsman enters the cottage.

Snow gives way to dried leaves in the entry. The leaves are so old that they do not crunch when he steps on them but simply turn to dust. Spiders have spun their webs throughout the cottage, connecting wall to wall and chair to wall and candlestick to bedpost, but there are no spiders. Nothing is alive here but the woodsman.

In the closing dark, he raises his hands to clear a path through the webbing to the bed. He stumbles only once over the fallen chair and he curses, though he had not wished to make a sound, as if his voice has power to raise the dead.

But, who here is dead? He finds the bed empty. He runs his hands over the length of the moldy quilt and then down underneath the bed frame. He lifts the quilt, the pillow, the mattress, all—nothing.

He moves to the fallen chair, rights it, and sits on it. He laughs. Bitterly, he laughs, hands clasping his hollow belly. How tired he must be, how hungry, that his starving mind would produce a vision of a body as if it believed he would feast upon the flesh of a fellow human. As if there would even be anything left for him. As if he might have boiled the bones for broth. But save some, oh, save some bones, the rib cage, to grind to make a loaf of bread. How many bodies, he wonders, lie buried in the village graveyard? How many bodies has the winter, like a root cellar, preserved? Could it work? Was it that simple? He has heard of such things. They were whispered to him as a young boy by his grandfather, a cunning man who sought his fortunes in distant lands only to return to the village with nothing to show for his efforts but a pretty, grinning wife and tall tales of foreign horrors. Now not so foreign, nor so horrible. Starvation births its own rationality.

Yes, it could work. It could be done. He could do it. Others would join. In mute acceptance, they would join him.

He lays his head on the table and sobs for nothing and for nobody but himself and how lost he has become in these woods.

But before he has time to taste the depth of his misery, there is a slight knocking on the still open door. One, two, three knocks. The woodsman jumps from the chair, sending it to the ground. In a heartbeat, he is at the threshold. He peers into the empty night. At the edge of the cottage clearing, he glimpses the flap of a cape, blood-red in the moonlight, and then it is gone, swallowed up by the trees.

"Hullo?" He tries to call out, but his weakened voice cannot penetrate the night.

Yet, as if in response, there is a groaning howl in the distance. Its echo peals through the snow-draped trees till it arrives at the woodsman. It tickles his ears like moths. Then there is another howl. A different beast. Closer. Then a third, a fourth. A devil's choir of howls. So thunderous that they fill the woodsman's skull, muting even the panicked thumping of his heart.

These must be the beasts who devoured the creatures of forest and farm alike. Who snatched infants from their cribs. Who gobbled up dutiful children from forest paths. Well, they would not gobble this child. The woodsman would get to her first.

He doesn't realize he is running until low branches tug at his cloak. Whether they would warn or detain him he neither knows nor cares but simply rips through them. Even with his hunger, he is faster than the girl, for he spies her cape up ahead, dodging trees and undergrowth. He believes he can hear the snow bite at her toes, although, in truth, all around him is howls. How different from the unwanted silence of that morning and of so many mornings before it. Others would surely quake at the sound, but not he. The howls quicken his blood even as they grow closer.

The woodsman enters a small clearing. It seems as though the trees were blasted backward to form a near perfect circle. The snowy floor is hard packed as if dozens of feet trampled it down to a smooth, icy surface upon which the woodsman slips and falls to his knees.

He rasps and coughs and heaves his empty gut. There is no sign of the girl. Above him, in the clear sky, is the moon, full and hearty like a pot of milk warming upon a hearth.

It is only when a twig snaps that the woodsman notices the howling has stopped. With bile still clinging to his chin, he gazes at the ring of trees around the clearing.

Out of the shadows to his right steps a wolf. Its fur is white and patchy, and on its head sits a ragged nightcap. It regards him blandly as a second wolf emerges beside it. Its fur is black and shimmers in the moonlight. Around its neck is a collar of lace. The wolf pants and paws at the ground, less patient than the first. Then there is a third wolf, a fourth, a fifth, more and more. Each a different shade of black or brown or grey, each wearing some item of clothing as if together they had ransacked a young woman's hope chest before her wedding day. Her pure white linens, her careful needlepoint.

Finally, a smaller wolf steps forward. Its fur is mousy and matted. The woodsman is not surprised to see that it wears a red cape around its slender shoulders. The young wolf sniffs the air, and, even in the darkness, the woodsman knows it is smiling.

He nods at it and laughs hollowly. He reaches to his belt and unclasps his small axe, his knife, and tosses them aside. They land in a pillow of snow. Useless now, perhaps always were.

The wolves circle him silently. Slowly, at first, as if bored, but then their pace quickens. Weaving from tree to tree, they pass from shadow into moonlight and back again. The woodsman tries to track the young wolf in red, but loses it among the rest of the pack.

And then they are upon him.

Teeth sharp and lips moist, snouts furry and claws sharp, yelps and gulps, flesh torn from muscle, fat ripped from bone, blood-stained snow, full bellies. Red cloak forgotten, unneeded, irrelevant, for the cold is not cold, and the night is not silent. And someone, at least, is no longer hungry.

Beware
the
knife

Hiding in shadows
Like wolves in the night
Traipsing over twigs
Preparing to bite

Catch him, slay him
And loot the prey
Fill their pockets
Collect their pay

Adorned in red
Cloaked in black
Beware the knife
Of the assassin's attack

Related to Thorn Tower *by Anne J. Hill*

SEQUEL TO *LOST NAMES*

DO YOU REMEMBER how utterly afraid you used to be of the dark?

How you used to cower under the covers, waiting for every creak, afraid that something might grab you?

All around the world, children fear the encroaching nighttime, as the sky dims and the moon warns them to be tucked away in their beds—*or else.*

I am the *or else.*

I am the monster under the bed, the reason why children fear to sleep with their legs dangling over the edge, lest I gobble them in the middle of the night.

And how *true* those fears are, despite the fact that parents tell their offspring otherwise.

"There is nothing to fear but fear itself," the adults whisper.

Which is correct—

But I am *fear itself.*

And when I mark a family for revenge, there is nothing they can do to escape.

And I have marked the Darling family.

Frost crawled up the glass with every breath as I stood outside the warm, familial scene that played out inside the lovely forest cottage. Two children played a board game while a third snoozed in a bassinet. Their parents, however, engaged in the most unusual of pastimes: fencing.

The father swiped at the mother, a rather clumsy attempt to end their duel, but the mother leaped onto a footstool and somehow managed to keep her balance as it teetered.

She grinned, a smart, vicious thing.

How I hated her—Wendy Darling, wendigo slayer, she called herself.

"Just a mite faster, Peter, or I'll be saving your neck again next time." Wendy placed one foot against his chest and pushed him backward.

He staggered before he caught himself on a chair. The children glanced up from their game and clapped a few times. The eldest, a little girl, chimed in, "You *almost* had Mummy that time, Daddy!"

Peter smirked and wiped the back of his neck. "It's all on purpose, you know. I like to stay just one smidgen behind your mother, so she can always keep me in check."

Wendy rolled her eyes as she took his weapon to hang up on the wall. "Ah, is that it? And here I thought I was just better than you."

"Never. Haven't you heard? I'm the best." A bit of cockiness slipped into Peter's voice—something I was familiar with, considering I'd taken that, as well as a bit of pride and loneliness, and twisted them to fit my needs when Peter had been my last host.

Ah, so many years ago since I'd last worn the guise of Peter Pan and feasted on the flesh of kidnapped children. Neverland, pixies, Lost Boys—so many rumors and lies that had kept me satiated.

But those good times were in the past, discarded like the name itself. Now, Peter went by Peter Darling—he'd taken his wife's name to further distance himself from the tales.

From *me.*

I scraped my shadowy claws across the windowpane. Without a corporeal body, they made no noise or impact, but the ice thickened near my mouth.

Wendy vaulted onto Peter's back, much to the glee of the children in the room. He spun her around as the children squeaked and fell in line behind, begging to "fly" with their father.

I flexed my paws and wished that I could tear into the familial bliss right then. But I had been patient thus far and would continue to be—though hunger gnawed at my stomach. Only hunger and cold could touch me in this form, but both were inescapable until my new host let me in.

"All right, all right. Enough flying." Wendy scrambled down from Peter's back. "Daddy and I really do have to leave. There are other children in danger all over the world, and it's up to us to save them."

"Can I come with you?" the eldest girl bleated. "Please, Mummy?"

"Not yet, Jane." Wendy picked up a bag and carried it to the door. I scooted into the bushes, to observe but not be seen. After all, my plan hinged on Peter and Wendy leaving as they had planned to do for weeks. "We need you to stay here and protect the house. Granny Mary doesn't know how to fight off nightmares like you do."

Jane puffed out her chest—apparently, she'd inherited a bit of her father's bravado. But other than that, Jane Darling seemed to possess only saccharine emotions that threatened to choke me if I partook in them too long. At six, her small world seemed perfect in her innocent eyes. A mummy and daddy that loved her, a little brother to play with, and a new little sister to adore. And though her parents had told her about the dangerous world they inhabited, I'd noticed one flaw in their plan: They tried to teach her not to fear.

That any creature she encountered could be defeated, if only she were clever and brave enough.

And in childish naïvety, Jane believed the rulers of her world.

Wendy and Peter hoisted their bags onto their shoulders, kissed their family goodbye, and moved toward the door. But Jane didn't take this parting as well as her brother and sister did. She chased after her parents, calling for them all the while.

"Jane, dear. Come back inside." An older woman with graying hair rushed after the child. "Come back inside with Nico and Sylvia."

"It's all right, Mother." Wendy smoothed back Jane's long, auburn hair, which fell in unruly waves past the young girl's shoulders. "I need to review the rules with Jane, anyway." Wendy held up five fingers. "What are they? No nightmare can catch you unaware if you follow them."

Jane poked Wendy's first finger. "Number one: don't be afraid. Mummy, Daddy, and I can fight any nightmares."

Wendy smiled and nodded.

Jane prodded the second finger. "Number two: don't open the bedroom window."

"Perfect." Wendy wiggled her three remaining fingers.

"Number three: don't take off my cloak if I go outside." Jane poked the fingers in order. "Number four: don't go into the woods. Number five: don't talk to strangers."

Wendy dropped a kiss onto Jane's freckled nose. Visions of biting that pert little nose off filled my head, and the hungry ache in my stomach grew deeper.

"Excellent." Wendy tightened the knots on the little red cloak Jane wore. Silver bells tinkled with every movement, and Wendy had stitched designs all over the fabric with silver thread.

I snarled. Frost dripped from my lips and made a plant shrivel underneath my incorporeal feet. Wendy had always been entirely too clever for her own good.

"Now, remember to be good for Granny Mary." Wendy rose and hugged her own mother, who had been tasked with babysitting while Wendy and Peter gadded about the globe to defeat creatures like me.

But yet, they had no idea the most dangerous wolf lurked in their own forested backyard.

"They're always good, Wendy dear," Granny Mary cooed.

Ugh. Such trite pleasantries.

I couldn't stomach them any longer.

I left the family and followed the long forest path to the village. It was far different from London and far removed from all the havoc I'd wreaked there. Did people here even know the name Peter Pan? Did they know who the strange family was that inhabited the cottage nestled in the heart of the forest?

But that was the past, and my future seemed full of only rage and starvation unless my plan came to fruition. Yes… what would my new name be?

I slipped under a crack in a tiny hovel, with "Woodcutter Jacobs" carved into a crude sign. Unlike the Darling house, which was filled with light and nauseatingly positive emotions, this place housed the opposite. And I had arrived at just the right time.

A large man wielded the broken handle of a wooden axe as he loomed over his small apprentice. The head of the axe thudded to the ground, and the man growled.

But the shaft must have been all he needed to carry about his discipline.

The burly, hairy man—the proprietor Woodcutter Jacobs himself—walloped the boy in the head with the jagged end of the shaft. The apprentice collapsed to the ground and braced himself as Jacobs whacked him on the back.

"You wasteful, ignorant dog!" Jacobs bellowed. "How am I supposed to do my job when you *break* all my equipment?"

The boy—Davey, as he went by—shivered. Blood ran from his lip, and one eye had swelled shut. Anger rolled off them both in droves, but there was something special about Davey's. Animosity, revenge, hatred—they coiled around each other and whet my appetite, in the way a nice soup might hold one over before a four-course meal.

"I didn't *mean* to break it," he snarled.

Jacobs rewarded Davey's honesty with another beating.

Davey curled inward and tried to protect his face as Jacobs clubbed him.

"Fix it!" Jacobs growled. He tossed the hilt at his apprentice; it slammed into Davey's stomach and ricocheted off.

Jacobs stomped away and slammed the door behind him. The whole hovel seemed to tremor, but the foul atmosphere didn't recede, even with his negative presence gone.

Davey quivered but didn't uncurl for a few seconds. Slowly, he peeked open his one good eye and unwound himself. He winced and hissed all the while as his fingers roamed over the sore spots on his body.

"I'll kill him one day," he muttered under his breath. He swiped at his busted lip and scowled at the path of blood it left on the back of his hand. "I swear I will."

I slithered closer to him, the shadow of a wolf with red eyes on the floor. "Who says you have to wait for one day?"

"You again?" Davey followed my lazy movements as I circled him. "I thought I told you to go."

And he had, for weeks and weeks. But I could not just leave such tantalizing hatred alone.

I lifted a paw to his scarred cheek. Though I could not touch him in the typical way, he shuddered as a bit of ice crawled up his skin. "Why don't you let me help you? You're in a lot of pain here. Just a little ice might help."

Davey frowned, but I could smell the subtle shift in his emotions as confusion and even a tiny bit of gratefulness mixed with the turmoil raging inside of him.

"You know," I began as I set about numbing the current injuries, "you have been awfully powerless to stop everything bad in your life thus far. Your parents' deaths . . . the master you were assigned . . . all the beatings."

"Shut up." Davey's face twisted into a sneer. "How do you know all that?"

I sniffed the air. Now that the memories were at the forefront of his mind, flavoring his emotions, I could taste even clearer pictures of what this young man had endured. "Ah, yes. Tuberculosis took them both. And then you suffered for so long at the orphanage . . . I dare say, you really hoped things might turn around when your master took you in two years ago, didn't you?"

Davey snorted. "At the time, I didn't see how they could get *worse*." He glared at me. "But how do you *know* that?"

"Because I have power. Power I have been trying to share with you, as I keep telling you." I glanced back at the door. It remained firmly shut. I hoped Jacobs would stay gone long enough for me to weave my web without his interference again.

"I don't wanna be some traveling kook who knows about people's pasts."

He groaned and grasped the dilapidated mantle to hoist himself up. He stretched out to his full height, a rather tall boy who had to be right on the cusp of adulthood, if not just past it. Quite a drastic change from my last host, who had been caught in neverending childhood until he'd thrust me from his mind—with help from a few whacks from a silver poker.

I chuckled. "That's not the extent of my powers. I can give you whatever you want. I can give you the power to change your circumstances. The power to get *revenge*."

I backed away from him and grew in size until I covered a whole wall of the hovel. Snow and wind began to whirl all around, and I bared my teeth. The howl of the gale raged, loud and vicious. The blackness of my body slithered across the windows and blotted them out. Small items shattered as the wind hurled them against the walls; shards exploded and got swept into the blizzard. The hovel trembled, and the apprentice's eyes widened as he clutched at his wooden lifeline.

"Do you think some traveling kook could do *this*?" I hissed, and icy snowflakes sputtered from my lips. "I'm not offering you the chance to be a sideshow attraction. I am offering you the chance to never be caught powerless again. All you have to do is let me possess you."

The young woodcutter's eyes widened. "I—"

The door flew open, and Jacobs barged in.

"What is going on here?" the older man yelled over the sound of my storm. "What did you do?"

His eyes fastened on Davey like a hunter might look at a deer—how *I* often looked at my own prey. Jacobs grabbed his second axe from the floor and stomped toward the boy. "You son of the devil! What demon did you invoke?"

Jacobs raised the weapon over his head as he charged forward. It was impossible to tell whether his intended target was me or his apprentice, but it mattered not—especially when Davey yelled, "I invite you! *I invite you*!"

He raised his hands over his head like they might be able to stop his master's deathly blow—but it never came.

I rushed inside Davey and grabbed hold of his consciousness. I filled every crevice of his body and mind the way water slowly conforms to a new container. Within a few seconds, my work was complete, and his shadow stretched out into a wolfish representation of himself. The blizzard around us stopped, and I smiled Davey's smile.

Jacobs stopped, the axe frozen in midswing. His face blanched. "No—"

I tilted my host's head—*my* head—and grinned. "Oh, *yes*."

I lurched for Jacobs and ripped the weapon out of his hands, tossing it to the ground. I had control now, though Davey's viciousness coursed through my veins as I pummeled his tormentor.

"*Return every blow he ever gave me*," he snarled.

I like your spunk, boy. I think we'll get along quite well with each other.

Jacobs groaned and struggled to reach his weapon. He strained as blood began to drip from his nose and mouth.

"Why go for that?" I chuckled. "It's made of iron. Only silver can help you now."

Jacobs groaned and thrashed. He must have realized the futility of his struggle, because he swung his hands back around and clobbered my ear. His beefy hands wrapped around my neck. Perhaps he thought I would be as easy to throttle as Davey had been. I smirked, wrenched out of his grip, and seized a burly arm. I brought it closer to my lips and inhaled deeply.

The *smell!* Ah, how many years had it been since I last tasted human flesh?

"*What are you doing?*" Davey questioned inside our shared mind. "*Kill him!*"

I shoved the boy to the back and willed him to sleep. Who cared if he didn't obey immediately—if this next part disturbed him, I could always edit his memories later, like I had with Peter for years.

I poked my tongue out and dragged it along Jacobs' wrist. Ugh—it tasted overcooked. I much preferred my meals to be tender and innocent, which made Jane Darling and other children like her magnificent feasts. But I could make do with the food in front of me.

"Monster!" Jacobs' face twisted in disgust as he writhed and struggled.

I opened my mouth and guided one solitary finger onto my tongue.

He screamed as I swallowed my appetizer.

Tears rolled down his face, and my body shuddered as my new host struggled to gain control. Davey's shock and revulsion coursed through my brain, and I could feel his desperation to be back in charge. "*Stop! No—just kill him! That's all I want! Just kill him!*"

My consciousness bit into his to keep him still. *That's not all I want.*

Jacobs wailed and struck at me with his free hand, but it didn't matter. I didn't stop until I'd left him only a stump at the wrist. His fear had added a nice bit of flavoring toward the end, but all in all, he'd been entirely too dry and thick for my liking. Still, my hunger abated slightly for the first time in years.

"What k-kind of devilish c-creature are you . . . ?" Fat tears rolled down the man's cheeks and mingled with the blood from my blows. Confusion and horror rolled off him in droves. I could sense his unspoken fear: was his time in this world almost up?

I grinned. I could feel the fangs in my smile and the blood that dripped off them. "Isn't it obvious? I'm the Big Bad Wolf."

And I dove for his face.

I ambled through the woods in my host's body. He'd been quiet since the earlier debacle. Even now, I could feel him trembling in the back of his consciousness. But whenever he tried to recall what happened, I twisted it just a little more and pushed the truth away from his grasp.

We only killed him. I pushed this narrative closer to his curious hands, conjured up scenes that reinforced this. *I got you your revenge.*

I chuckled under my breath. Ahead, the Darling house loomed, and little Jane picked some flowers, though she never left the path her parents had made.

"Hello," I called.

Jane peeked up, her blue eyes bright underneath that scarlet hood.

"Hullo." Her eyes widened, and she gestured to me. "What happened to your face, mister? Did you get into a fight?"

"Of sorts, but don't worry. I'm okay." I knelt down and plucked a yellow flower from the ground and twirled the stem about in my fingers. "What's your name?"

Would she remember her precious rule number five?

She opened her mouth, but then closed it. It seemed she might recall her blasted rules after all.

With a sniff, she ran to the cottage door and knocked on it. "Granny!"

Granny Mary appeared in just a few seconds. She wiped some flour off her apron and attempted to tuck a loose strand of auburn-gray hair back into her bun. I could tell when she took notice of my host's injuries—she started and bit off a gasp. "Can I help you? Are you unwell?"

"This?" I touched my eyes. "Ah, I'm fine. Just some of the local boys that like to pick on me. But regardless, I actually want to help you, ma'am." How polite I could be, when it suited my needs. "My name's Davey. I'm a woodcutter from town, and I wondered if you might need my services." I slipped my hands under my suspenders and dipped my head. "I could build a nice fence in the backyard for the little girl to play in. Or I could chop some wood and collect it so that, come winter, you're not left in the cold. Or if you've got trees that need branches sawed off…" I swallowed and tried to make myself feel contrite. "My master just died, you see."

My stomach gurgled as if the master in question wanted to protest being mentioned in such a manner.

"Oh, you poor thing." Granny Mary looked about. "I suppose a backyard fence might be nice to surprise Peter and Wendy with. As for the cost… I'll pay you with my own money, and I'll offer you some meals as well. Does that sound fair to you?"

I smiled.

She'd offer me some meals, all right—although I doubt she could imagine what type I truly wanted. "Fair enough, ma'am. Thank you."

I dared not venture back to the village after I struck my bargain with Granny Mary. I'd put up a note on the door of Jacobs' hovel that he'd been summoned out of town before I left. I hoped that would suffice to curb any nosy neighbors that might enquire to his whereabouts. As far as they needed to know, Davey, the apprentice woodcutter, had gone with his master.

So I set about my job. Davey was quite accomplished, and I could easily call upon his muscle memory to help me complete the tasks set before me. I started with the fence in the back. I scarcely minded it when sweat dripped down my human host's body, or when I felt a prick of pain from a splinter. After all, pain meant I had a host, I had a plan, and I'd had my first meal.

And my second meal had warmed up to me as well, now that I was no stranger.

But she still wore that blasted red-and-silver hood everywhere.

"Davey!" Jane skipped out with a plate of cookies and water. She barely noticed that with every hop, a little more of the liquid sloshed over the rim of the glass and the silver bells on her cloak jingled. "Granny sent you some food. She just got done baking them!"

Jane settled down on one of the logs I'd cut and sized but had yet to put up.

I nodded my head and took the human food. "Why, thank you. That was ever so kind of her."

Jane giggled. "I helped her make them. Are they good?"

I licked my lips. "Delicious." I reached for the glass of water. "Say, Jane. You must be awfully hot in that little hood of yours. Why don't you take it off?"

"Oh, I can't. Mummy says I mustn't." Jane crossed her legs and ate her own sugary dessert. The tiny granules caught on her fingertips, and she licked them. "There are things in the wood that want to hurt me, and this protects me from them until I can fight them all by myself, like Mummy and Daddy."

"But I'm here right now. I could keep you safe." I puffed out my chest and flexed to show off my host's burgeoning biceps. "See?"

Jane poked my muscle. "You *are* very strong."

"I know." I leaned in closer. I could smell her flesh—mine for the taking, if only she'd take off that blasted garment! "See? I'll watch you. You don't have to be afraid."

"Well..." Jane fingered the tassels around her neck.

Yes—yes—*yes*!

But she shook her head and dropped her hands. "No, I better not. I don't want to disobey Mummy." She stood back up then and blew me a kiss. "I'll be back in a little. Do you want more food?"

"Yes," I growled. "I do."

But I still watched as my next meal bounced back inside.

The following days seemed to pass in tortured monotony. Both Jane and her brother Nico eventually decided I was a good playmate and often rushed outside to see me when I arrived in the morning. But Jane wore her hood, and Nico had a coat stitched with silver. Granny Mary wore silver hairpins and a bracelet when she went outside; even Baby Sylvia had a locket made of that blasted material.

After the first week, a letter came from Wendy and Peter. They'd arrived safely at their destination and described how they'd faced the latest set of foes. The older children found this delightful and decided to make *me* a monster. They "vanquished" me every hour with little sticks, and I had to pantomime dying at the hands of a Darling countless times each day.

I'd make them pay for their cruelty soon.

How I wished that I could turn over control of day-to-day operations to the woodcutter, but I sensed his displeasure with my actions. He sulked and hardly left his little mind-corner, except to stew over recent events.

He seemed more moody than ever the morning Jane had left me a big bouquet of flowers. She dropped them off and skipped away with Nico in tow to do whatever childish things she had in mind.

"*You're going to eat them too, aren't you?*" the woodcutter's mental voice said dully. I could see his scarred form as it paced at the edge of our consciousness.

You got your revenge. I'll get mine. If it's too unsettling for you, don't watch. I brought down the blade of an axe on a slab of wood and cut it clean in half.

"*Those children didn't do anything to you. They adore you—me—us. They're sweet and innocent.*"

I snorted. *They're the offspring of my enemies. They know too much. And—they're lunch.*

The woodcutter grumbled and fell silent again. I tried to erase more of his memory as I set about my work. But, even when I'd finished the fence, I felt some strange sense of resentment. Granted, Peter had been much younger when I had used him as host, but he'd willingly believed all my lies and let me alter his memories often.

But Peter had also been filled with loneliness, desperate to be wanted. He'd told himself so many lies along the way that I hardly had to do anything to keep him in eternal youthful bliss.

"Hullo!" Jane bounded up to me right as I sat down to wipe my brow. "I saw you from the window. You're all done with the fence, aren't you?"

I gestured around the perimeter and bit back my sarcastic reply. "Good eye. Yes, I am."

Jane rocked back and forth—really, did the child never sit still? "I knew it! And guess what? Granny Mary has a big surprise for you! She made a huge dinner to thank you for the fence."

I mopped up the rest of my damp face. "That was nice. I suppose you can bring it out whenever you want."

Jane shook her head. "No—you get to come inside!" She clasped her hands together, and I fought the urge to keep my shadow under control. It wanted to dance with delight, though I had enough experience with humans to know that their shadows did not move of their own will as often as mine could.

I stood up and tucked my handkerchief into my back pocket. "Well. That certainly is a pleasant surprise, Miss Jane. I'd be happy to join you for dinner."

Jane skipped over to the back door and tossed it open. She beckoned me in, and as I crossed the threshold, a shiver crossed my back.

This house was filled to the brim with silver. That might have prevented my entry in my natural form, but so long as my host didn't touch it, I would be all right. More than all right, actually—today, I could feast upon the Darling family, who would soon shed their garments and trinkets of protection. Or—as the most brutal irony of all—maybe I'd somehow possess Granny Mary's body and lie in wait for Wendy and Peter to come home. They'd suspect nothing until I pounced on them.

Jane led me to the table. Nico and Granny Mary had already gathered around, and Baby Sylvia babbled in her high chair.

"We wanted to thank you for all your hard work, Davey." Granny Mary reached out and patted my hand. "I hope that we can help you as much as you've helped us."

"Oh." I dipped my head and smirked. "You already have."

And then—

Little Jane slipped out of her red hood and hung it on a coat rack by the door.

She smiled and slid into the seat next to me, and I reached out and gripped her arm.

"Davey?" Her brow furrowed in confusion. "That's—that's a little tight."

Granny glanced over. "Careful, Davey. You're a lot stronger than her."

I tightened my grasp and leaned in closer. "You don't say?"

Jane's blue eyes widened as her face paled. Oh, yes. At last, I'd taught this child what her parents neglected to teach her: *fear*.

I wrenched her away from the table with a cackle. Her knees hit the floor, and she cried out. Her tiny fingers clawed at mine as I dragged her away.

"Davey—*Jane*!" Granny Mary screeched. She fumbled upward and grabbed a spoon. Perhaps she intended to ladle me to death? The confusion around the room was so palpable—and palatable.

Granny Mary stumbled after me but smacked her knee into the chair. Both woman and furniture clattered to the ground, and the spoon fell out of her hand. Nico—well, I'd lost sight of him. I was far too consumed with Jane now.

I hoisted her up into the air and inhaled the childish fragrance that wafted from her. It mingled with the terror in the air, as sweet as chocolate.

I opened my mouth and lowered it toward Jane's arm. Saliva dripped from my teeth onto her skin and rolled down her elbow. She shuddered, screamed, and punched at me with her fist. How I wanted to savor this moment, but I could not spare any dramatics. I had to kill them all on such a short time limit.

I caught the first bit of flesh between my teeth—only to be bashed in the face by a shoe.

I yowled and dropped Jane. I stumbled back, cradling my face.

Nico stood, another silver-tipped boot held in the air. "Don't you touch my sister!"

"Do you Darlings make everything in this world out of blasted silver?" I bellowed.

Jane scrambled back to the table and snatched a fork. I lurched toward her with the intent to grab her again, but she dug her cutlery into my shin.

I howled as my flesh burned.

"You little—" I kicked her off. Her head slammed against the leg of a chair. I raised my foot to bash her skull in—only for my whole body to go rigid and topple backward.

"*I won't let you hurt them! They didn't do anything to you!*" Davey dove at my consciousness in our mental battlefield.

I writhed on the floor as Davey's spirit shook me back and forth. He pinned my paws and dragged me away from the front of his mind.

I snapped and snarled at him. I managed to bite into his shoulder, though, as a spirit, pain registered differently inside this playground. Still, he hissed and tackled me. We rolled, and I felt our body convulse.

We tumbled together, but somehow, Davey's spirit overpowered me enough to cry, "Help!" I bit his arm and scratched at his face; he walloped me with his fists and tore clumps of my black fur out. "Help me!"

How could I not overpower him? True, maybe my power had not recovered completely since Wendy Darling had defeated me. But I thought it had recovered enough to at least stave off the attacks of one pathetic human.

I managed to seize control of the lips again. "I've waited too long for my revenge against the Darling family to stop now! I'll kill them! I'll kill them all!"

"Get the fireplace poker!" Jane yelled to her grandmother.

The little girl grabbed a serving spoon and began to pelt me. I screamed and lurched for her—Davey grabbed my soul and jerked me away. Our hand fell limp before I could touch the girl, though she beat it a few times with her makeshift weapon for good measure.

How utterly humiliating to be brought low by *kitchen utensils.*

Mary Darling brandished the silver fireplace poker as she approached. Her hair had fallen from her bun, but her eyes had an inner fire I recognized. She'd passed it on to her daughter.

"Be careful, Jane." Granny Mary thrust the tip of the poker against my throat until it burned. I snarled, impotent against two snot-nosed brats and an elderly lady who baked cookies. "You said *revenge.*" Granny Mary's voice quavered. "Are you that beast that ate my son?"

My frustration boiled over, but I chuckled nonetheless. My one victory so far tonight, and a surge of pride boiled up in me. *Yes.*

And though I wasn't sure if I said it or if Davey said it, someone spoke the word into existence.

"You abomination." Granny Mary dug the poker in deeper. Her face flushed, which made her seem even more frazzled. Her words, though, were anything but. "My daughter defeated you years ago. I'm glad I'll get the pleasure this time around."

Davey tackled me in our mental arena before I could say anything else.

Our body lurched left as the woodcutter dragged my consciousness to the side. Then we rolled back to the right as I bit into his neck and held him still so I could continue my tête-à-tête with Granny Mary. "Your daughter only *thought* she killed me all those years ago. She weakened me, yes, but I can never be killed."

Not unless they killed me while I inhabited a host's body. But since that would kill the poor soul who shared the body with me, most humans were far too sentimental to do so.

But *I* would never share that with the Darlings.

Davey chuckled. "*No. But good thing your thoughts aren't exactly your own right now.*"

I snarled; he wrestled my consciousness out of the way, just enough to scream: "Kill—me—! Host—dies, wendigo dies!"

"The host has to die…?" Granny Mary murmured. I could taste the emotion that dripped from her—a bit of resolve that hardened the fear and anger all around me. It stiffened them like bread that had gone stale.

Nico charged at me with a pair of silver daggers.

With what little control I had left, I smacked them out of his hand and lunged for him. The weapons skittered into the leg of a chair. Davey grabbed my wolfish ears and jerked me back. Our body collapsed once more, close enough to the daggers to deter any other Darlings from claiming them.

"*Get out of my head!*" Davey thrashed at me, and our body spasmed as he did.

Stop this! We'll never be able to accomplish anything if we keep fighting each other. We must work together!

Davey snarled at my suggestion and managed to scream out loud, "Run! Take the kids—go—"

I wrestled him away. Our body flailed and flipped over onto its face, but he still managed to keep control.

"I won't let you hurt those kids!" Davey yelled, his voice muffled. "I never should have let you in. Get out of my body!"

"Yes." Granny Mary said softly. "Get out of his body."

She brought down the silver poker on my back with a large *thwack*. Davey winced, and for a moment, I could see hatred flash through the eyes of his soul. I could even see the memory that popped to the forefront of our brain, could taste the confused emotions as Davey re-lived being beaten by his master, day after day.

We killed the man. Isn't that better? Remember what I've done for you. I can do so much more, but all you have to do is let me have this one moment. Let me kill the Darlings, and history will remember you as a powerful creature. No one will ever forget the legacy of the Big Bad Wolf!

Our body shuddered, and Granny Mary slammed the silver into our back again. Davey and I both screamed.

"I don't want to be a Big Bad Wolf! I don't even want to have power if it's to abuse it. All I want is the power to stop people like you from hurting anyone else!" Davey howled, once again in control of our mouth.

"Do you hear the boy? Get out of him right now." Granny Mary took a deep breath. I tasted some new emotions: her heavy acceptance and internal resolve. "Enter me instead. Leave that poor child alone."

Davey and I ceased our mental fight. I opened my mouth and let his soul's arm slide out from between my teeth. "What?" we asked in unison.

"You heard me." Granny Mary lifted her head. "Get out of that poor boy. I'd much rather you fight with me than cause him any more torment."

"A Darling is offering to be my host?" I raised an eyebrow. "You do realize I am attempting to kill your entire family?"

Granny Mary straightened her back. Her eyes bled fire. "I do. I also know that you are causing this boy misery, and *I* am strong enough to keep you in control."

I cackled. "Do you really think that, old woman? I've conquered the will of the Baba Yaga. I've destroyed entire towns. I've eaten countless children under the guise of your son-in-law! And you think you can stop the Big Bad Wolf?"

Granny Mary spread her arms out wide. "I do."

Well.

That certainly changed things. How delicious revenge would feel when I used the body of the mother to slaughter the daughter.

Granny Mary leaned down and whispered something into little Jane's ear. Jane burst into tears and shook her head.

"No, Granny, no! I can't—I can't—"

Granny Mary kissed Jane's nose—the very item I fantasized about eating. "You must. You are brave."

Davey jerked my soul away from our body's eyes, so I didn't see what happened next. I could only see the passion inside of Davey's soul as he pinned me to the ground. "*I'll never stop fighting you,*" Davey hissed.

I chuckled. *How about a rematch in my new body, boy?*

The air grew cold as I peeled my soul away from Davy's piece by piece. I began to crawl out of his mouth. Davey gave a choked scream as his consciousness regained control of the body, and he rolled over onto his back. His chest heaved from exhaustion as sweat poured down his face, dampening his hair.

The upper half of my torso wafted into the air: red eyes, a wolfish shadow. *A wendigo.* A creature of winter and death, emerging from its human husk.

"If you want me—" I began, only to choke as a silver dagger sliced through my abdomen.

My legs and stomach—they hadn't fully detached from Davey's body yet. I could almost feel him tug me back into place as our souls merged once again.

His eyes glittered as he pulled the dagger from his stomach; he delivered a second blow right between the sternum.

"No! Davey, no!" Granny Mary yelled. She rushed over, but he shook his head weakly. I howled as his spirit reattached with mine, dragging me back inside.

"I can't let him—us—hurt anyone else," Davey whispered. Blood dribbled out of his mouth—out of *our* mouth.

His hands trembled, though he managed to pull the dagger out again. With shaking hands, he aimed it over his heart.

Our heart.

"I'm sorry," he whispered, right before he plunged the sliver blade into his chest.

I howled as night closed in on me. *No*—I was never supposed to endure death. Wendigos were made to be immortal, as long-lasting as time itself. A herald every winter, a curse—

Davey's heart slowed.

My heart slowed.

Another stab, weak but still effective.

He'd done it.

Somehow, that little powerless woodcutter had managed to recover a sliver of power.

He'd never be abused or taken advantage of again.

And, as I took my last breath, I cursed his name, cursed every Darling child from now until eternity, but it didn't matter. Davey's one choice to decide to die had stolen every ounce of power from me.

And I...

The Baba Yaga…
The Pied Piper…
Peter Pan…
The Big Bad Wolf…
The wendigo with many lost names…
Died.

Wendy Darling jotted down the last of the battle notes she'd been told into a notebook. Jane sniffled as she recounted everything she'd been through and snuggled closer to Peter's chest.

"Davey was a hero, Mummy," she whispered.

Tears burned in Wendy's eyes, and she nodded. "He was. He was a true wendigo slayer if there ever was one. And we won't forget his sacrifice. Ever."

Peter pulled a blanket over Jane's legs and kissed the top of her head. Wendy longed to pry the thoughts that kept her husband silent out of his head. Did he wish that the sacrifice had been his to make? Did he feel regret that they'd failed to stop the wendigo completely in their childhood?

Wendy had done the best she could with the information she'd had as a little girl during their last encounter. Clearly, though, her resources had been outdated. By the wendigo's own admission, he could only be killed when in the host's body.

Time would tell if that was the truth, but with Davey's sacrifice, things certainly seemed quiet. Wendy's mother had recounted how, as she'd gone to bury the body, the wolfish shadow still stayed attached—unlike when it had dissipated last time.

"The world's knowledge on monsters is sorely lacking," Wendy whispered. "And no matter how many monsters we fight, there will always be more to hunt. Someone has to protect those children and let them sleep easily—and there will be nurseries worth defending until time itself stops. Someone has to live up to Davey's legacy."

"And yours, Wendy." Peter wiped away a tear on Jane's cheek. "Don't undermine all the good you've done. You've given so many children sweet dreams, even if you've had to work in the shadows. Even if you've never had to sacrifice what Davey had to sacrifice."

Wendy tapped her pencil against the leatherbound book. "Okay—*our* legacy. Yours, mine, ours. Someone has to keep the future safe, and it can't always be us. We can't go to Neverland and pause time forever." She tried to smile, though it didn't reach her eyes.

Now, more than ever, she understood her husband's fanciful desire for a place where age couldn't touch them. The stories had tantalized her as a child—up until she'd been traumatized by the truth—and that desire still lived inside her. Especially as she gazed at her children and yearned for time to slow down, just a little bit, to let her cherish them just a few hours more.

Mary Darling shifted in her seat. She, more than the rest of them, seemed haunted. She'd confessed to Wendy that her plan had been just like Davey's. She'd arranged to have Jane stab her, but Jane had fussed and refused to kill her grandmother. Mary thought perhaps Davey had overheard her scheme and executed it himself.

"What do you propose, then?"

"I can fight." Jane's eyes latched onto Wendy's. "I can fight, Mummy. And so can Nico and Sylvia. Well—maybe Sylvia has to get a little bit older."

Four-year-old Nico lifted his chin. "I can fight like Davey, too!"

Wendy traced his chubby, childish jaw. "I don't doubt it at all, my brave little man. But who comes after us?"

"Well . . ." Jane tapped her lips. "I think our children can. When I'm a mummy, I'll tell my babies about the nightmares and how to stop them. And when Nico's a daddy, he can tell his kids. And Sylvia, too, when she's a mummy."

Wendy paused. Thought. Rapped her pencil against the edge of her journal.

And slowly sat up straighter. "Yes—yes, Jane, I think that's a marvelous idea. We'll write it ourselves—"

"Write what?" Peter interrupted.

"Why, isn't it obvious?" Wendy grinned. "A book! A guide, if you will—how to fight monsters. How to *really* fight monsters so that no one ever has to be caught unaware like we were. There will be no surprises. No more innocent people like Davey hurt."

"A guidebook for monster hunting?" The rocking chair creaked as Mary leaned forward. "For just our family?"

"Or perhaps anyone that our family trusts enough." Wendy opened the book and began to write down the rules that she'd taught to Jane and Nico. That seemed like a simple enough place to start. "And we'll pass it down, and each new generation can learn more and more about these nightmares and how to fight them."

For years, she'd called herself Wendy Darling, wendigo slayer. But that didn't really fit now that her horizons had expanded. Wendigos were not the only danger that threatened the sweet dreams of children.

And so, after a moment of pause, Wendy Darling tilted and signed the first page of her journal and held it up for the rest of her family to see.

The Nightmare Hunter Guidebook

By: Wendy Darling

Nightmare Hunter.

MIGHTIER
THAN
MAGIC
PART FOUR

Cinderella

The Blue
doesn't get the
final say.

THE WISHING TREE

Beka Gremikova

THE WISHING TREE stood right where Ella had said it would. Ryn stumbled through the graveyard, stopping before a small white headstone. Behind it, a tall, slender tree stood, its dark green leaves veined in gold. Doves cooed in its branches, nestled close to one another as they slept.

It won't grant every wish, Ella had warned her. *But*... Her eyes had gone soft, her lips trembling ever so slightly. *Sometimes, it offers more than a wish.*

More than a wish? What could that be? Ryn didn't need anything like that. She just wanted to get rid of the Blue. She rubbed at her aching eyes. She hadn't slept a wink in the two weeks since she'd returned from her travels for Moma's funeral. In the haze of funeral arrangements, she hadn't even seen any of Ella and Charlin's children yet.

She sat before the little tree. Its leaves rustled in a soft, chill breeze that sent tingles down Ryn's neck in the evening quiet. It was still so small... Perhaps too small for her request. But Ella had wished for and received three gorgeous dresses to catch Charlin's eye five years ago...

She had to try.

The Blue kept its grip on her as tightly as ever, making every word she uttered feel so much heavier. She glanced down at her trembling hands, at the midnight-blue smudge that perpetually tinted her skin. The Blue. Only Moma had ever seen her body's outward reflection of her inner, haunting sadness—because Moma had the Blue, too.

It will be all right, Ryn, Moma would tell her. *The Blue doesn't get the final say—you can still thrive despite it. You will have many hard days, but you can also help spread hope to so many suffering in silence.*

But Moma was gone now, and it was difficult to believe her words when those closest to Ryn—Ella and Charlin—could sleep soundly every night. When they weren't struck by sudden, unprompted attacks of sadness.... How could she ever be anything like them?

Ryn's throat closed. She missed sleep. She missed her job, traveling to collect and share stories with everyone she met. She missed Moma so much she could barely breathe. She knew she needed to keep going, to leave again, to travel the world and spread her stories. She just didn't know how. She felt...stuck.

And it was the Blue's fault.

She inhaled, exhaled, shook out her arms. She'd never wished upon a tree before. What if she did it wrong?

Something rustled close behind her, disturbing the peace of the graveyard. Ryn leaped to her feet, spinning around.

A little girl in an oversized purple dress gazed up at her with large, doleful eyes. Nirabeth, Ella's youngest daughter. "Auntie Ryn," she whispered, "Moma said to let you have some alone time here, but..." She swallowed and ducked her head. "I haven't gotten to see you yet."

Ryn clutched her chest, sinking to the ground. "Oh, Ira, I'm so sorry." She stretched out her arms, and Ira ran to her, clasping Ryn's neck.

"Is this my moma's wishing tree?" Ira pressed her cheek against Ryn's. Her skin was clammy. "The one that gave her all the beautiful dresses for Doda's ball?"

"Yes, it is," Ryn said absently, leaning back to take a careful look at Ira's face. Her heart hammered. Three years ago, when Ryn left for her latest storytelling voyage, Nirabeth's cheeks had been rosy-red and gleaming with health. She'd been a bouncy two-year-old. Now, her face was sunken, and her skin a light, mottled cobalt. "Ira, my darling..." She stroked her niece's hair. "How are you feeling?"

Ira squirmed. "I don't know, Auntie. I feel...sad, sometimes." Her lips pursed and wobbled. "A lot of the times. And I don't know why." Her eyes met Ryn's.

"My skin's like yours now, Auntie. All *blue*." Ira's eyes were glazed, almost vacant. As though she were terrified to feel too deeply. Terrified of a wave of emotion that might drag her too far into despair to return. "Can the wishing tree take it away?" Ira whispered. "Is that why you came?"

Ryn shivered. "I don't know. But... we can try." She sat down with her back against the smooth tree trunk, and Ira settled in her lap. The silence in the graveyard deepened. "I—no, we—wish—"

"—for the Blue to go away!" Ira burst out. "*Please*!"

Please, Ryn echoed silently, and her arms tightened around Ira. Together, they looked up into the branches.

The tree seemed to straighten, and a bright, golden light encompassed its shimmering leaves. That same light surrounded Ira and Ryn, brushing their skin, caressing their hair. Power tingled through Ryn's limbs... but her skin remained as before.

The Blue didn't go away.

Ira sobbed quietly.

"Why?" Ryn whispered. "Why couldn't you...?" She trailed off as light-sluiced leaves drifted from the tree, twirling into her lap, brushing her skin. A tingling sensation tickled wherever the leaves touched—through her fingers, coursing up her limbs, nestling into every aching nook and cranny of her body.

Ira's sobs quieted, and she sat up, her eyes wide. She stretched out her hands to catch the falling leaves, gasping.

"Do you feel it?" Ryn whispered. "That... tingling?"

Ira nodded emphatically. "It feels tickly, like feathers!"

Ryn trembled under a sudden weight and warmth—overwhelming assurance of comfort and love. Something surrounded her.... Something she didn't dare to name. She shut her eyes tight, but the presence didn't leave. It lingered, soothing the cracks in her soul, whispering against the crushing weight of her mind.

Ryn sighed, resting her head back against the tree trunk. Ira jumped up and frolicked amongst the falling leaves, her blue face bright. Hopeful. Alive. *Assured*. Despite the truth of her condition. Despite the sorrow that would come.

"More than a wish," Ryn whispered. "Moma was right." *The Blue doesn't get the final say.*

But I've been
my own fairy in
darkness

DON'T HAVE A FAIRY GODMOTHER

Anne J. Hill

I don't have a fairy godmother
No magic will get me through this
No glass slippers or talking mice
To inspire my journey in the wilderness

Grief hits you like a ton of bricks
Stacked upon each other on your chest
But you smile as your rib cage cracks
Or they won't let you into the dance

So, there I glide, blood dripping
But no one else can see my wound
All they glimpse is my lovely figure and face
And no magic will get me through this

I've got no godmother, no pumpkin carriage
No one can see the blood beneath
No prince charming bowing at the waist
No one watching in awe as I glide with grace

They'd be gasping and cheering in shock
Seeing a knife sticking out of my back
At all that I can do with a bunch of bricks
If they understood how heavy this is

But all they see is the smile and beauty
And the stories of a magical godmother
Twirling a wand and making this bliss
But I've been my own fairy in darkness

Under my dress, I've strapped a dagger
I'm armed and ready for the next fight
Because grief makes you unsettled
Primed to leave when the clock strikes

So find me a fairy godmother to hold my hand
Because though I might be a warrior,
On my own, I can't carry wounds or bricks
Tell me how to soothe this ache in my chest

Related to Thorn Tower *by Anne J. Hill*

After Midnight

Hannah Carter

NOBODY EVER TALKED about what happened after the clock struck midnight.

After the ball finished, when the pretty dresses disappeared.

When the glass slipper broke, and Ella found herself walking on shards of broken glass.

"I—I don't understand." Ella stumbled away from the fairy in the royal bedroom—the bedroom Ella had shared with Prince Flor since their marriage a year ago. Now, it felt more like a nightmarish prison cell. "I thought you wanted to help me."

"Oh, I do." The woman who had once claimed to be her fairy godmother giggled and floated closer, the bloody knife clutched in her hand.

And Prince Flor lay dead on the floor.

Blood pooled around his body and leaked toward Ella's feet, the same dainty toes that had once danced in enchanted slippers. Ella's head spun, and she grasped for something, anything, but came up short. She staggered backward and almost lost her balance.

"I have *always* wanted to help you. What mother wouldn't want to help their own child, dearest Ella?" The fairy godmother sighed, a dreamy smile on her face. "My own little fairy changeling."

Ella jerked away as her fairy godmother reached for her cheek. "I'm *not* your child."

"Aren't you?" The fairy chuckled. "Why do you think I've been here to help you every step of the way, watch over you from birth? Why else would I make sure you snagged the prince at the ball? Why would I waste my time on someone other than my own daughter?"

Ella choked on a sob, but the tears slipped out of her eyes. "You're lying."

She had to be—the young, smooth skin of the fairy godmother seemed to belong to someone Ella's age. But then again, everyone knew the fairies didn't age as humans did.

"I have no reason to lie anymore. Here we stand, on the cusp of victory." Magic sparked between the fairy godmother's fingers as she swept Prince Flor's body out of the way with a wave of her hand. The magic that had so effortlessly changed Ella's rags into a ballgown now seemed much more malicious.

Ella glanced around but could see nothing to protect herself with as the fairy godmother inched closer. But Ella couldn't even find a glass slipper she could use as a bludgeon.

"I've waited so long for this time to come. From the moment I placed you in a human crib, I knew what you would become. What *we* would become: the saviors of the fairies." The fairy held out her arms as if she expected Ella to run into them.

Or perhaps she just wanted an easier target to stab.

"I want no part in this. This—this is *evil,* regardless of who or what you think you are." Ella wrapped her arms around her trembling body and stepped back until she felt the stone wall against her spine.

"Evil?" A spasm of anger twisted the fairy godmother's face into a sneer that promised death and destruction. "Ella, dear—you should know more than anyone that the true evils in this world are the people that seek to enslave others. For years, our kind has lived in magical servitude to humans, just as the woman who dared call herself your stepmother enslaved you. But we can liberate them, just like I liberated you."

"I didn't ask you to." Tears wet Ella's lashes. "And I wouldn't have, if I knew you'd kill Flor like this."

"But I couldn't just leave you there! I couldn't watch you—*my child*—grovel in front of any human, stepmother or otherwise. I did it out of love."

"If you love me, why did you kill my husband?" Ella tiptoed closer to the bed. The only weapon in her arsenal was a pillow against a fairy godmother who had maimed or killed at least four people already. "He loved me—and I loved him."

The fairy clucked her tongue. "Oh, Ella, dear. With him in the picture, you could never truly be in power. You would simply be a wife, resigned to dote on your husband as his broodmare to awful *half* children. But you were meant for so much more, my love." The fairy placed an icy hand against Ella's wet cheek. Blood dripped off the poisoned dagger as the fairy leaned in closer. "You, my child...were destined to be queen."

SLEEPING BEAUTY

WORLD WITHIN A WORLD

Emily Barnett

WHAT IF WAKING is merely a dream?

I drift from my tower and pass faces who are nothing more than strangers. Strangers not only from another land but another world.

How long did I sleep in briar and stone, with the hands of time guarding me?

It was a kiss that pulled me from the sorceresses' deep enchantment. Away from the husband I adored, the children I loved as fiercely as sunlight. A world of magic and ever-twilight only found in dreaming.

I can still taste the prince's proud, coarse lips on mine when he woke me. Wanting to take, not give. The thief smiled down at me as if he'd just rescued me. But he hadn't. He'd stolen me from the life that I loved. The people who still needed me in my sleeping realm.

Each night I travel back, peeling back realities' skin. My dreams are a gateway to other worlds that only I can find—a gift from the enchantment that had meant to hurt me, but instead, healed me. Perhaps the sorceress had known, had seen my cold existence, and had sent me through the stars to another. To them.

Closing my eyes, I drift from sleep-walking to sleep-waking, to find my world within a world.

I have found many since the prince woke me, but none have been the right realm. But I will keep searching and yearning for the door, the place, where they call me loved.

Where they call me home.

AT FIRST SIGHT

Anne J. Hill

Beautiful... I hated you at first sight
You're proud, the world falling around you

You prance about waving swords
And act like you have something to prove

But no one is even questioning you
So put away your pride, you fool

You think I spend my time watching
As if I have nothing better to do

Well, honey, not everything is about you
And I'm done paying you for my sins

Maybe you should close your eyes
Lay your head and sleep for a while

You've got too much soul and it shows
Blaming others for undone wrongs

I'm horrible, you say, and maybe that's okay
At least I know who I am, hope you understand

I won't come visit you while you sleep
A briar rose, face soft and sweet

But don't forget you mean nothing to me
Even if you catch me staring at you

Gorgeous, shut your mouth and go to sleep
No one wants to hear you prove yourself

Sleep the days away and maybe even pray
Some prince will come to wake you

But, honey, he won't be me, even though
I've admired you from first sight

Related to Thorn Tower *by Anne J. Hill*

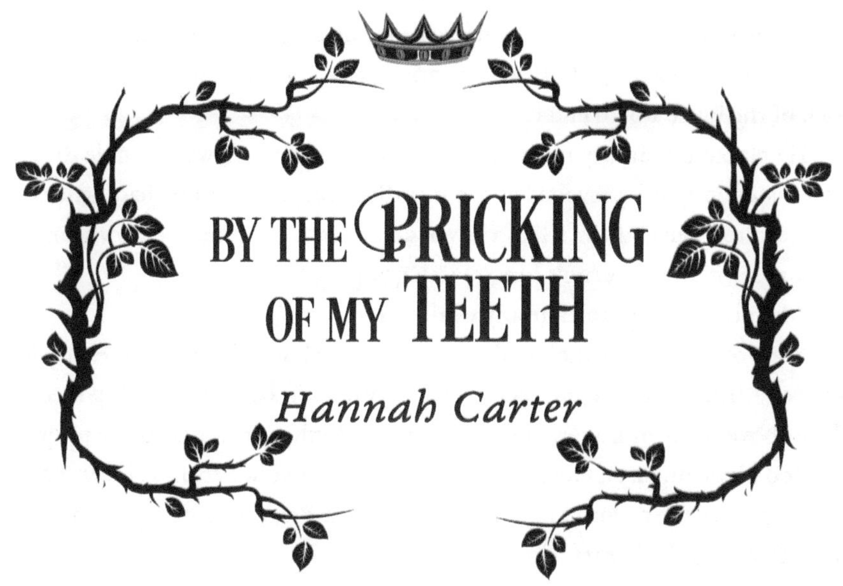

BY THE PRICKING OF MY TEETH

Hannah Carter

THE RUMORS SAY that she went mad for beauty.

Alistair remembered the tales of his childhood. Desperate to keep her youth, Princess Briar first sought the fairies. When they declared they could offer nothing past her christening gifts, well...

Princess Briar had searched for other ways to achieve her goals—unnatural ways. Ways that involved the blood of innocents and dark arts and threatened to destroy the kingdom if left unchecked.

The fairies could not turn a deaf ear to the terrified screams of Venzura's citizens. After all, they felt responsible for the fairy-blessed princess. When reasoning failed to work, they placed a curse upon a spindle and attacked Princess Briar with it. But even the fairies, with all the power they possessed, could only curse her—not kill. So they had to spread a rumor.

"*Only true love's kiss can save her now.*"

For a hundred years, people had believed that lie. It seemed more palatable than the truth, and anyway—the fairies hoped that it would prevent anyone imbecilic enough to search for Princess Briar from waking her.

But Alistair knew the fairies had hidden away the truth, swathed in coffin lining, pale as death, in the tallest tower of the Castle of Roses, where thorns twisted their way around its once grand magnificent facade.

He pressed the tip of his dagger against the finger of the sleeping princess until he drew just a drop of blood. The prick of a spindle had started this curse. A prick of the knife would end it.

He placed her dainty little finger in his lips and swallowed a single drop of blood. Most might be revolted at the metallic taste, but Alistair had little time to be revolted. Sensibilities fell by the wayside when the future, the crown, and all Venzura hung in the current king's weak grasp.

Alistair could not tolerate any weakness.

Years of wartime turmoil under the ineffective leadership of King Henry had whetted Alistair's resolve, sharper than any weapon he could wield. He poised the blade above his own finger, pressed it into his flesh, and watched the pinprick of blood blossom, just enough to equal what he'd siphoned from Princess Briar.

He pressed the crimson liquid against Princess Briar's mouth, soft and plump even after a hundred years of rest.

Her still chest came to life as she took a deep breath. Her tongue peeked out from between her teeth, and she licked her lips.

Two crimson eyes flickered open.

A fearsome, fanged smile twisted her visage into a beautiful horror story.

"You dare to wake me?" Princess Briar whispered. "Brave man. Brave—but foolish."

The vampire rose from her coffin and dove for him, her hands extended for his neck.

Alistair put out his arm in defense, and her sharp teeth sank into his skin. He smirked. Let her sink her fangs into him—the impotence of her venom humored him.

Using her close position, he grasped her neck and pinned her against the wall. He jerked the fangs free with only a slight wince. Blood dripped free, and Princess Briar salivated.

"On the contrary. I took a calculated risk—with absolutely no room for error." Alistair smirked. A weaker man might cave to the sharp, pricking pain in their arms, but Alistair could not let the vampire think she could hurt him. "I have researched your curse quite thoroughly. And vampirism has no effect on those that have consumed just a single drop of vampire blood." He nodded to her finger, where he'd stolen one drop of her life force. "You cannot turn me, nor can I kill you after I willingly gave you my blood, or so the stories go."

Princess Briar growled, more feral than fairy-blessed princess at that moment.

"Now, Princess Briar...much has changed in a hundred years." Lowering his voice, he ran his finger over her pale cheek. "How would you like to help me murder a king?"

RAPUNZEL

What sort of
Queen
are you?

A Taste of Grace

Beka Gremikova

THE CRUNCHY BITTERNESS of the *riptalion* leaf takes a slight edge off my craving. As I grasp my swollen stomach, shoulders hunched, I glance back toward the castle, pushing strands of golden hair out of my face. Here in our private garden, my husband and I grow the dark green, large-leafed lettuce that has plagued my family since my grandmother first started chewing it.

Now, like my mother and grandmother before me, the craving gnaws at my thoughts. *More.*

What are you doing? You can't!

I must.

You want your child born with this dependency?

Of course not. I don't want it to ruin her life even as it claws its way through mine. My fingers quiver as I stuff the riptalion in my mouth. Healer Lief claims relapses are common during the struggle to break a dependency, but he can't understand how it really feels—as if I've claimed a kingdom only to break it with my own hands.

What sort of queen are you?

Shame sharpens against my tongue like rancid milk. *Think of something else!* I picture strawberries and clotted cream, and icy-sour longing fills me. I sigh. Over the years, I've learned how to cope with my magical ability to taste emotions, but simple distraction doesn't always work.

The warm, rich tang of venison—excited recognition—suddenly envelops me. I frown. It's not *my* emotion I'm tasting. I glance over my shoulder.

A stranger lurks near the riptalion patch, his shoulders hunched, his bright golden hair streaked with grey. "Your High—" He swallows. "Riptalion..."

The venison flavor melts into a muddle: fishy fear, searing-spice uncertainty—all mingled with the tartness of... *desperation.*

This man knows me.

"Grace is my name." I stand. Riptalion is the name Witch Hellen gave me, that of a woman enslaved to a plant and held captive by a sorceress.

Grace is the name I gave myself.

His eyes shimmer.

My tongue tingles with cumin and nutmeg, his anticipation. The same flavors *I* taste when I'm about to gnaw on riptalion after going through withdrawal.

"Grace," he murmurs. "Your mother..."

That hair. Those hunched shoulders. Details I see in the mirror every day. "You're my... father?" The words are charcoal, gritty.

He nods.

"You gave me over to a witch!" I gasp for breath. "Hellen *locked me up in a tower* because I was *growing up.*" She didn't want to lose me like her little Peter, who flew off to some land she couldn't reach. She cursed me to taste emotions, as if knowing her every feeling would bind me to her.

But I *did* grow up, fell in love...

I cradle my stomach and gaze back at the castle. My eldest children are probably pestering their governess for riptalion while I scrounge in the garden. I've forbidden them from it, but I can't resist it myself. I blink back tears.

What sort of queen are you?

The man shuffles forward. Resignation exudes from him in waves of pickle brine as he sits cross-legged on the ground. "There is no excuse. Your mother..."

"Craves it still? Did she send you here to steal some from *me* now?" As I say it, rotten egg putrefies in my mouth.

"She wanted me to see you." His voice, honeysuckle-soft, breaks. My eyes sting at his devotion to the woman who traded me for lettuce before I was even born. His stinging-pine regret and salty-sweet longing chase the heated words from my lips.

Perhaps he wishes to have been better than he was.

Just as I long to be better than I am.

"Does she regret giving me up?"

"She couldn't face you. She still struggles so much. She hates herself for what happened, but the craving..." His gaze slides across the riptalion patch to my green-smudged fingers. His sorrow is cold summer rain on my tongue. "You understand, I see."

"I haven't given up my children."

"I'm glad you don't have to." Though his tone sounds sad and not reproving, the words still scald. I'm privileged to garden my own riptalion—to not have to resort to stealing, to giving up my children to satisfy my hunger. "I pray every day you might break the cycle."

I suck in a breath. If he only knew how often I pray the very same.

He stands. "Thank you for letting me see you, Grace." He stuffs his hands in his pockets. "Your mother will be happy to hear you've grown into a strong queen." He starts to shuffle away.

I bite my lip. I wonder—when will I hear of him next? When he steals from the wrong person and lands himself and his wife in *jail*?

"Wait." The word bursts out of me before I can bite it back.

The man's steps falter. He stops next to a particularly large batch of riptalion.

"If..." I swallow, then plow on. "If you *must* have the stuff, I'd rather you not steal. You may collect from my garden... but I ask a favor in return."

His shoulders slump, and my cheeks burn. My words must remind him of Hellen's, when he bartered me away to her. "What's that?" he asks, his tone tasting vile with suspicion.

"You join me in my visits to Healer Lief." Perhaps he and I can attempt to heal our wounds together through Healer Lief's counsel.

The man's eyes widen. "That's it?"

That's it? I nearly bark out a bitter laugh. As if the road I've chosen—to fight for my children, to fight for *myself*—is so easy. As if it hasn't brought with it moments of utter agony and hopelessness.

And grace, Healer Lief's voice breaks in, gently reproving yet encouraging. *You need to have grace for yourself, Your Highness, or the dependency will feed on your despair and make itself stronger.*

The man's voice interrupts my ponderings. "I thought you hated us. Why be so generous?"

I swallow a lump in my throat. "I—I'm trying not to hate you." *If I hate you, I hate myself.* I knot my fingers together. "If you accept my offer, I will see you at Healer Lief's house at the week's end." My voice comes out stiffer than I wanted it to.

The man gives a rigid bow, his shoulders tense. "Yes, Your Highness."

His sharpness hurts. I clench my fingers, clear my throat. Let the words out gently, so he can see that I want to attempt *some* sort of relationship between us. Even if it can never match the ideal in my mind. "Tell your wife... there's nothing to fear from me. I haven't had a real mother in a long time. I don't know if she can ever be that for me, but...." My anticipation and longing surprise me with the warm comforts of clotted cream and strawberry jam. "Perhaps she can still be a grandmother to my children... and you can still be their grandfather."

The man's jaw drops. His shoulders straighten; his face smooths in a smile. Before he can speak, I say hurriedly, "I must go now. I'm to help my husband look over our roses."

The man, my *father,* nods and hurries off toward the garden gate. He passes my husband halfway down the next row but offers him only a furtive glance.

My husband beckons me to join him deeper in the garden, and I gladly leave the lettuce patch behind. "Who was that man?" he asks as we wander amongst the roses. Here, our mutual love and affection mingle in the crisp, clean tastes of spring and autumn, our favorite seasons.

I gaze behind me. The craving that tugs at me now is not for the riptalion plants fluttering in the breeze. "An... acquaintance." *Perhaps, one day... something more than that.*

Because I know what sort of queen I want to be. One who knows when and how to fight for those she loves....

One who has grace for others—and for herself.

WAITING TO BE SAVED

Anne J. Hill

He sits in his tower in the treetops
Waiting and wishing to be set free

His heart is trapped, his mind is stolen
He won't try to get out on his own

He once was full of life and love
But now he's chained to these walls

Will anyone come to save him?
Some princess to call him by name?

He's built a stronghold around his heart
To hopefully keep the darkness out

But when she climbs the tower
And slips through the hidden cracks

She dares to whisper his name
He starts to feel like himself again

And he's no longer alone up in the tower
She has saved him, that's all he knows

She brushes his hair, tells him she cares
Holds his hand and helps him climb down

She'll help, but she can't be his savior, she says
That's not a fair title for any mortal soul

It locks you and binds you and drives you mad
Makes you responsible for someone you're not

She tells him he shouldn't lock his heart up
To learn to climb down his towers another way

Related to Thorn Tower *by Anne J. Hill*

WARM WELCOME

Beka Gremikova

"Hello, stranger." There is a catch
in her voice, a stutter in her breath
that catches me.
My grip tightens on my cane,
and I blink back tears. That voice
seeps through my skin
and reminds me I'm no stranger.
Before I can speak, she is in my arms—
or am I in hers—
and my fingers no longer clutch a cane.
Instead my palms press into rough, woolen fabric
and my face buries against a bare
shoulder slick with sweat yet
still soft
to the touch.

In the distance I hear the cries of children,
the bleating of sheep. Scorching desert
sunshine beats down on my head,
but I cannot bear to push her
away.

In the long-ago distance bird cries sang
me through her tower window.
The nights should have chased
me out, but she always pulled me
closer.

I lift my head to find her face,
to brush my lips against her cheek—
She turns my head so our mouths press
together, and she holds me there until
I can taste salt. She trembles as I drink
her tears, and when we part
her arms will not release me.
Though I can no longer
gaze upon her beauty, I feel its pulse
in the hands that cradle my face,
and in the warm wetness that slides
into the gaping holes
where once upon a time my eyes
used to lie—

before the witch's thorns plucked them out

—and when sight staggers through me—
as if her tears have formed new eyes—
she does not see the miracle. She turns
and calls to the children
to come meet their father.
A boy and girl toddle toward me
and wrap skinny arms
around my legs.

She stands before me, and finally
sees the sight in my eyes
as I meet her gaze. I notice her hair,
short and drifting along her shoulders
in a jagged cut.
I still cannot believe
she is real.
I still cannot believe
we have survived.

She brushes the shortened ends with
a finger. "It will grow back," she says.

READ ON FOR AN EXCLUSIVE SNEAK PEAK FROM

THORN TOWER

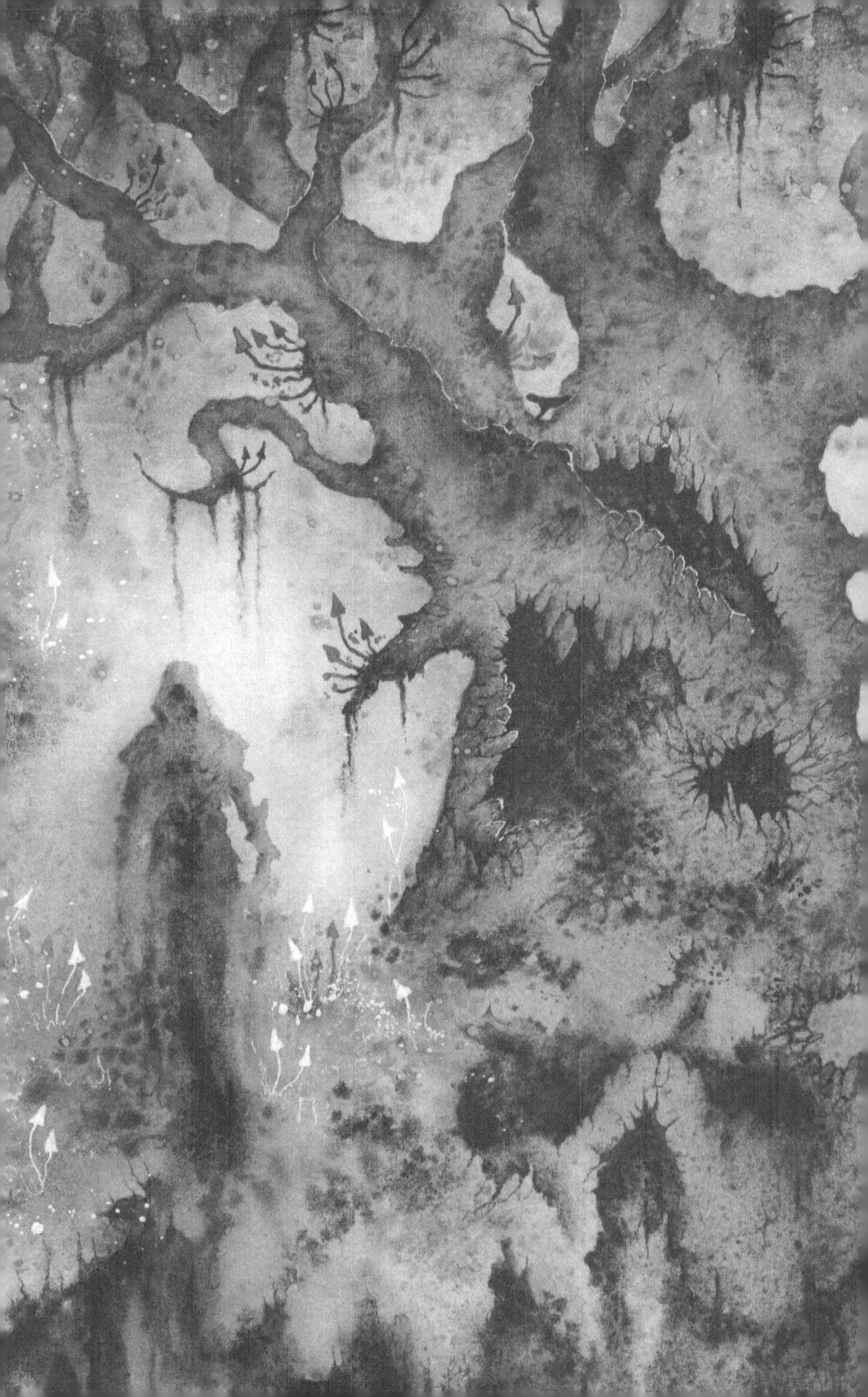

THE RED X

Anne J. Hill

THORN TOWER CHARACTER INTRODUCTION

BOYER WASN'T CERTAIN about much in life, but he knew for a fact that the man standing before him was going to die. He ran his thumb along the flat side of his dagger, the hard metal cold in the night air as his hooded elvish partner circled the man.

Boyer almost felt bad watching him squirm under their gaze, crunching forest leaves beneath his feet. Tight ginger curls pooled down their target's forehead, stuck in sweat, and swept over his ears. A thick scar ran through his left eye, too jagged to be from a blade. Boyer's partner had already stripped Scar-eye of his sword, and he looked naked without it.

Getting the elegantly-dressed man with clean cuffs out this far into the empty forest at night had been all their client's doing. The woman Scar-eye was sleeping with had asked him to come alone on the promise of running away with her—leaving his wife behind. Boyer's eyes moved from the shivering man to scan the shadows for hidden guards. He knew Scar-eye would have to be a fool to leave his guards at home.

"What is he going to do with that knife?" Scar-eye blubbered.

The hilt was embedded with a red jewel, the only aspect of the weapon that resembled the beautiful elf that had gifted it to him with a kiss before Boyer left for this mission. The recent memory lifted the corner of his lips, and he was sure it looked sinister to Scar-eye.

Waldren, Boyer's accomplice, smiled from under his hood and paced around Scar-eye. He held his hands behind his back, not a weapon to be seen on him. "That's a fine elven dagger. Slices through skin like soft-turned butter."

Boyer spun the dagger around in his hand, his finger looping in the intricately weaved hilt. His hood flapped over his cheeks.

"What's a human doing with an elvish blade? You some sort of elf-lovers come to rob me?" Scar-eye crossed his arms over his chest.

Boyer's core tightened at the thought of what this man had done. Boyer may be an assassin, but he would never dare stoop to Scar-eye's type of low.

Waldren paused in front of the man. "I don't really think that's what you should be worried about. Seeing as we're going to kill you, and all."

A cloud drifted over the moon, darkening what little light they had. No one moved, the sound of a distant river trickling over rocks. Their horses nickered from where they'd left them a stone's throw away. A bird took flight from a tree to Boyer's left, and crickets chirped like nothing was amiss. Like no one was about to die.

"No. You would have by now if you meant to." Scar-eye's voice trembled.

Boyer narrowed his eyes at the tree on his left. Something had made the bird take flight.

"You would think that, wouldn't you?" Waldren cocked his head with a pitying smile. "But how I see it is, a cat plays with a mouse before eating it, eh?"

To an untrained ear, Waldren sounded as human as anyone. But after working beside him for five years, Boyer could pick out the smooth honey-coated elvish way he ended some of his sentences and the slight roll on his Rs learned from his hometown. Years of practice had almost eradicated the accent.

Scar-eye swallowed, glancing briefly to the trees. His good eye twitched as Waldren's words seemed to sink in.

He was going to die.

"My friend here could slice your throat; that'd be a decent way to go," Waldren continued, circling him like a kitten ready to pounce. "There are longer ways to leave this earth. But it's not exactly fast, either. You'd sputter and feel the pain, but then all you'd know is suffocation as air no longer travels to your head. You'd tumble over, writhing on the forest floor, not a breath left to beg with."

"Please, please don't kill me! I haven't done anything!" Scar-eye held his hands out as if to present his clean palms. His skin was smooth and pampered, unlike Boyer's, which grated against the metal.

Boyer suppressed an eye roll at his partner's threats. If he had things his way, the man would be told his crimes and then beheaded with no grandeur, no long speeches, no pompous threatening. But it was Waldren's turn to take the lead.

Waldren gave Scar-eye a smile that would be comforting in any other circumstance. "We truly are sorry, but your head is worth my weight in Crown Silver."

Leaves drifted out of the left tree and tumbled to the forest floor.

And Boyer waited.

The man ran a shaky hand through his ginger hair. "Look. I can pay you. Whatever I'm worth, I can pay more Crown Silver. Trust me."

Waldren's head tilted ever-so-slightly in a look that Boyer knew all too well. He sighed. If it weren't for Boyer, they'd be hunted down for betraying their clients for higher pay many times over.

Waldren's mouth opened, and Boyer cleared his throat.

"Fine." Waldren huffed, straightened himself, and looked back at the man. "Sorry, chap."

Scar-eye's good eye widened, and he stepped away from them. "Please. Just tell me why and maybe we can talk this out? Do you even know who I am?"

Boyer held his hand up, and Waldren moved aside. He walked over to Scar-eye and finally spoke. "A rich monster who's never used his hands for anything other than to beat and ravage women. Never again." Switching his dagger into his left hand, Boyer pulled another knife from his pant leg and tapped the two blades together. Waldren wanted a show, after all.

Scar-eye stared at the knives in Boyer's hands and shuddered. His face grew paler, and his one eye widened, lips quivering.

Boyer worked his jaw. He'd witnessed this look of horror so many times before a kill. Seeing his targets fully acknowledge their fate for their corrupt ways had been his favorite part... before he watched the woman he once loved die. The look always took him back to her brown eyes filled with confusion and then terror, just before the blade sunk into her stomach.

Boyer blinked, pushing her lifeless form to the back of his mind. Scar-eye's screams jolted him to the present.

"I've never done that! You have to believe me!"

And part of Boyer did, the part that once thought people could be trusted. His naive, youthful self begged him to hear Scar-eye out, to tell his tale, and let fate play through. But that child was silenced after seeing how cruel the world was, filled with war and betrayal. After his fellow humans took over elvish land and tossed them into slavery just for a few coins. After he'd vowed to assassinate barnacles like Scar-eye...

The clouds drifted away from the moon.

That was all the light he needed.

Boyer flipped the knife in his right hand, eyes darting to the tree on his left. Finally, what he'd been waiting for—

He caught sight of a shiny elbow sticking out from behind the early autumn leaves. He snapped his throwing knife through the air, a clear path to the tree in question, and sliced through the leaves.

A gasp came from the tree, and a bow and arrow fell...followed by an armored body. With the knife embedded in his bloody throat.

Boyer suppressed a wince, knowing he killed a likely innocent guard just doing his job to feed his family.

But then again, so was Boyer.

Scar-eye shrieked and staggered back, bumping into Waldren.

"Careful there. Would hate for you to be next *so* soon," Waldren soothed.

Something slammed into Boyer's shoulder, and he jerked forward. The all-too-familiar feel of an arrow ripped through his right shoulder muscle, with a resounding *crack* when it shattered through his collarbone, and the arrowhead emerged on the other side.

The dagger slipped from his hand and tumbled in dry leaves. His head spun, and his knees felt weak. Boyer wheezed and paused a moment, assessing if he was about to die. While the arrow shaft stuck in his upper shoulder hurt like Belok's claws, nothing but flesh, muscle, and bone seemed touched. He knew all too well what a nicked lung felt like, and this wasn't it. Though the blood loss could do him in....

Waldren grabbed Scar-eye's hands and yanked them to his back, using his body as a shield and restraining him from lashing out. Waldren's hood slid off his head, revealing his red cloth tied on like a cap.

Boyer glanced over his shoulder, spotting a figure perched in the treetops, an arrow trained on him. His eyes never left the second archer, even as his vision blurred. Though he could not recall all the injuries he'd endured in this trade, the pain never lessened. He only got better at ignoring it each time.

His teeth ground together at the throbbing ache in his shoulder.

Knife throwing was much harder with his left hand. If his elvish partner had brought his bow instead of leaving it on his horse, this would be an easy target. But no. Waldren had insisted he didn't need them, that it would ruin the whole suspenseful atmosphere he'd cultivated for this kill.

"Bastard," Boyer mumbled. The shooter shifted slightly, and Boyer jumped aside just as the arrow released, too late for the archer to change his aim.

He tumbled, landing on his left arm, and rolled behind a tree, blocked from the shooter. He stood up with his back pressed to the trunk, though his shoulders stuck out and could be visible to a trained eye.

Curse my broad shoulders.

He shifted sideways, cutting off any view of him from the shooter's angle, and faced Waldren, who gave him a concerned eyebrow raise. Boyer nodded his reassurance.

His whole right arm was stiff and screaming from the stunt he just pulled. He didn't reach behind and touch his shoulder, though he wanted to. The less he knew of the damage right then, the better. He couldn't throw with that arm, that much he was aware of. But Belok burn them all, he wanted to.

"Please," Scar-eye yelled. "Kill them! Save me! Save me!"

Boyer thought that was a wonderful idea. *Yes, archer. Get out of the tree and try to save the rich scabby sea bass.* If he could get Waldren away from Scar-eye and let the archer think it was safe to come save him, they'd be able to take the men down with ease. Boyer let out two short bird calls, signaling Waldren. Silence. Then, in response, Waldren dragged Scar-eye toward Boyer, still using him as a shield.

"What are you doing? Let me go!" Scar-eye pleaded and tried to toss his body against Waldren, but to no avail.

Boyer heard the archer jump to a new branch like a squirrel, getting closer to Waldren.

"Shut up, slime," Waldren growled as he pulled. "Trust me, I'm not happy with how things are going either, but sometimes we have to work with what we have, so stop your complaining." He paused with his back against the tree opposite Boyer, and took a gamble that Boyer was all too aware of. He slipped a dagger out, held it to Scar-eye's throat, and whispered something in his ear—his forearm exposed for the taking.

Either the archer was a lousy shot and Boyer was lucky it hadn't penetrated any vital organs, or he knew exactly what he was doing and Waldren's arm would be an easy target.

Whatever Waldren whispered worked, and Scar-eye stiffened and nodded. "Good," Waldren said with a smile and patted the flat edge of his dagger against his cheek. "On you go then."

Scar-eye turned his head to the treetops and with a shaking breath, said, "Let this man go freely. That's an order. Or else his friend will kill my wife and pin it on you. Come down, Kilm."

Boyer's breath caught. He knew that name. Kilm was once a guard of a nobleman named Friddan, who they killed. Kilm helped Boyer out in a pinch a time or two. And Waldren had stolen gold off him once.

Kilm could either be their saving grace, or the noose around their necks.

Boyer leaned his temple against the tree, using it to support his throbbing head. They needed to get this sorted fast so Waldren could heal his shoulder before he lost too much blood.

Kilm shifted in the trees and shot an arrow between Scar-eye's feet. "I'm no fool. Boyer, come on out and play. I could use a good target practice."

"Kilm! That was an order. Put that arrow away." Scar-eye kicked at the arrow between his legs like a toddler who lost his toy soldier.

"Sorry, but I don't trust a word these two say," Kilm replied. "My arrow goes down, and they're likely to run me through with some hidden scheme. The Red X doesn't play around." An arrow skimmed past Boyer's shoe.

Boyer shifted back behind the tree more. He breathed in sharply when the arrow in his back bumped against the tree trunk.

Waldren laughed from behind Scar-eye. "We don't play around? I would have thought that's all we do. Well. Me at least. It's lovely to see you again. How's that gold treating you?"

Boyer inwardly groaned. Waldren sure knew how to make himself even more of a target.

The tree branch creaked, Kilm's feet repositioning. "It's likely lining your stomachs now."

A loose stone caught Boyer's eye. He wedged his boot under it best he could and kicked it into the air, sending it flying away from him.

Kilm's arrow fired after it, scraping a tree. "Look, why don't we work out some sort of deal here?"

Boyer could hear the underlying tremor in the guard's voice. Kilm knew Boyer enough to know the Red X worked like a shadow in the night, undetectable and ready to spring from nowhere.

"I thought you *don't trust a word we say*?" Waldren clipped his words, mocking Kilm's Conwell accent.

"Listen and shut your talk-hole, pisspot. I don't trust you, but you two owe me one, don't you?"

Boyer ran his tongue between his teeth. Kilm wasn't wrong, and he knew far too well that Boyer couldn't stand owing people.

He'd be playing into his hand if he replied, but he couldn't kill the innocent man now that he knew who he was. *Some* assassins still had morals.

"Or we could just kill you, send you straight to hell. We don't owe you a damn thing," Waldren retorted, and Boyer almost laughed at the expected reply.

Kilm let an arrow slice past Waldren, bouncing off the tree at his back.

He had good aim, after all.

Scar-eye let out a helpless cry.

"I think you swear far too much, half-elf," Kilm said.

Scar-eye peered over his shoulder at Waldren. "You're an elf?" He looked twice as scared now.

Boyer could almost feel the wave of annoyance roll off Waldren. "Well then, fern you, you dandelion seedling! Take your ferning arrows and shove them up your acorn," he yelled at Kilm.

"You little—"

"What deal did you have in mind, Kilm?" Boyer spoke from behind the tree. It was a risk, but Boyer was in the business of risk-taking.

Kilm's words were doused in a smile. "Ah, so you can talk, Boyer."

"In the name of Belok above! What is going on?" Scar-eye thrashed against Waldren.

"Get on with it, Kilm." Boyer scooped up a rock. He paused as he straightened, pain shooting down his back and almost sending him tumbling into the leaves. He bit down hard on his lip and pushed himself to stand fully. The taste of blood touched his tongue.

"Well, I know your names. I could easily report you, get your necks hung once and for all..."

Boyer thumbed the smooth edge of the stone. "But you won't."

"Did you all forget I'm here!" Scar-eye groaned, but no one looked at him.

"Very clever, Boyer. You don't miss a thing. Instead, I'll allow you to finish your job and let you run free, *again*. But this time, I don't want any gold in return. I want you to find someone."

Boyer's fingers tightened. "I'm not in the business of killing just *anyone*."

"And you may have killed my fellow guard, but you won't kill *me*. You're not much of an assassin, are you? I don't need her dead. I just need her found."

Waldren laughed. "Who could *you* possibly need found?"

The trickling river and enduring crickets filled the air, seeming louder in the silence between them. Boyer usually wouldn't mind waiting forever for Kilm to answer if needed, but he could feel the blood seeping from his veins.

"Well?" Waldren snapped.

Kilm cleared his throat. "My niece. She's gone missing. She's...part elf. Last seen near the Skull Sea coast."

Boyer sighed and stepped out from behind the tree. "Put your toy bow away, Kilm. You don't have to threaten us for something like that. Deal."

"What?" Waldren gasped. "Blast it, Boyer! Give a man a chance to think something through first. We could have just killed him and saved ourselves a payless job."

Boyer sighed. "He's right, you know. Isn't much of a deal if we aren't getting anything out of it." He eyed the tip of Kilm's arrow.

"You get to walk freely. That's payment enough," Kilm reasoned.

Boyer smiled. "Is that so? See, how I look at it is, we'd get away one way or another. Really, you're bargaining for your own life here, my friend. So climb on down before I change my mind and end you."

"I think I'm done taking my chances with you, Boyer." Kilm's elbow pulled back ever so slightly, his aim adjusting a fraction....

But before he could take another shot, Boyer threw his rock at Kilm's head. The jolt it took to get the right momentum sent a wave of shock through Boyer's body, and he stumbled, slamming his left hand against a tree to stabilize himself.

The rock knocked Kilm in the helmet; a clatter of armor and metal tumbled through the tree branches, and he landed on his back.

Waldren dropped his grip on Scar-eye and dashed through the falling leaves. Knife in hand, he climbed on top of the guard and secured his arms under his knees, popped his helmet off, and pressed the blade to his throat.

Boyer slipped back, grabbed Scar-eye by the scruff and dragged him over to Waldren.

Kilm breathed rapidly. "Waldren, don't."

"Don't kill my *friend*, Wally." Boyer chuckled through his shoulder's throbbing pain.

"I thought *I* was your only friend?" Waldren stuck out his lower lip, his knife drawing a drop of blood from Kilm's throat.

"I think we define 'friend' differently."

Scar-eye's arms flailed like a windmill, smacking Boyer's lower back. "Let me go!"

Boyer's jaw clenched. If one more thing jostled him...

"We have a job to do, Wally. Stay focused." Boyer tied a gag around Scar-eye's mouth, done listening to his pleadings. His right hand felt numb as he worked the gag.

Waldren's knife cut in just a little deeper. "Yes, and he ruined my whole plan. I was going to sneak up behind the human and slice his head off just as he thought we would let him go. But no. Sir Noble Uncle here had to step in."

"You don't make any extra coin if you kill him," Boyer pointed out.

Waldren froze. "Well, fern you, Boyer. Seeds, you're right. So how much can you pay me if I let you live?" Waldren smiled down at Kilm.

"I have 50 Crown Silver on me," he sputtered.

Waldren's face screwed up. "That's all?" But he fished around until he found a pouch and smiled.

"Now we're even. We get your 50 Crown Silver for Waldren to waste on ale and your vowed silence, and you get to walk another day and we'll *keep an eye out* for your niece." Boyer chose his words carefully. "Deal?"

"What's to stop him from blabbering?" Waldren asked.

Boyer gave his best malicious smile. "He knows we can outrun anyone. If we find he's gone blackening our name, we'll make sure we do more than just find this niece of his." He hoped Kilm couldn't see how sick the thought made him. But Kilm needed to believe it.

Kilm took a shuddering breath. "Deal."

"Good choice. Waldren?"

The elf pulled his knife off Kilm's neck. "Now remember your promises when you wake. I'd hate to make this a killing blow next time I see you." He slammed the butt of his knife into Kilm's temple. "That oughta do it." Kilm lay still, chest rising and falling steadily. Blood trickled down his head and onto the dirt.

Scar-eye whimpered under his gag.

"Now, where were we?" Boyer straightened the quivering man.

Shaking his head fast, Scar-eye begged with his eyes while Waldren slipped out of sight.

Boyer leaned his left shoulder against a nearby tree. He ran his tongue over the blood on his lip. "I sure hope you've made your peace with Belok, or else he'll devour your soul in fire. Or whichever dragon-god you serve." Just because Scar-eye had sworn by Belok didn't mean he worshiped him. Boyer knew that better than most.

A shadow fell behind Scar-eye, and Boyer whispered, "Sweet dreams."

Two blades crossed and slashed through Scar-eye's neck from behind, and his head toppled to the ground, blood pasting leaves to his cheeks. His body hesitated as if taking a moment to realize something was missing and then crumpled, landing inches beside the stunned head.

"Who do you think he was?" Waldren asked, pulling out a cloth and cleaning the blood from his blades.

Boyer took out an empty pouch, grabbed Scar-eye by the hair, and shoved the bloody head inside. "I don't want to know."

Waldren rolled his eyes and slid his shortswords onto his back. He'd stashed them behind a tree earlier for the look of his performance. "You never do." He whistled, and the distant sound of horse hooves plodded their way.

Boyer crouched down and gently folded the man's arms over his chest. He may be a monster, but even filthy swabs deserved a tinge of respect. He grunted, his head spinning. "Keep anonymous jobs anonymous. Not knowing means we can deny it. You know that."

"But where's the fun in that? Live on the edge some, Boyer." Waldren pranced over to the first fallen guard and weeded through him for coin.

"Sorry, I thought being an illegal assassin was risk enough. Clearly, I need to up my game." Boyer stroked his horse's muzzle when she trotted over.

"Whatever brings in coin, eh?" Waldren grinned when he found a pouch.

"Not *whatever*. Some things aren't worth it. Get this blasted arrow out of me."

"Oh, come on. Can't you handle it?" Waldren smiled slyly but nodded for Boyer to sit. He pocketed the pouch and bounded back over to Boyer. Waldren carefully snapped the feathers off the end. "Lucky the arrowhead went the whole way through."

"We don't have time to make it pretty. Just—"

Waldren gripped just above the arrowhead and yanked the shaft through. Boyer dug his fingers into the dirt, screaming curses.

Tossing the bloody arrow, Waldren pressed his hands on either side of the wound. Boyer closed his eyes, his head flopping back against a tree. Waldren's hands sputtered in a red glow as his energy drained and passed into the wound. Boyer could feel his muscles slowly knit themselves back together.

A distant whinny filled the air. Both assassins looked up, and Boyer filled with dread.

"Belok's rainfire," Boyer swore under his breath.

Waldren jumped up. "That'll have to do for now." He pulled him to his feet, snatched Boyer's jeweled dagger from where he'd dropped it earlier, and climbed onto his steed.

Boyer's shoulder ached with every jolt through the forest, but he pushed it aside. He knew Waldren would finish healing him once they were safe.

They rode off before the coming riders could glimpse them—shadows drifting into the night.

To be continued in Thorn Tower *by Anne J. Hill*

Acknowledgments

FAIRY TALES AND friends...what a lovely, soul-stirring combination. We want to thank the authors and poets in this collection for your patience, encouragement, and understanding as we've put this anthology together. It's been an honor to work with you.

Thank you to the authors who helped with edits, and especially, Meseeha Seedat, Crystal Grant, Hannah Carter, Emily Barnett, and Rachael Katharine Elliott, who gave feedback on most if not all the pieces. Also, the outside beta readers who offered their valuable insight. You all are fantastic, and we're so grateful for the support you offered us.

We'd like to thank all our close friends who also helped with brainstorming and reading over our stories—we love you, and your enthusiasm is always a balm to our tired minds.

Thank you to everyone who helped with the cover reveal and spreading the news about this book's existence. Huzzah for fairy tale lovers!

Most of all, thank you to God, whose love and redemption can be found reflected in so many of the fairytales we know.

And to Perrault, the Brothers Grimm, Gabrielle-Suzanne de Villeneuve, and Andrew Lang, who collected and wrote the tales so that we might retell them...Please don't come for us.

-Anne J. Hill and Beka Gremikova

About the Authors

ANNE J. HILL

Anne J. Hill is an author who enjoys writing fantasy for all ages. Her love of words has also led to her career as a freelance writer and editor. She spends her days dreaming up fantastical realms, talking out loud to the characters in her head, and rearranging her personal library, which has been affectionately dubbed the "Book Dungeon."

Instagram @anne.j.hill.editing
Twitter @AnneJHillAuthor
www.annejhill.com

BEKA GREMIKOVA

Beka Gremikova writes folkloric fantasy from her nook in the Ottawa Valley, Ontario, Canada. When she's not traveling, playing video games, or dabbling in art, she can be found curled up with a mystery novel. Her work is featured in the Havok collections *Bingeworthy, Sensational, Prismatic*, and *Casting Call* as well as the anthologies *Aphotic Love, Fool's Honor, Tales From the Tower, Moonlight* and *Claws*, and more. Currently, she's plotting a plethora of dark fantasy fairy tales. *Photo credit Sarah-Ann Wijngaarden.*

Instagram @beka.gremikova
Twitter @DreamofWriting

LARA E. MADDEN

She might be crazy—the jury's still out—but Lara E. Madden would consider herself to be widely fascinated, with an affinity for wonder. She is madly in love with Jesus, with storytelling, and with the tribe of colorful characters that is her family and friends. When her feet are on the ground, she lives in Lancaster, PA with her housemate, Anne J. Hill, without whom she would likely never finish any project she starts. She is a novelist at heart but is currently focused on creating short fiction as she hones her writing craft.

Instagram @lara.e.madden
Facebook @Lara Madden
LaraTheWanderer.blogspot.com

EMILY BARNETT

Emily Barnett resides in Colorado with her husband and two sons writing young adult fantasy full of feels. She has had short stories published in *Spark Flash Fiction*, *Havok*, and *What Darkness Fears*.

Instagram @embarnettauthor
Facebook @emilybarnettauthor
Twitter @embarnettauthor
www.emilybarnettauthor.com

HANNAH CARTER

Hannah Carter is just a girl who loves to dream and write and still wakes up every day hoping to figure out she's secretly a mermaid. Her short stories and award-winning flash fiction pieces have been published in anthologies such as: *Whispers From Before, Prismatic, The Depth's We'll Go To, Aphotic Love,* and *The Willow Tree Swing*. She also won a competition with her short story, "Lara." She currently has two published novellas, *Amir and the Moon* and *Seashells.* In addition to fiction, she also has had over a dozen devotionals published in various magazines.

Instagram @introvertedmermaid3
introvertedmermaid3.mailerpage.com

MASEEHA SEEDAT

Maseeha Seedat is a 17-year-old author, born and raised in sunny South Africa. She made her publishing debut in *What Darkness Fears*, then went on to be the chief editor of the medical podcast Journey through a Stethoscope and the screenplay writer of Maskerade Mystery. Her latest publishing adventure is *Fool's Honor.* When she's not writing, Maseeha can be found chasing after her toddler cousin, hitting the padel courts, or clawing her way toward a degree in physiotherapy.

Instagram @sincerelymaseeha
Twitter @maseeha_writer
sincerelymaseeha.weebly.com

BERNADETTE LAMB

Bernadette Lamb is an author and illustrator based in St. Louis, Missouri. Her work for young people often deals with relational healing, the fantastical, and the complicated business of growing up. Like the keeper of a lighthouse, she wants to guide her readers to shore. When she's not telling stories, you'll probably find her re-watching *The Incredibles* or in a thrift store searching for the latest addition to her library.

bernadettelamb.com

CRYSTAL GRANT

Crystal Grant grew up loving stories and often spent more time in her imaginary worlds than the real one. She's had multiple short stories published through Havok Publishing, including their *Season Six: Casting Call* anthology. Her poems and short stories have also appeared in the Twenty Hills Publishing anthologies, *What Darkness Fears, Fools Honor,* and *Sharper Than Thorns*. She also works as a copy/line editor for Twenty Hills. During the day, Crystal shares her love of books and writing with her kindergarten and first-grade students. She spends her spare time doing jigsaw puzzles, watching old movies and TV shows, or reading books that sweep her away to other places.

Instagram @crystalgrantauthor
Facebook @crystalgrantauthor
www.crystalgrantauthor.com

JULIA SKINNER

Julia Skinner is a nineteen-year-old, modern day hobbit, with a love for good stories and chocolate ice cream. She lives in South Texas with her family and two miniature Australian Shepherds (and a ton of other animals!). When she's not working on one of her many fantasy novels or flash fictions, she can be found juggling college, playing video games, dreaming up yet another entrepreneurial project, or happy-ranting about Brandon Sanderson's books. She is a sinner saved by Jesus, and if any good comes from her journey, it's because of Him. Her published works include *Prismatic, Fool's Honor, Casting Call, Darkness & Moonlight*, and more!

Instagram @litaflameblog

ERIN DELLA MATTIA

Erin Della Mattia is a writer, editor, and amateur tarot card reader from Brampton, Ontario, Canada. She is currently working on a speculative novel about teenage girls and witchcraft in early Canadian history.
You can connect with her at:

erindellamattia.com

ANNIE KAY

Annie is an aspiring author and accidental poet. She began writing poetry as an outlet, which quickly became a passion. She is a 7th grade English teacher. During her free time, you can catch Annie reading, bullet journaling, embroidering, and playing with her beloved cat, Louis. You can find her on Instagram at:

Instagram @anniekay.reads

MORIAH CHAVIS

Moriah is the author of the short stories *The Assassin's Kiss* (Phantom House Press, August 2022) and *Thorns of Winter* (Twenty-Hills Publishing, July 2022). A two-time graduate from the University of South Carolina, she holds a Bachelor's in Liberal Arts and a Master's in Library and Information Science. She indulges in her love of all things bookish by spreading that passion to others as an elementary school librarian. When not reading or writing, she can be found at the bookstore, adding another book to my endless TBR, sewing, or drafting something new.

Instagram @moriah.chavis

CASSANDRA HAMM

Cassandra Hamm is a psychology nerd, art collector, jigsaw puzzler, and hopeless romantic who spends most of her time lost in another realm. As a mental health advocate with a passion for social justice, she writes about shattered girls finding their way in the world. Her two kittens, named after her favorite middle grade heroes, are the lights of her life, and she suspects she may end up as a cat lady (or the owner of a Warrior Clan). Her work appears in various anthologies, including several of Havok Publishing's collections, ***Warriors Against the Storm, When Your Beauty is the Beast, The Depths We'll Go To, Aphotic Love, Exquisite Poison***, and ***The Lady in the Tower.***

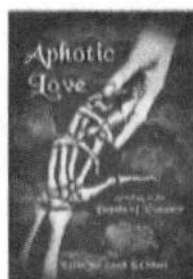

T.H. FORSTER

T.H. Forster is an author and illustrator from Whidbey Island, Washington. She recently earned her M.F.A in Illustration and Visual Culture from Washington University in St. Louis, and has a passion for all book-related things. When she isn't writing or drawing, she can be found baking, watching movies, and walking the family dog, Cider.

KAITLYN EMERY

Kaitlyn Emery was obsessed with dragons and fantasy at a young age. When she grew up, she learned reality was darker than anything she read in a book. Through writing, she learned to cope with the world around her and find a voice in fiction. Kaitlyn has written short stories for various magazines, Flash Fiction for Havok Publishing, and been published in several anthologies including *Rebirth, Sensational, Prismatic, When Your Beauty is the Beast, Moonlight and Claws, Tales From The Tower, The Depths We'll Go To*, and *Aphotic Love.*

Instagram @kaitlyn_scribbling
Kaitlyn-Emery.com

RACHAEL KATHARINE ELLIOTT

Rachael Katharine Elliott is a middle school English teacher from northern Indiana. In her spare time, she sews costumes to wear to renaissance fairs and convinces her friends to read classic British literature. Her debut novel, a solarpunk retelling of Rapunzel, is scheduled to release in 2023.

TASHA KAZANJIAN

Tasha Kazanjian is currently pursuing her masters in clinical counseling and writes fantasy to escape APA citations. She loves losing herself in books, especially very old ones that smell strongly of ink and dust, and has been known to disappear into used book shops for hours at a time. Tasha's writing process usually involves stacks of historical nonfiction, a hundred index cards stuck up on her wall, and copious amounts of coffee, tea, and colored pens. She is currently revising a dark fantasy novel involving ice age dragons.

Instagram @tnkazanjian.writer

AJ SKELLY

AJ Skelly is an author, blogger, and lover of all things fantasy, medieval, and fairy-tale-romance. And werewolves. An avid reader and a former high school English teacher, she lives with her husband, children, and many imaginary friends who often find their way into her stories. They all drink copious amounts of tea together and stay up reading far later than they should.

Instagram @a.j.skelly
www.ajskelly.com

EVERLY HAYWOOD

Everly Haywood imagines herself to be a shieldmaiden of great prowess...but you're more likely to find her in a dusty library than on the battlefield slaying monsters from the underworld. She seeks to combine dark fantasy worlds with clean, sweet romance. She loves strong but sweet leading ladies and smoldering, tragic heroes. She lives in the country with her husband, two daughters and their protective dog nanny.

Facebook @authoreverlyhaywood
www.everlyhaywood.com

Other Books by

Twenty Hills Publishing

What Darkness Fears

Fool's Honor

The Never Tales: Volume I

www.annejhill.com/twenty-hills-publishing
Instagram @twenty_hills